Table of Contents

Introduction

What would your life be like if you achieved all your dreams? What about even half of them? Different to your life now? Are your dreams so buried they are now forgotten?.

Fact is, a lot of us give up the dreams we had as small children, bogged down by the 'normality' and 'routine' of life. Our elementary school years encouraged vision, creativity and imagination; we all remember the stories we wrote and the pictures we drew of ourselves flying planes, driving fast cars and living as princesses in castles. So what happened? Our high school curriculums crushed those dreams. They didn't teach us 'entrepreneurialism'. They didn't teach us how to develop millionaire mindsets. School taught us to get a career, to follow a plan and to work for others. So, how do some people break free? Who taught the dreamers, the bosses, the company owners, the millionaires? Simple. They taught themselves!

Driven by Passion brings you a collaboration of 15 conversations with people that possess a true drive to succeed. Throughout this book, you will discover and explore what drives them to push beyond what they learnt in high school and how they broke free of those invisible shackles. You'll learn how they pushed through their self-limiting beliefs that were cultivated during those vital years of their lives. You'll learn how to dream big again and reignite the passion you had as a child to live a life beyond that expected of you. Personal and financial freedom can be yours, if you open your mind and embrace the behaviours and habits practiced by successful people.

Enjoy the ride as you too are Driven by Passion!

Message from The Author

Welcome to Driven By Passion. I have a belief; passion is the key to achievement. Throughout this book you will engage with successful people and gain insight into the traits that have unleashed their individual passion to succeed.

We hear time and again there is no secret to success. However, my years as an entrepreneur and successful network marketer working with some of the world's most sought after leaders has shown me there is a secret, and that secret is passion! A common theme you will identify through the chapters of this book.

My own internal passion is what I believe to be the secret behind all of my achievements, be they sport, education or business related. I consider myself to be a passionate individual committed to being the best I can be and to enjoying the journey along the way. There is a great power in personal triumph; it is about succeeding in what we set out to do and reaping the rewards of getting things done.

I believe our life is for living and that we live in a world of abundance. I know that if we find what we love doing, and are passionate about our chosen field, we never in theory will work another day in our life because when you are passionate, when you are in love with what you do, you will enjoy the moments and you will enjoy giving value without need of compensation. I remember my Mum once saying to me "Craig, if you don't enjoy doing it, find something else to do. You have to love what you do". How right she was. When you truly love something, it is far easier to stay focused on your activity, knowing the results will follow. Doing something you don't love quickly leads to complacency when results don't happen overnight. We rarely get good at things we hate.

People passionate about what they do share 7 key habits and by understanding and learning these, you too can unleash the power of success. So, what are the 7 habits of highly passionate people?

HABIT 1. Passionate, successful people are in touch with a deeper motivation. It's our guiding principles and values that enable us to make important decisions and stay on track, keep focused and attain what it is we truly yearn for. When you are passionate about what you do, you are buzzing and the endorphins bouncing round your body, through your bloodstream enable you to unlock that ability to focus on success.

HABIT 2. Passionate, successful people have learned to prioritise. We all know the human mind collects thousands upon thousands of bits of information coming in from all different avenues. Some people let the volume of information coming in overwhelm them and fail to prioritise effectively. They get sidetracked from goals and are poor time keepers often doing trivial things before the things that truly matter. Those that are passionate about achieving their goals successfully train their 'internal executive secretary' to take in the information and funnel it in line with what they wish to achieve and where they want to be in life.

HABIT 3. Passionate people are doers. What excites them isn't just talking about their dreams, their passions, the giving value, it's about the doing, it is about the 'sweat equity'. It's the act of making it happen. What I mean by making it happen, is taking the action that you know is required; blood, sweat and tears in order to achieve your dreams and goals. Passionate people are devoted and the devoted will do what it takes to achieve their dreams and their passions. Procrastination never gets anyone anywhere!

HABIT 4. Passionate people expect the best. I learned long ago that in life, we may not always get what we want but we will always get what we expect. We effectively programme our own lives by the expectations that we have. I personally live my life with what I call the three E's; Energy, Excitement and Expectation.

To achieve anything, you have to possess energy. Nobody ever achieves goals by staying in bed. Period. Being excited about your goals and the fear of not achieving them is all part of the fun-fuelled journey. Expecting to succeed is essential to actually succeeding. It's a simple philosophy; if you think you can, you can and if you think you can't you're probably right! Having low expectations of yourself and of life limits your possibilities.

Passionate people light up a room when they walk in, because they are happy, and they give off a great vibe, a vibe of expectation and good will.

HABIT 5. Passionate people understand the power of association. Whether you realise this or not, you are always being influenced from outside forces. We are a sum of the 5 people we spend most of our time with. You need to learn to engage with those that raise you up and energise you, rather than those that drain you.

Connect with others that share your vision and share your joy for life. Positive people create an uplifting environment of belief and high expectations. Associate with yourself with those that won't distract you from your goal.

You want to be an entrepreneur? Mix with entrepreneurs. Associate with those on the same journey, not others who will encourage you to deviate from your path.

HABIT 6. Passionate people love to grow and develop. Our mind is the most powerful possession we have. Passionate people love to learn and to expand their knowledge and horizons. They always look for ways to improve themselves, improve their surroundings and their contribution to others. They have a childlike wonder about life and knowledge. They read, they ask questions, they join communities of people like themselves in order to satisfy their thirst for knowledge. In this book you'll hear people say you are either learning, or you are dying, and that rings true for so many people.

We live in a world that is forever growing, forever changing and we are built to grow, it is what we are here for. Our capacity on the inside is there to help us develop. If we don't learn and grow, we quite simply get left behind, whilst others take leaps and bounds forwards as they embrace and acquire new experiences and knowledge. I watch my girls every day, the questions they ask, the new challenges they undertake. They inspire me constantly as they grow and develop not only in years, but in wisdom through their inquisitive natures, taking in information. Adults need to not stop learning; the journey is never over until the end!

HABIT 7. Passionate people savour the journey. You see too many people focus on the destination, on the results and the required compensation. I believe true satisfaction comes from loving what you do and enjoying the rollercoaster ride. You only have to speak to anyone passionate about what they are doing to realise it's the process that is often more thrilling than the result. They get up out of bed everyday, they give value without compensation, and enjoy the pursuit of their dreams.

Developing these 7 habits isn't hard, but you have to learn to live and breath them. They need to become second nature to you.

Once you start working on your habits, you'll find that one feeds the other, and by developing them fully you enter into a self fulfilling circle.

Mastering these habits will help you create the bedrock of your journey to success, and feed your passion to succeed.

CHAPTER 1

Transformational Leadership Secrets

Are you unhappy in your current job? Are you unhappy where you live or how your life has panned out? What is preventing you from making more money and why are some people more successful than others?

In today's society, we can go where we want, live where we want, study what we want and even choose any profession that we want. Your choices are neither right or wrong but the profession you choose is going to be more apt to make a million Pounds / Dollars than the other.

Chris uncovers the excuses we are making that are limiting our choices for success. Chris believes that the primary key for success is choice. Successful people understand the power of choice. Where ever you are right now being the sum of the choices you've made up until now. Let Chris empower you to choose the rest of your life, which can be your dream life.

CRAIG WHITE:

Just a free show, which has well over 30,000 downloads and continues to provide some amazing insights on how we can become more and contribute more. Over the year, though, we have some superb shows and some extremely inspiring and influential individuals, and today is certainly no different. I get the opportunity to bring a great man, a great pleasure to chat with and give you an opportunity to listen to a man that's had over 25 years of making a difference to the lives of millions of people worldwide.

Chris Widener is a successful businessman, author, mentor and coach and some of you know him well. He's worked with two of the world's greatest legends, Jim Rohn and Zig Ziglar, in the world of personal development. And Chris has been an author of over 12 books. Some of my favourites, are the likes of The Angel Inside and I found myself on a trip to Florence, you know, looking for the David statue. The Art of Influence is something I have just finished reading and he co-authored one of my personal favourites, Twelve Pillars, as well as the sequel, Above All Else. Certainly, Chris is one of the foremost experts on Leadership and Influence and it really does give me great pleasure to bring this successful man to our show today. How are you today, Chris?

CHRIS WIDENER:

I'm doing fantastic. Thanks so much for having me. You mentioned going to Florence. I made my first trip to Florence a couple of weeks ago, so I wrote a bestselling book that was based there and I've never actually been there, so it was exciting to be able to be there, and of course, see the artwork and the David and the likes, so it was a lot of fun.

Craig White:

Wow, that's pretty fantastic. To be honest, it was only three to four weeks ago that I actually took the trip myself when I read your book. It feels like a few years ago, but yeah, it was an amazing city.

Chris Widener:

Yeah, it's beautiful. Amazing.

Craig White:

Did you get a chance to venture around the area?

Chris Widener:

We did a day trip there from Rome, so we were in Rome for five days and we took one of the days and we did a day trip up there. So, we were only there for maybe five hours.

Craig White:

Beautiful city out there, the pleasure of spending three or four days there, it's a beautiful part of the country, a beautiful part of the world even.

I do really appreciate you giving us some of your valuable time. I know you're a very busy man Chris, a lot of the listeners listening to our show will be fully aware of who you are, certainly, guys I work with very closely. I know they've just been reading a book or some of the guys that lived the life you've always dreamed of, and we were talking just now as well about, I would say living in your dream home and it was your dream home for 21 years. How did it all start for you? How did all this come about?

Chris Widener:

I actually sold about four years ago to my business partner and he still runs it and runs a terrific business online, iTunes etc.

I actually got started right out of high schools, speaking to summer camps, high schools, youth groups, colleges, because I had a really rough upbringing and got my life turned around, and so people were interested in having me coming on and talk to teenagers and then from there, sort of navigated over to doing time management seminars. And then, from there, I got online really early 1997, I think and started building some list there and wrote my first book, which was just a compilation of a series of articles that I've written for that email list.

And then, I ended up putting on some conferences, got to know some different folks, and then I worked with Jim Rohn and we did a lot of work the last seven years of his life. And from there, I got my own TV show, and then got asked to co-host a TV show with Zig Ziglar. So it's been an interesting ride over the last number of years since 1998 when I graduated college.

Craig White:

Wow, that certainly sounds like a fantastic adventure. You mentioned you had a rough upbringing in your life and it was turned around, what was the turning point? Was there a certain point or was it a series of events?

Chris Widener:

Yeah, actually, my dad died when I was four and I got into a lot of trouble growing up. My mom went into real estate. She was flipping houses long before it was popular or on television. And we would buy a house, move in, move on, and I tell people I went to 11 different schools and lived in 28 different homes. And because I was such a handful, my mom shipped me off to relatives a couple of times when I was growing up, once in the 4th grade and once in the 9th grade, and I just really couldn't figure it out.

And then, the summer before my senior year in high school, I guess it was probably my sophomore year in high school, I was invited by a friend to go to this little youth group at this little Lutheran church. I mean, it's a little, tiny Lutheran church, but they had a youth minister. He was a really cool guy and I didn't know anything about God. I didn't know anything about life and I've never really had a male role model. My dad died when I was young. One of my grandfathers had disappeared and the other one died and I didn't know him very well either. I never really had any male role model, so this youth minister really became two-fold: One, a male role model. He was from Montana and you might not know too much about the United States, but Montana's where all the rough and tumble cowboys live; Montana and Texas, right? He was a guy who just kicks you in the butt and told you to get your act together, and so he was good and taught me all about God and purpose and just a bigger picture of life than just this myopic focus on what is currently and momentarily important. So, that was a real significant change in point in my life.

Craig White:

Wow, you certainly shifted your thinking to a whole new kind of direction.

Chris Widener:

Yeah, totally.

Craig White:

One of the questions you've talked about and I've followed you and read a lot of your books and watched some of your videos on

YouTube and the stuff that you get out there to influence other people, I know you've talked about a question that's driven you for 25 years, you know, what separates the successful from the unsuccessful, what kind of answers have you come across to allow you to develop what you've developed yourself from your own successes, but also to positively influence other people to maybe follow that lead?

Chris Widener:

You know, when I find that things turned around, I didn't realise it but I wanted the same thing everybody else wanted in life and back in my seminars, I will regularly ask a series of questions. I'll say, "How many of you would like a million dollars in your bank account?" And, of course, everybody raises their hand, like I was just saying now, I spoke in Barcelona and Gothenburg, so I said, "How many of you would like a million euros in your bank account?" The funny thing is they all still raise their hands, even in euros. They wanted euros in their bank account.

Everybody wants financial stability, wealth, financial security and the like. Then I'll say, "How many of you would like to have a loving relationship, life-long relationship, finding somebody you can share your life with?" And everybody's hand goes up. Nobody wants to be single and alone every night for the rest of their life, eating TV dinners and watching reruns of old television shows. No, you want somebody you can share your life with.

And then I'll say, "Okay, how many of you would have children or want children? How many of you would like their children to grow up and be productive members of society?" Well, everybody's hand goes up. Nobody says, "I hope Little Johnny grows up and go to prison." Everybody wants their children to do better and to do great. I would love for my kids to even go further beyond what I've accomplished and to live a healthy, productive life.

And then I'll say, "How many of you would like to be physically fit and live to a ripe old age?" And everybody's hand goes up. What that tells me is that everybody wants essentially the same thing. Now the specifics of it might be different. If everybody wants a million dollars, but some might buy a Ferrari and some might just stick it in and buy gold and silver and just stick it away somewhere. What you might do with it might be different from person to person, but it was intriguing to me to see that everybody wants the same thing.

And then, couple that with the fact that we live in a free society. You and I both live in Western culture. We live in a free society and there are certain things about free societies. We can go where we want. We can live where we want. Nobody accidentally ended up living where they live, right? You chose the house. You're telling me you bought this old farmhouse and renovate it. You chose that house, I chose my house. I didn't accidentally end up, waking up one day and then go, "Wow, how did I end up here?" I chose to live here. I chose my profession. We can go where we want, live where we want. We can marry who we want.

I always ask, "How many people in the audience accidentally got married?" And there's always one smart aleck who raises his hand and says, "Yeah, one night in Las Vegas," right? But making a note of that is we choose everything that we do. So, you couple those two things together and it's fascinating to me.

Everybody wants the same thing and we live in a culture where you can have exactly what you want, you can make any choices you want, and yet some people do and some people don't. That, to me, is the profound question there is; everybody wants a million dollars, anybody can have a million dollars, but some people can do it, but some people don't.

What is it about the people who do and what is it about the people that don't? And I find that question has brought me to a lot of the answers. I mean, there's lots of answers that will come into success, but the primary thing would be choice. It's that successful people understand the power of choice.

Now, for example, I was getting my hair cut. I love my barber and he cuts my hair all the time. We've become friends. We haven't done anything outside the barber shop, but we'd grab a cup of coffee or something, it's not like we'd go on vacation together or anything, but super good guy and I like him a lot, and the other day, he said something to me about and I'm paraphrasing, "I wish I made the money that you make." And I said, "Well, you could." And he said, "How could I, you know?" And he basically played the victim card. "I'm a barber," and I said, "You chose to be a barber." There aren't a whole lot of barbers making, you know, 500 grand a year unless they own a chain of barber shops, right?

And so, he chose to do that and it pays him a certain amount of money. You know, when you're going to college, for those people who go to college, they make a choice. Am I going to major in Finance and go work on Wall Street where even the dumbest guy can make a million dollars a year, or you're going to go to be a teacher, an elementary education major? That's just a choice. Neither one is right; neither one is wrong, but one is going to be more apt to make a million dollars than the other one. And people don't understand that the choices they make determine to a great degree whether or not they're going to be successful in their endeavour.

What they want to do is they want to make a bad place and gripe about the fact that the result didn't end up the way they ended up picking. So, they'll say, "Well I'm a school teacher. I don't make any money." Well, it's fantastic you're a school teacher. You're making a difference in the lives of children. You're helping kids. You're a productive member of society, but don't gripe about the fact that you don't make much money because if you wanted to make money, there are other choices you could make that would make you the money. And so, I think that that's just a really big idea that most people never get their eyes around.

You know, you're probably aware of my Invisible Profit System CD where I talk about the difference between working for profits or working for wages. And it's based on an old Jim Rohn quote, "Profits are better than wages."

Most people want to be wealthy, but they work in a wage system. And nobody gets rich are working for wages. Very, very few people who get rich working for wages. I have to have something.

Professional athletes can get rich trading time for money. You'd get to play football for a year, you make $2 million. If you'd go on tour for 6 months and you're a musician, you might make $20 million. If you are an actor, an entertainer, if you're a sports star, you can trade time for money. Work a period of time, get paid a certain amount of money. If you're a high-ranking CEO in a very large company, you can get rich trading time for money.

But the reality is the average person chooses to work in a wage system and they don't make the kind of wealth that they want. Instead, they need to choose to not be in the wage system and get into a profit system where they own their own business, whether it's network marketing or its traditional business like opening up a chain of ice cream stores or shops or dry cleaners or whatever it might be. But most people choose to be in a wage system and yet complain that they don't get rich, complain that they don't have enough money.

They won't get into the profit system because there's too much risk and people don't want to take that risk. Is it fine that they work in a wage system? Absolutely, the bulk of the world is in a wage system. Fun, kind, loving, terrific, wonderful people, but don't complain that you don't have a million dollars in your bank account because you're never going to get there, because of that choice. And people, they're disconnected from how their choices produce results and how the results don't match up with what they really want in life.

Craig White:

This basically amazes me that I'd realised, although not recently, about 100 years ago, 90% of the world were entrepreneurs. They were self-employed. And now we fast forward to today and 90% of the world are working for somebody else. It kind of marries up with me how, obviously, how generally people are not going to get wealthy other than that kind of pointed out, working for somebody else. And it certainly is here in Europe, 90 to 95% of Europe need some kind of extra income to live the lifestyle they've become accustomed to, and I'm sure it's the same worldwide. Certainly, for me, go back a hundred years and I think there wasn't the poverty that there is today. There was more wealth. There was more entrepreneurialism. And it seems like society has influenced people, in some cases, into that negative thinking where they don't believe they can make choices.

And I come across people, everyday people, creating new relationships for the people that I've been working with for years, and it's trying to get them to see exactly what you said already, but it's the choices we make. I mean, how do we, can we get people to embrace change, to embrace or believe the fact that actually it is about the things that they choose? It's the six inches between their ears maybe having a paradigm shift. Is there a way we can influence people to do that?

Chris Widener:

I think it's just a matter of helping them see and walking through, if you're in a personal coaching relationship with somebody, you know, maybe over a cup of coffee they're griping and complaining and just say, "Okay, let's take a look at how you ended up here." Let's say they say, "Well, I'm broke and barely pay my mortgage and my car is eight years old and the transmission just went out and I don't know where I'm going to get the $2,000 to afford the repair.

Well let's just sit down with them and say, "Okay, let's take a look at how you got here." Let's back up and let's see the choices you made to get here to where you're financially struggling. And then, let's see if we can make some different choices that would produce different results. So, somehow, that's what I usually do is I tell people, "Wherever you are right now, for better or for worse, wherever you are right now is the sum of the choices you've made up until right now." Now here's usually where somebody says, "No, you don't know, Chris. You don't know my parents." "Oh, yes, I do. I have a dad who died and my mom--god, I love her--but she was not the best mom in the world." I can beat what every single long and flexible thing you can possibly think of, from power cords to Hot Wheels tracks, to switches, you name it.

I had a mom who wasn't the kindest and loving and nurturing woman. Yeah, I love her and we ended up having a good relationship toward the end of her life, but that it doesn't matter what your parents were like. If that's going to be your choice and that's going to be your excuse, then that's what's going to be.

I gave a seminar once and I said, "You know where you are right now is the sum of the choices you made up until right now," and this woman came up to me afterwards and she said, "Well I didn't choose my husband to cheat on me and run off with another woman and divorce me." I said, "You're right, you didn't choose that, but let's think through a couple of things. Number one, you did choose him and so you chose a guy, who did that, and of course, you didn't know and you wouldn't have chosen him, but you were a part and you're engaged there, right? And I don't know and I'm not going to place blame on one or the other, but you probably had some marital issues that could have been resolved." And, of course, she doesn't ever, you know, you can't blame her, a spouse, for a cheating spouse. But, you know, theirs probably was not the best marriage and how did your involvement form a marriage that was conducive to that and, again, I'm not placing the blame on her at all, but just understanding that all of these things add up.

But then I said something to her that created a stunned look on her face. And I said, "And my last question to you is, are you going to use the excuse that your husband cheated on you, to never achieve anything in the future?" And that's just a really simple question.

He did a horrible thing. He cheated on you. He run off with another woman, left you and your children. Now is that going to be your excuse for the rest of your life, because if that is, it doesn't have to be. There are all sorts of women who've been dumped by men, you know, bad guys, who said, "I'm going to do something in spite of this," and that's a choice. She is now presented with a choice.

I got a horrible thing happen to me, now I have a choice. Am I going to hold on to that as a warm, fuzzy excuse for the rest of my life or--and that's a choice--or am I going to choose to say, "In spite of the fact that I had something really negative happen to me, in spite of the fact that I have been left a single mom, in spite of the fact that I am struggling, I am still going to go out and succeed," and that is a choice. And that's what I confronted her with. I just held up the mirror and I said, "Is that going to be your excuse?" Because, the fact is most people, they use it as an excuse. "My mom was bad." "My spouse cheated on me." "I started a business and it failed and I'm bankrupt."

Do you know how many bankrupt billionaires there are? There's all sorts of billionaires that went bankrupt. I have a good friend named Bill Bartmann. Bill would be a good guy for you to get on. Look him up. He was at one time the 23rd richest man in

America. He was one spot ahead of Ross Perot. He's a well-known billionaire.

Bill, he owned a company and he had 3500 employees. He was partners with his high school friend and I think Bill owned about 80% of the company and his best friend owned 20% of the company, and to make a long story short, his best friend was cooking the books. The Federal agents raided the place. They bankrupt him. He literally went from being worth $3.6 billion to losing his entire company, losing all the employees and being worth nothing a couple of years later.

Now, he could have said, "Woe is me. I'm never going to be able to..." But Bill is back on his feet, building businesses, learning from his past. That's choice.

Some people would say, "Well, I invested $50,000 in my life's dream to start an ice cream shop and it went bankrupt and now I'm just going to work for the man for the rest of my life." That's just a choice; it's just an excuse.

And what I try to do is tell people we all have made choices up until now and we all get to make new choices from here on out, regardless of whether you suffered an injustice or you suffered, you know, at the hands of another person or a bankrupted business or something like that. Most people don't want to accept responsibility for their choices, but here's the power and this is what I explain to people.

If you're willing to accept the responsibility, if you're willing to stand where you are today and say, "I am now, right now, exactly where I've chosen to be." That's hard for a lot of people to do that, but if they will, if where I've come from is the result of the choices I made back here, then it's also true that wherever I want to go is simply the choices I'm going to make from hereon now.

That's the real power. If you can get over the responsibility of accepting that your choices have brought you this life that you don't like, then you actually empowered yourself to choose the rest of your life which can be your dream life. It can be whatever you want it to be and that's a pretty amazing thing.

Craig White:

I really do love that, it's taking responsibility and certainly, in my own experience and listening to you, and the story about your colleague friend, Bill Bartmann, it's amazing. Again, it's a belief of mine, I've read it somewhere, I've been influenced with it, somebody suggested that if you divided all the wealth equally to everyone in the world--every penny, euro, dime, yen--to all the individuals, eventually, it will end up back in the same pockets because people don't realise their self-worth.

People say is that footballer worth that volume of money? Well I think, yeah, he's made himself worth that for what he provides and what he gets.

Chris Widener:

You may disagree with the footballer getting paid $2 million a year, and that's when a lot of them say, "Oh, you know, that guy, all he does is throw a ball through a hoop." He's a basketball player. All he does is throw a ball. He's playing a kid's game. But the reality is that these same people or their friends or family will go spend 200 euros to sit in the front row and watch that guy throw a ball through the hoop, right? So, he's creating value in the market place, and then, the owners who own the companies, they charge people this money to come and they put 50,000 people in a stadium, they have to pay somebody else who can do it very well. In order to get the best, they have to pay them most. It's the gaming business. It just happens to be a large-scale business and the larger the scale, the more money you get to make.

Craig White:

Yeah, it makes perfect sense to me, you know, I've just been reading one of your books The Art of Influence, which is a fabulous story about, obviously, a young guy yet to go through business school and then gets the opportunity to spend the time with one of America's wealthiest men, Bobby, and he talks about the four golden rules.

Now you were talking about Bill Bartmann and losing his money, and then acquiring that wealth back. It kind of just felt right to maybe ask you about these four golden rules of business and influence, really. Are you happy to share them with the listeners?

Chris Widener:

Sure. The premise of the book is that, and this is actually kind of funny, but the Art of Influence is about my third or fourth best-selling book, but it's about 95% of all the speeches I did, and so that's what I talk about most is The Art of Influence. And it's really based on four things.

If you want to have a good life, if you want to build a big business, if you want to build a big team, if you want to be a great leader, if you want to sell a lot, you have to gain four things from other people, and the four things that you have to gain are trust, admiration, loyalty and respect—Trust, admiration, loyalty and respect. So I'll ask my seminar attendees, "Do you think you'd make more money if people trust you more?" The answer is yes. "Do you think that you'd make more money if people admired you more?" The answer is yes. "Do you think that you'd make more money if your employees and your clients are more loyal to you?" The answer is obviously yes. "Do you think that you'd make more money if people respected you more?" And the answer is yes.

So how do you gain trust, admiration, loyalty and respect? Well you do it through four correlating character traits and The Art of Influence is not so much about persuading other people like what do I do? What do I say to you to get you to buy from me? It's really at a deeper level. It's what will I do to myself so that you want to do business with me, so that you're attracted to doing the business with me, so that you're attracted to buying from me?

And the way you do that is, in order to gain trust, you have to live a life of integrity. And so, if people think that you're going to lie to them, then they're not going to trust you. If people think that you're not honest, they're not going to trust you. If people see that you do one thing one place and another thing another place, they're not going to trust you. They see that you say one thing, one place and another thing in another place they're not going to trust you.

So, what it means is that you can work on yourself and work on your integrity and say I'm going to be a trustworthy, honest person with integrity. And when you make those choices about the way that you're going to live your life, other people are going to see and they're going to say, "I trust that person."

How do you gain admiration? I believe that we gain admiration by being positive, optimistic people, and it starts with the words that we use. It starts with the way that we talk from the very, very basic level. Somebody comes in and they'd say, "How are you doing?" And they just asked a simple question, "How are you doing, today?" And you say, "Well, pretty good under the circumstances," you know. Nobody wants to be with you if you're under the circumstances. Nobody's ever going to go, "Hey, you're under the circumstances, can I come under there with you?" "No, he's under the circumstances, let's get out of here."

The fact is that people want to see people who are overcoming and they're positive and they view life as something that they can win at in spite of the circumstances. I have a friend of mine, he used to live in and just sold it, a $9 million house, and the first time I ever met him, we went over to his house. This friend of mine brought me over there and he gave me his business card, so they called me in a couple of days and started to talk about doing some business and I go, "Okay."

So, I called him a couple of days later and he answered the phone and I said, "Hey Dave, how's it going?" He said, "Man, if I wasn't any better I have to be twins and I'd be somebody else, I'd be jealous of me." And I go, "Okay, if that works for you." And obviously, I did, he's quite successful, but somewhere between "another day, another dollar," and "If I wasn't any better I have to be twins," you know, somewhere in that continuum, we have to find our own unique personality where we are going to project a positive, optimistic person.

You know, if people are listening today, we have some people who are introverts. If they were to walk into their office and start talking like Tony Robbins, people will say, "Whoa, what happened there? What happened to him?"

Be yourself, but ask yourself and listen to yourself, what am I saying? How am I talking? What am I projecting? Yesterday I put on my Facebook page if people want to join me they can go to Facebook.com/ChrisWidenerspeaker. I put on there, there are two kinds of people, the kind that brighten the room when they walk in and the kind that brighten the room when they walk out.

And the reality is that there's a lot of people who brighten the room when they walk out. People go, "Man, I'm glad that guy left," because all they do is talk about, "Hey, how's everything going?" "Whatever, it's terrible. The economy sucks and the Republicans are bad," you know, there's whining about life all the time and people don't admire people like that. They admire people who are optimistic, who can see the best in the world around them.

And so, I always encourage people; make sure you're talking positively. Make sure you're thinking positively. Make sure that you're reading people positively. You gain admiration from people.

The third one is loyalty. How do you gain loyalty? You gain loyalty by serving other people, by considering other people's interest more important than your own. I was just speaking in Gothenburg, Sweden and I was speaking to a network marketing company. It was a company that give away a car when they reach a certain level. They'd get a car and different companies have different rewards that they give, and this one just happened to be cars.

There's a whole bunch of cars sitting over there and it's up on the side of the stage and I said, "How many of you would like to get that car?" And, of course, everyone went "Woo-hoo, I want that car." And they're focused on what they can get for themselves and I said, "Okay, let me ask you a question. Instead of just thinking about how I can get my car, what if you said I'm going to help five other people get their car, would you get your car? Would you get your car if you help five other people get their car?" And of course, everybody said, "Yeah, absolutely."

And it doesn't matter if the company you're in gives away trips or cars or cash bonus. They've done that if you can get a $50,000 on cash bonus in your company, great. Help five other people get their $50,000 cash bonus and guess what you're going to get? You'll probably get $250,000 cash bonus or if it's a trip, you know, if you can help 20 other people get a cruise and you're going to get a cruise, they'll probably put you in a suite.

So, it's about focusing on other people and when other people realise that you're out to help them, that creates this bond of loyalty. They're like, "He helped me get something out of life." And it always reminds me of that famous quote my mentor, Zig Ziglar, it's one of his most famous quotes, "You can have anything you want in life if you help enough other people get what they want in life." And that's really what it's all about.

How can I help a lot of people get out of life what it is that they want out of life? And, you know, we talked about footballers. A lot of people, they want to go on a Saturday night and watch just an amazing game of football and paint their faces. I've seen your European crowds. I've seen how you guys do it. You guys are way more out of control than us, Americans, and we always think that you Brits are the stodgy ones. I've seen those European soccer matches, flags waving and faces painted and people going crazy, and they'd love that, and they're willing to pay money to go do that.

So, if you can become a great footballer and you can help 50,000 people or 100,000 people go out every weekend and have a blast at the game, you help enough other people get what they want out of life and you get what you want in life. And it doesn't matter if you're selling ice cream or books or network marketing or football. It doesn't matter. The more people you help, the more you get back, and most people are just living like this, "How can I get what I want out of life? How can I get what I want?" They got this tunnel vision and instead of thinking how can I help other people get what they want in life? And that creates loyalty.

Then the last one is respect. How do you gain respect? You gain respect through excellence, and if you can just take your life and increase excellence a little bit more at every single level, in your spirituality, in your emotional state, in your intellectual state, in your physical presence, in the way you communicate, in the way that you relate to other people. If you can take that game up a notch or two or three or four, and create a state of excellence in your life, then other people will be attracted to you. They're going to seek you out and they're going to respect you.

I'll give you simple analogies. If you want to lose weight, do you go to the big fat guy and say, "Hey, what are you eating? What's your diet like?" No, you'd go to the totally robust people and go, "Hey tell me, how do you eat? What do you do and what's your regiment?" or regime?

If you want to get rich, do you go to the guy who stands on the end of the off ramp with the little card board sign that says, "Will work for food," and pull up and roll down your window and say, "Hey, tell me your secret?" No, you'd go to the guy that's made millions of dollars in real estate or network marketing or building big businesses.

If your marriage is falling apart, do you look for a couple that fights all the time and say, "Hey, can we get together and you can teach us how to do it?" Or do you go to the couple that's been married for 40 years and say, "How did you last? What did you do? How did you make it through the hard times?" Excellence attracts.

And so, when we hold up the mirror and have people look into it, we just ask, are you living a life of excellence? And does that attract other people? So, you gain trust through integrity. You gain admiration through optimism. You gain loyalty through service. And you gain respect through excellence.

Craig White:

I see, amazing really. These characteristics are obviously key attributes to be successful, key attributes in leadership and positively influencing in other people. And that's what you've been doing for years now. From your personal journey, these kinds of four characteristics, is there any others that you felt are things that you've acquired. I know you've spent a lot of time with Jim Rohn and as you said, he very much took you under his wing and before he passed away, he was certainly very proud of what you had become and what you had to offer moving forward to the future, and I know you said and you spoke of that, and obviously, you had a chance of working with Zig Ziglar. Is there any other lesson from these great guys that has helped shape you in becoming the person that you've become?

Chris Widener:

You know, at the top of my head, I'll tell you a couple of things. Nice guys finish first. There are a lot of jerks in the world and people can point to the jerks and say, "Oh, look at him, he made a bunch of money." But, you know what? Making money doesn't tell me that you're successful. It tells me you learned how to make money. And by far and away, most of the people who I've met and I know billionaires and successful sports stars and you name it, successful people in all the industries, and most of them are pretty nice people.

Most of them have realised that it doesn't pay to be a jerk. I mean, for every Kanye West, there's a few other guys who are pretty nice guys, right? There are some bad people who make it, but most of the people who succeed long-term are nice people. They're good people and that's why they succeed because business isn't done in a vacuum. Business is done face to face. It's done working with people.

You know, Kanye West can be a jerk because he just puts a song out and people download it. He doesn't have to interact with people. If his interactions were any indicator, he probably wouldn't have made all the money that he makes because he doesn't seem to be the kind of guy that people can really get along with, but I might be wrong, but that has been my perception as I've seen. But most people have to do business interacting personally, and so they have to be nice; they have to be forgiving. They have to be patient. They have to be kind. They have to be gentle. They have to work with other people and people aren't perfect, and certainly we aren't perfect.

And so, when you're doing business in the real world, as opposed to big music stars and things like that, it can be done from a stage, or in a recording studio, you really have to be good people. And that's one of the things that I really realised about Jim Rohn and Zig Ziglar is they're just terrific, kind people. And it was a great illustration for me to see that they were humble people, they were kind people, they were good people. And I want to tell people now, I want to be the easiest speaker you've ever worked with. And I cannot tell you and I focus on that, on being very, very easy to work with when people bring me in to speaking engagements, and I tell them that. I want to be the easiest person you've ever worked with.

I cannot tell you how many people come to me after they hired me and the event is over and they'd say, "You know what? You told me that you want to be the easiest speaker that I ever worked with and I'm telling you, you are the easiest speaker that I've ever worked with." And then they'd tell me horror stories of famous people who they demand all these, just purely little things that really have no bearing on whether they can do their job or not. It's more on just to prove their own self-worth and stuff like that. I see it all the time, you know, a lot of famous people and behind the scenes they're not necessarily the greatest people.

So, that's one thing, and then I want to really tie one thing up, a question that I get asked a lot and that is, "What's the skill? What's the number one skill that I have to learn?" The number one character trait is integrity, but the number one skill is communication; to learn to communicate because, again, you have to do business with other people. And to do business with other people, you have to be able to communicate.

So, to me, it's really important for us to understand that we have to learn how to communicate concisely, clearly, passionately, so that other people get it. So they learn, so they grow, so they understand, so we connect, so we build rapport, and all these kinds of things.

And so that takes practice and it takes learning how to communicate more effectively.

I encourage people, to take a public speaking course at a local community college or take a creative writing course at a local community. These are usually very inexpensive, a few hundred dollars, usually at a community college or something like that. Or Join Toastmasters. Toastmasters has places all over the world where you can go once a week and meet with 10 or 15 other people and learn to speak more articulately and those kinds of things.

So take a drama class, I mean, really break out and take like an impromptu comedy class or something, anything to help you learn how to communicate more effectively that's going to stretch you and grow you and teach you how to do these things. It's a really good idea to learn how to communicate more effectively.

Craig White:

It's just being sincere, being honest and being true to yourself, and as you said, putting other people first. From a people skills perspective, I supposed, it's something you can read and study, but it takes a lifetime to master. I have a vibe or feeling about people skills and I think if you're honest and you care about other people, it's the beginning, the foundation of having good people skills and building rapport with people, showing an interest, genuinely caring about others. Like you said about Zig Ziglar, positively influence other people's lives and in turn, you'll positively influence yours.

Chris Widener:

Yeah, the word that I use all the time is authenticity. It's real, if you watch one of these pawn stars shows, these shows on TV where people go in and they try and sell something to a pawn shop or something, and occasionally they'll bring in a ball autographed by a famous player or something. And what's the first thing that the pawnshop wants to do? They want to authenticate it. They want to make sure that it's real because the value is in being real. The fakes aren't worth anything, but the authenticated baseball or bat or letter with the autograph, that's worth a lot.

And I think that's what people are really looking for and, frankly, as our society has become more educated and more in tune, people can sniff out a phoney a lot easier than they used to be able to. And people who've been burned a lot, and so they really are looking for authentic people, and that's what I tell people--to be authentic. Be yourself. Be a voice, not an echo. Do not try to be somebody else.

I learned this lesson early on my speaking career. I was watching some videos. I think it was the 2001 General Weekend Leadership Event and they had a couple. There are a number of speakers there, but one was Jeffrey Gitomer and one was Jim Rohn. And Jeffrey Gitomer, you know, he's a New York Jewish guy and he's just hard charging and straight talking. He's just an aggressive speaking kind of guy. I thought, "Man, it would be great to be a speaker like Jeffrey Gitomer" because people love Jeffrey Gitomer, I mean, "Man, look at him. He's amazing."

And then the next speaker was Jim Rohn who was very soft-spoken and he would take his glasses and he'd put them down and he'd talk like this and then he'd pull his glasses off and he'd give you these little bits of wisdom, and I thought, "Boy, wouldn't it be great to be like Jim Rohn," you know, wise old man. And then what I realised was Jeffrey's successful because he's being Jeffrey and Jim is successful because he's being Jim. And I'm going to be successful by being Chris, not by trying to be a fake Jeffrey or a fake Jim or a knock off of Zig Ziglar or a knock off of Tony Robbins. Chris Widener is going to be successful by being Chris Widener. And you're going to be successful by being yourself and the people who are listening to this are going to be most successful when they're being authentic and being themselves instead of trying to be somebody else.

Craig White:

Yeah, I love that. I certainly believe everyone's got something special inside them. They just, more often than not, I mean, obviously yourself, you had a rough upbringing and there was events that allowed you if you're going to the church and being influenced by your male role model, to change your thinking.

Tony Robbins talks about the power of association. It's something that made a huge difference in my life over the last 12 years and I just think, sometimes, that you can get people to understand that they can make the choices, they can associate with like-minded, positive, optimistic, hungry individuals, you know, honest people. At the same time, they're so much accessible now. You don't necessarily have to be in that environment. You can choose that environment through audios, books, YouTube. You can almost influence yourself with your choice because there's so much out there. There's so much so that people can discover themselves, and what's within through that association.

Chris Widener:

Yeah, you know, Charlie Tremendous Jones, I don't know if you remember Charlie or ever heard of Charlie. He was a contemporary of Zig Ziglar and Jim Rohn. He passed away a couple of years ago. He was the most amazing personality I ever met. You ought to just look him up and watch some of his videos.

Charlie Tremendous Jones, he was an amazing guy, just a big booming, amazing personality and Charlie, he used to say that in the next five years, you will become the product of the books you read and the people you hang around with. And, of course, you could say the audio books that you listen to and the YouTube videos that you listen to and the people that you hang around with, and Jim and I, in the book 12 Pillars, we talked about your associations and there's three categories. And this is what I teach in my seminars as well.

Now, that Jim has passed, there's three categories of association. One is expanded association. These are the people you want to expand your association with. These are good people. They're win-win people, they're mutually beneficial and they can teach you. You can learn from them. You can help them. They can help you. You want to expand that relationship and that association. You want to spend more time with those people.

The second one is what we call limited association and that is the people that you have to have an association with, but you have to limit it or they're going to drag you into the depths of despair. This is like a crazy brother-in-law, you know, the guy that you have to have over for Thanksgiving and Christmas, but you don't have to have him over any other time because he's just a bad dude or whatever, or the lady in the cubicle next to you who just whines about life all the time and the whole extent of their life is the 12 cats she lives with and all this kind of stuff, right? You'd limit that association. You have to work with them but you're not going to the crazy guy down the hall at work and say, "Hey, let's go to lunch three days a week." You're going into the meetings, you have to be in with that guy, and then you're staying away from him the rest of the time. And this doesn't mean that you have to be mean or anything like that. You just extract yourself from the relationship and you limit it to what is required.

And then the last one is disassociation and this one's the hardest for people and that means you just disassociate with some people. And, again, you don't call them up and go, "Hey, I made a decision. You're a jerk and you're out of my life because you're horrible and I'm good." You know, I'm not suggesting that you have to be mean-spirited about it, but it does mean that you have to disassociate with them.

I realised that a lot of people are friends by convenience. They're friends of convenience and why am I friends with them? Well, because I've been friends with them since high school. Was he good to be in a relationship with? Probably not, he's going nowhere and he's not doing much. "Well, why are you friends with him?" "Well, because I've been friends with him since high school." Okay, that's a friend by convenience and you need to let go, and it's okay to let go.

If he's going in a different direction, that's fine. Let him go in a different direction. It's like I live in Seattle and if you'll look at the United States of America, if you'll look at a map, we're in the upper left hand corner. Straight down from us, along the coast, is Los Angeles. Straight east from us, for the most parts, it's almost directly east, but if you were to go east, is Chicago. If I'd get in a car and I'd say, "I want to go to Chicago." I have to get on I-90 East and that's my choice; I'm going to Chicago.

If somebody else meets me and says, "Hey, I'm going to Los Angeles." I'll say, "That's great. You can go to Los Angeles but I'm on I-90 East. You need to be on the I-5 South." Go to Los Angeles, it's totally fine, you're a terrific person. Love yah, have fun. Best of luck to you, but I'm not going to be in the car with you because I'm going on I-90 East, you need to go on I-5 South.

We need to take that mentality and look at the way we're living our lives. Where am I going? Am I going to abundance or am I going to wealth or am I going to difference making? Am I going through an extraordinary life? If so, I don't want to be in the car with the people who are going to scarcity, who are going to drama, who are going to broke relationships. I'm not going to be in the same car with them, the same way I wouldn't be in the car with somebody going to Los Angeles if I wanted to go to Chicago. And that's the blunt reality.

And a lot of people, you know, most people who are listening to this, you're nice people and you're going to go, "Well, I don't want to break up with him. I don't want to not be friends with them anymore." Okay, that's fine, circling to that to what we've talked about in the past, but it's a choice.

Who are you going to hang around with? And the people who you hang around with are going to determine to a great degree what kind of person you'd become. Now I've become pretty successful in my life, but you know what? I'm one of the least successful people in my circle of influence. I love being the least successful guy in my circle of influence. I love having friends who I think are smarter than me, richer than me, better than me. You know why, because it means I'm moving up. I don't know why they hang around with me. It's like I want to hang around with people who are better than me and I don't want to hang around with people who are going to drag me down.

Now let me just give a paradigm statement here because sometimes people mistake what I'm saying. They'll say, "Do you mean we shouldn't help the poor?" "Do you mean we shouldn't help the downtrodden?" No, I'm not saying that at all. We should help the poor. We should help the downtrodden. We should help people who suffered injustices and things like that. But, we don't make them our colleagues. We don't put them in our inner circle and ask them to influence us.

So we can have a relationship but it's a relationship where we're mentoring them or we're helping them or we're being charitable to them. We're not viewing them as peers and colleagues who speak into our life and have an effect on what kind of life we live. It's an important distinction there.

Craig White:

Yeah, I think it's that association, again, what you are talking about that some of the people we spend most of our time with and it just gets me thinking as well. I love the fact that you're obviously very successful but your circle of influence are at the next level. But I suppose that helps you aspire and learn and associate with people maybe where you kind of want to keep growing and keep it coming and keep giving and keep influencing.

Chris Widener:

Yeah, one of my best mentors is a very successful real estate investor and I knew he had a lot of money and I didn't know how much until he ran for the United States Senate and he had to discuss his financial situation and they were on the front cover of the local newspaper. I looked at the newspaper that morning and I said, "$50 million," and I told him that and I said, "You're buying lunch next time, pal."

Well, I want to hang around with guys that have a lot of money and they're not giving me any of their money. It's not about, "Hey, will you buy lunch for me?" It's more about people who succeed and achieve those things. They've achieved certain things in their life and they have the right mindset. They have the right actions. They have the right discipline. Those are the things that I want to incorporate into my life.

Craig White:

I really get that. Chris, I really, really do appreciate your time and I'm sure all the listeners have gained great value. We have listeners from every walk of life all over the world and from people that study, people that are entrepreneurs involved in traditional business and I think these characteristics you've talked about and these traits to be successful and positively influence other people, well, are certainly transferable from any success in life. So, I'm really, really grateful. I thank you very much for your time on this Monday evening or Monday morning I think it may be for you.

And just for people that want to connect with you, Chris, where is best for them, if they're not already connected, I'm sure many are, but for those that aren't connected with you or maybe coming across you for the first time, where is it best for them to connect with you?

Chris Widener:

Well, the first thing I always like is to give people something for free, so I got a free video. It's about 23 minutes long. It's on how to influence and persuade other people, which if you're in sales or leadership, you have to get. And in order to get it for free, you have to go to this address. It's www.widenerleadership.com/chris. That will take you to a landing page. It will give you the free one. On Twitter, you can reach me at chriswidener, it's @chriswidener. And on Facebook, you can go to Facebook.com/chriswidenerspeaker. And then, of course on the web, just chriswidener.com.

Craig White:

That's absolutely fantastic. I will certainly make sure that this web link for this free video is on the resource on the website as well.

Chris, I thank you very much for your time. I hope you have an absolutely magical Monday. I'm very grateful and I'm sure the listeners will really appreciate your time as well, so thanks again Chris and wish you a good day.

Chris Widener is widely reccognised as one of the top speakers in the world today. He has spoken all over the world in places like Germany, Spain, Russia, China, Egypt, Singapore, Australia and of course, all over the United States and Canada. Chris speaks to groups as small as 100 and as large as 25,000 people. His clients are a "who's who" of American businesses and organisations, including notables like General Electric, Cisco Systems, Microsoft and the Harvard Business School. Chris' dynamic, practical and engaging speeches will have your audience laughing one minute and learning timeless truths of success the next. Chris was hand selected by two of the legends of the speaking world to work with them and he now carries on their legacy. Jim Rohn, one of the most successful speakers of the last 50 years, and also known for being Tony Robbins first mentor, made Chris his last protege and worked with Chris the last seven years of his life. Chris and Jim co-authored the Jim Rohn One Year Success Plan as well as Jim's last book, The Twelve Pillars, which has become an international best-seller.

www.chriswidener.com

CHAPTER 2

How To Be The Best Version Of You

What does 'living the dream' look like to you? A successful, thriving career? Supporting and spending time with your children? Maybe leaving everything behind for a blissful home in the sun. Well, Adele has achieved ALL of the above, and is about to share with you the secret behind her success.

Discover how someone with no confidence or self-belief learnt to unleash their entrepreneurial spirit to eventually become an influential author in personal development. Specialising in helping people deal with unwanted shyness, Adele is a firm believer of staying true to yourself, and teaches people exactly how to use their undesirable attributes to their advantage – without needing to alter themselves in any way.

ADELE'S PASSION FOR INSPIRING OTHERS IS WHAT SHINES THROUGH THE MOST, SO DON'T MISS THIS AMAZING OPPORTUNITY TO SOAK UP HER KNOWLEDGE.

Craig White:

Welcome and hello again, I'm Craig White. This podcast show is proudly brought to you by Passion to Succeed. I'm stoked today, I'm so excited to have such a wonderful lady on our show. Do you know, at the beginning of every show, I'd just like to ask you a question, and a question for you I have is: How do you keep true to being yourself, yet developing into becoming much, much more? You see, on today's show we have a fantastic lady, Adele De Caso. Adele is a wonderful mother to three great children and her husband Jaime, if you can count him. She is a successful entrepreneur, a two-time successful author of *Shy People Can Be Successful Too, and 52 Tips to a Fantastic Year!*

As well as being a sought after international speaker, Adele is a prime example of how you balance your life, you balance your mission of contribution and living the dream with her family in Spain and experiencing all the great things that this abundant life has to offer. I'm really stoked, as I said, and I'm really happy to have Adele with us today. Welcome to today's show, Adele De Caso.

Adele De Caso:

Hi, Craig. Yes, it's absolutely fantastic to be back. Yes, the weather is great. I'm in Spain at the moment and I hate to tell you, but the sun is shining and it's very, very hot.

Craig White:

I'm always forever jealous, yet inspired by your adventure and your opportunity that you've created to live the dream in Spain with your journey. Tell us a little bit about your journey, Adele. Knowing you as I do, I know a little bit of where you're from, what you've achieved, the challenges you've gone through, and the lifestyle you live, and how you continue to work hard on yourself and having an influence. But, for our listeners, for people that maybe stumbled across the show for the first time or for people that even know you, that have connected with you in the past, tell us a little bit about yourself and about your journey.

Adele De Caso:

Okay. I'd love to. Going back to when I was a child, I was always really, really shy and lacking in confidence. That sort of stayed with me until I was at school and college, even university. After university, not really knowing what I wanted to do—and I didn't really have any sort of major careers in mind, to be honest with you—so, I started a job in a hospital in a laboratory. To be honest, I didn't really enjoy it that much. I did make some nice friends, but I didn't really enjoy the job. I was sort of, constantly looking around me for other opportunities and luckily, an opportunity did come along the way for me to start a business based from home. Which I still work today and I love that business with a passion.

What the business did for me, was not only give me this extra income, I eventually built up to a full-time income, so that I could leave the job that I didn't really enjoy, which was fantastic. But, as well as that, it also gave me the introduction to personal development, which is something I've become really passionate about over the years. Because I read so many books at university and college, I sort of got fed up of reading and I didn't really want to pick up another book if I didn't have to. But, when I got introduced to this other form of reading it was like, where has this been hiding? I was into it straight away and it just became eager to get the next book and the next book.

It was all about how to live a better life and how to become a successful person. Just generally, be a better person. Me and Jaime both got into the personal development thing and the first set of tapes we ever listened to was a set by Jim Rohn a guy from

America who just had these really, really fantastic philosophies on how to live a great life. That's where it all started. Over the years as I said, I just read more and more, went to different events. There were lots of events put on by the company that we were working with and we just met successful people and wanted to just, increase our level of success.

So, I got to the point where - I mean, all along the way I was building my confidence as well. Which was great and it got to the point where I had to give a talk on stage in front of a few thousand people and I thought, it was something I never thought I would be able to do. Because of all this development that I was doing, it actually went well as far as I'm concerned, anyway. I don't what the audience thought, but I enjoyed it. It was after speaking on that day that I just, somebody asked me, oh what are you going to do next? I said, I'm going to write a book and it was just, it just came out of the blue really. I just thought yeah, I really want to write a book just to show what's happened to somebody like me who could never ever dream of doing that kind of thing. From what I went from. The kind of person I was before I started out.

I thought surely, there's got to be other people out there that were like I was and they could learn from this, too. So, I just decided I'd put everything I knew and everything I learned into a book and share it with other people, so that they could have the same experience as me because looking back, I was always ambitious. I always had that entrepreneurial sort of, spirit in me but I never had the confidence to pursue anything. That's why I thought, there's lots of people out there that also have that and they can benefit from knowing what to do with it. You know what I mean? Just knowing how to go about it and how to push themselves forward a little bit.

Yeah, the first book came along. It's very, very sort of, a simple and easy to read book and so is the one that follows because I feel that's important for people who have never been introduced to personal development before. The books are really easy to read. You can just pick them up, read a couple pages, and put it down again if that's what you want to do.

Craig White:

I agree. Having read both of your books and I remember when you brought out your first book, *Shy People Can Be Successful Too*, which I guess is the message that you're sharing with us now about how you never thought you'd be able to deliver that talk on the stage or even become the success that you have and work for the successes of the future. I guess, success is different to every one of us and we'll probably talk about that. I know in the book, *Shy People Can Be Successful Too*, and to discuss first, it is a very simple read. It's a very strong read. What I mean by that is it is simple to read, which is great, but it has so many strong points of focus in there. One of them I love. You talk about how to remain true to yourself.

Adele De Caso:

Yeah.

Craig White:

Which, I think is really important. I think sometimes people say, well I'm happy with who I am. I don't want to change.

Adele De Caso:

Sure.

Craig White:

Well, it's not necessarily changing who we are, is it?

De Caso:

No, not at all. It's being you, but enhancing that you so that you're the best version of yourself that you can be. One of my messages is I even think people should embrace whatever they are. Whether it's shyness, whatever it is about them because a lot of people have some things about their personality that they feel is stopping them. Whatever it is about your personality, that is you and that makes you unique. So, you should embrace whatever that is and for me, it's embracing the shyness and that's what I try to sort of, get across to people. If they are shy, they should not try and get rid of that at all. They should just embrace it and use it to their advantage because shy people have a lot of good qualities that they can bring to the table in business. I really feel that that's important that you don't actually start trying to change who you are because you wouldn't have been made like that. Do you know what I mean?

If you were meant to change, you wouldn't have been the way you were to start with. Then there's lots of things that we can do to just make ourselves a better version of ourselves. So, that's what - I do concentrate on in the book. All the little skills that you can put to use, just to make sure that you put across the best self that you are. If that makes sense.

Craig White:

Yeah. For me, totally. I just hope that more and more people can understand and actually be proud of the attributes that they have, but do take on this philosophy of learning more, to become the very best version of yourself. What a great way to put it and even have - there's a quote. Maybe people should get this all around them. The very best version of yourself because I think you're right. People do have I guess, that internal magic within them. A passion, a purpose. I guess like the rainbow, we need all the colours just like we need all the personalities to make them glow.

Adele De Caso:

Exactly. Yeah.

Craig White:

Obviously, you're a successful lady. What does success mean to you now? I mean, you've been successful in business. You've been successful in developing yourself. You've been successful in bringing up your children. I know that they're very young and I guess challenging, and fun, and everything that comes with being a mum. But you are a successful lady. A mum-trepreneur, an author, and I guess I am trying to get some of the things that you're passionate about. Maybe habits that you feel highly passionate people possess. What springs to your mind? What are you passionate about? What keeps you on song? What keeps you in the game, kind of contributing and wanting to continually learn and become more? What are you passionate about?

Adele De Caso:

Okay. I'm still to this day, really passionate about learning. Just learning about how to be a better person. How to be a successful person and also, sharing what I've learned. That gives me great satisfaction. Coming across information that I feel is beneficial to me and then sharing it with everybody else. So, that is a big part of what I do. To be honest with you, I spent quite a number of years because I read lots of books and they were all saying, find out what your passion is, what is your purpose, what were you put here to do? To be honest, I think I spent quite a lot of time - I don't know about wasted time. It's probably wrong to say that, but I kept thinking, there's something out there that I'm meant to be doing.

Even when I'd written the books and everything, I kept thinking there's something else there. Actually, it was right in front of me. It was staring me in the face because it was the fact that I'm absolutely passionate about learning about other successful people and what they're doing to create that success. Then I'm passionate about sharing what I've learned with as many people as possible. That's where my passion lies and what I'm going to do, what I'm working on at the moment is putting together a course to share more knowledge with people. Again, showing entrepreneurs that perhaps, want to make a difference in the world but don't really know what is the next step. They're too shy, lacking in confidence to go out there and do something about it. So, that's what I'm working on at the moment and that's what I'm really passionate about.

The other thing I'm passionate about is just taking a little step back and just enjoying the moment, living a great life. The kids grow up so fast. You know what it's like. Children grow up so fast and it's all about spending time with them now and just creating as many memories as we can with them, while they're still young enough to want to be with us because they're growing up. The eldest one's starting college in September. It's just really important to me now, that we spend as much time as a family as we can. That we do make every day count and some part of every day is enjoyable in some way as a family. So, that's really, really important.

Craig White:

Yeah, totally. I think it's getting that balance. Which is what I mentioned earlier about how you've got that balance of contribution. When you were talking earlier, it just reminded me of how so many successful entrepreneurs, millionaires, billionaires, leaders, other authors, people that are the very best of the best in the game. I heard someone say recently, being the best of the best, but no better than the rest. What a great concept. They always talk about learning and contribution, and making a difference to other people. That's what you're doing. You said you're kind of looking for your calling. Which I guess, we'll talk about a little bit later. You were looking for that purpose, that reason why. As you said, you stumbled across it, but you're almost doing what I guess is true to contribution. It's almost giving value without need of compensation. It's about doing it because you love it.

ADELE DE CASO:

That's right.

CRAIG WHITE:

You can hear that in your voice, Adele. It's just, it's very inspiring. How did you manage to - because you know what? Everyone in life comes up with these goals, these ambitions, things to do, lose weight, get fit, eat better, drink less, run more, spend more time with the family, write a book, or succeed in this area in life. For me, one of the habits of successful, passionate individuals is passionate people learn to prioritize and focus. Within your busy schedule of running a business, running a family, and also learning and developing, how have you become a successful author? How have you managed to produce two fantastic books in, I guess such a short space of time? How have you managed to stay on track and actually, almost deliver the goods, so to speak?

ADELE DE CASO:

Okay. I was very, very fortunate with the first book because it was the first time we'd actually come to Spain. So, we came for nine months the first time. The children were in school from 9:00 AM to 5:00 PM every day. Which was slightly different to how it works down in this area, but I had sort of, quite a lot of time to put into that. It still needed to be prioritised. I did still need to set aside time, which I did, so that I wrote a little bit every day. Probably spent an hour a day on it. Then got the sort of, the basics of the book together during that nine-month period. However, then it got put on the back burner for a time after we returned from Spain because our third child came along. We got even busier than we were. Having three children.

So, yes. It did get put on the back burner for a short while. But then again, when I took it back up again when the little one was sort of old enough to go off to nursery, I gave myself a deadline for the book. I said, right, we can spend so long on things. You've got to give yourself a deadline. I gave myself a deadline. I think it was about a three-month period and I decided that every Wednesday that I was working on the book and that was all I was doing because it is easy to get distracted when you've got lots of things going on. You've got perhaps two or three different business things going on. I know a lot of people, deal with multiple streams of income. So, people are juggling lots of different business.

If you can just set aside time for each one at some point during the week, and it's in the plan and nothing else gets in the way of that, then that's how that I feel that it works. For sure, it works for me that way. Yeah, Wednesday was book day and that involved in the morning it was writing, so it was sort of getting the final writing together. Then in the afternoon it was dealing with anything else that needed to be dealt with on the publishing side. It was ringing printers and ringing about the ISBN numbers, for example, and things like that.

Whatever there was to deal with the book was done on that day. I managed to complete it for the time that I said just simply because I prioritised it on that day and nothing else got in the way. I was reading a book from a lady that's successful and she was saying the same thing. She got children, if ever the children were at nursery, she'd be doing the housework. She found herself hoovering or putting a wash in or something. Somebody turned around to her and said look, when the kids are at nursery, that's when you spend time on the business or on your work because the cleaning can be done at any time, can't it? The household chores can be done at any time. Your time to work on that business is there and now so, you've got to take advantage of that time.

Again, it's prioritizing. Not letting anything get you distracted. That's why I find, even now to this day, I don't work in the house if I don't have to. I go out and I work in a coffee shop because I know that if I'm there and I'm concentrating on the task at hand, then I'm not going to get distracted by things that need doing in the house. There's nothing worse than sitting there writing and looking at a pile of something that needs to be done. Whether it's dishes that need to be loaded into the dishwasher or a washing that needs to go in. It's distracting. Whatever it is, I need to get out of the way and just do it when I'm on my own and nothing else can get in the way. That's where I work best and that's what I recommend to people.

Craig White:

I totally agree. I think when you're working at home, sometimes people think that working from home it's about being stuck at home. It's actually about your base is at home, but getting out in the environment. I sometimes go and sit by a lake not so far away from me. It's a rowing lake., surrounding by woodland and nature. There's a hotel, a bar and restaurant there, though I can sometimes just go drive down there in my car and even just sit in my car if the weather's not great because it's just a different and empowering environment. It's an environment without distraction. It's nice to get out in nature. I think when we're in motion, it helps us to find that motivation as well.

Adele De Caso:

Yeah, definitely.

Craig White:

As you move forward, there was some key principals in your book and there's some really great techniques in there. I guess, what I want to talk about is some other things that are happening because I think if people can make a commitment to get both the books. *Shy People Can Be Successful Too*, because there's some really basic, great focus techniques in there. The fundamentals, if that's even the right word for people to follow and start to work to implement in their life. Then your second book is almost giving people a tip a week.

Adele De Caso:

Yes.

Craig White:

Well, it is a tip a week. They just get the chance to read them all at the same time. However, it's a fantastic way for people to really get some foundational, personal development in place and start to maybe find out what their purpose is or discover it by just being in that environment. With your course, what are the key kind of areas that you're looking to concentrate on? Is there anything in particular that you've discovered or you feel now that's focal to peoples' success?

Adele De Caso:

Yeah, there is. I've come up with sort of, the four key areas that I believe helped me a lot and that sort of, split everything. All the different parts of the course into these four areas. So, the four areas basically what I feel. Generally, for people, anybody that wants to be successful but more importantly, for people that are coming from a shy background, I feel. These are key for me. The first one was confidence. Building up that confidence and belief in yourself, that you can do what it is that you set out to do. The second is just a few simple communication skills. I mean, people think it's a really sort of, hard thing to become a great conversationalist or that they've got to be able to deal with people, it takes a lot. It's actually a few simple things that you need to know.

I do talk about communication because if you want to succeed in business, you have got to be good at communicating. Although these days, obviously with technology, it's a lot easier. Just some key little things about how to deal with people in there. That's things that I learned, just from dealing with people in my business and giving little testimonial talks and then presenting the business to different people. It's just little things that I came across. I then talk about your calling. Like I was saying earlier, what is it that drives you? What is your why? What is your reason for doing it and just talk a little bit about that. You have to search for what you believe is the real reason that's what you're meant to do. It's all about just looking a little closer to yourself and finding something that you actually, you love doing. That could well be your purpose and your reason why. So, we talk about that.

Then the last thing is developing a consciousness for success. It's just about getting your head right and getting the right mindset for success because that's something that again, it's one of my major passions. It's mindset because I think somebody with the right mindset, anybody can accomplish anything. I really do. That's the four key areas that we talk about and it all takes the form of different little things. Some will be videos, some will be little key exercises and worksheets and things for people to go away and do. So, yeah. I'm really excited about it all.

Craig White:

Right. It sounds really exciting. I think that consciousness for success is more often than not, sometimes the missing element. Isn't it? I guess in a way that almost the philosophy of, I guess slightly different but a same sort of principal is people win the national lottery. Usually within a couple of years they completely skint. It's that philosophy if you shared out every penny, dollar, dime, yen, euro, whatever, equally to the human beings on the world, eventually they'll end up back in the same pockets because people have got a consciousness of wealth. They've got a mindset of wealth. They've become worthy and I guess they know what to do with it. I think sometimes people can be working hard.

It's when to put that blood, sweat, and tears in. Maybe be great at communicating. Maybe know what our motivation is and maybe even having an element of confidence as well. Which, I can see why they're all really vital. That consciousness to success, I think can sometimes be the trigger getting the mindset right.

Adele De Caso:

Yeah. I think you're right. Definitely.

Craig White:

Again, that sinks in to actually be successful. Sort of mind, body, and soul before it happens.

Adele De Caso:

Yes, because if you've got the right mindset, then you'll perform the action in the right way. You can have people doing the same actions and if they aren't, they aren't isn't doing it with the right frame of mind and the right attitude, then they actually will have different results depending on who's carrying it out.

Craig White:

Yeah, totally. It's about being true to yourself. Isn't it? Being the greatest version of yourself and just having good values, contributing to others without need of compensation, as you said. Doing it because you love it. Which is really, really cool. What are you up to for the rest of the day? It's been an absolute pleasure talking to you. What are you up to today? Don't tell me you're going to the beach [laughs].

Adele De Caso:

That's tempting, actually. We did that last night. We went to the beach at dusk. So, beautiful. It was just a really nice time because it's so hot now during the day. It's nice to go to the beach at night time when it's started to cool down. So, we did that last night. I feel that might be a possibility today.

Craig White:

Hey well, you deserve to be living the dream and enjoying yourself, Adele, for your consistent contribution. I do hope everyone's enjoyed today's show. I guess, this wealth of knowledge from yourself and people can connect with you at your website, adeledecaso.com and this course sounds really exciting, so I'm looking forward to hearing more about that when you're ready to launch. Thanks again. It's been great to have you on the Passion to Succeed Show and I'll look forward to speaking to you soon, Adele.

Adele De Caso:

Thanks, Craig. I think it's a great thing that you're doing with this as well. So, well done.

Adele de Caso was born in Staffordshire in1972. She embarked on a career with a network marketing company when she was 24 and is still involved in that business today. She thanks the business for introducing her to the world of personal development. Adele was very shy growing up and never believed she could be successful, however she found personal development to be fascinating and studied the subject so much so that she made a transformation and went on to enjoy success in lots of areas. In her first book, Adele shares with readers how she made this change using some simple ideas and techniques that she discovered on her personal development journey.

You can buy both Adele's first book Shy People Can Be Successful Too! - How to achieve your dreams without changing your personality, and her second book 52 Tips For A Fantastic Year! - Simple Ideas Big Impact on her website www.adeledecaso.com

To receive your copy of Adele's free ebook, 'The Top 10 Things That Hold Shy People Back From Achieving Success' go to www.shypeoplecanbesuccessfultoo.com

To find out about Adele's new course 'Success Formula For Shy People' go to http://adeledecaso.com/courses

Facebook
https://www.facebook.com/adele.decaso

Twitter
https://twitter.com/AdeledeCaso

CHAPTER 3 The Mindset Of A Billionaire

When faced with adversity, are we programmed to accept the future that is laid before us or do we build the foundations we believe we are destined for?

Inspired by the success of his father and with the support of his loving wife and children John Rochon Jr is determined to positively influence those he meets by sharing his own personal story when he too was at the depths of despair. For John failure is not an option, he is testimony that with the right attitude, determination and work ethic you too can influence people around you.

IN THIS PODCAST JOHN REVEALS HIS RECIPE FOR SUCCESS AND THE LEGACY HE WOULD LIKE TO LEAVE BEHIND FOR THE NEXT GENERATION !!

CRAIG WHITE:

Welcome and hello again, I'm Craig White. Our show, as always, is proudly brought to you by Passion to Succeed, and I'm feeling passionate today. I'm buzzing, and I've got a question for you listeners? What's your culture for success? What environment do you find yourself in? What is your environment that you're in and you look to create for success and influence on a daily basis? I'm buzzing for today's show, and we have a truly inspirational guy, a guy that has a wealth and background of success, a billionaire in business and a billionaire in contribution. Today, we have a show with the fantastic guy, Mr. John Rushton, Jr.

Now, for me, John is most certainly the blueprint for success. I've been very lucky to have partnered with John and spent some quality time with him all over the world, to date, and this guy gives ownership, his leadership, his focus is about giving ownership. He gives power to the people, bringing them together as one force, as one family, and stepping out of the way, and side by side. Now, for me, that is true leadership. So, welcome to today's show, Mr. John Rochon.

JOHN ROCHON JR:

First of all, it's a pleasure to be with you. Today I'm actually in Seaside, Florida, a place with probably some of the prettiest beaches in the world.

CRAIG WHITE:

Wow, there's somewhere I've still yet to visit. My personal experience of the U.S. at the moment is New York, which is a beautiful city, and then Miami which is just mind-blowing. I went there and decided I need an apartment in Miami. But Florida and going to that Seaside area and that part of Florida you were talking about, I think would be a fantastic achievement. So, you're talking to us from the beach, then, John?

John Rochon Jr:

I am looking at it as I speak. It's gorgeous. There is a storm rolling in but it's beautiful to see it against the sun. Absolutely gorgeous.

Craig White:

John, as I said, I've spent some time with you in a few different countries around the world, getting to know you a little bit. I believe, like myself, you've had an amazing family around you. My first meeting was actually with your father, prior to meeting you, John Rochon Sr. Do you know what bizarre thing I remember, and it'll always stay with me for the rest of my life, because for me, people skills and leadership and feeling valuable and also making others feel valuable was really important.

I'll never forget that the day I met your father when, from a simple handshake, the guy took my breath away, made me feel warm, and you know, it's just amazing, really how a simple action can actually almost hand over power. Not power, maybe that's the wrong word, but just make you feel welcome, make you feel warm. Since then, I've learned a little about your family, the values you share, the culture that I mentioned previously, the environment that not only you create and contribute to, but like me, you were born into such an empowering environment of "John, yes you can." Tell us a little bit about your environment. I know, as I say, of you contributing and creating this environment and taking it to a new level, but tell me a little bit about your life and what's engrained some of your key philosophies and values.

John Rochon Jr:

Well, I think that's probably the most important question you can ask anybody. For me, it's always intriguing to see and hear the stories of where people come from, successful or on their way to being successful. So many people look at not having successful parents as a potential hurdle in life. I actually embraced it, and when I say my parents were and are successful but not only were they really good parents, but they were hard-working and have taught all their kids that hard work is in the core of being successful. But, with my dad, who is my inspiration, he's who I look up to, who I pattern my daily life after, how he treats people and how he cares for people, that even if he's known them for one second he treats them with dignity and respect. I learned that because my father was never home when I was growing up. He was always working, he was going around the world, but his system was to call me every day, check in, listen to me, make sure that my childhood stories were not falling on deaf ears. My dad was a phenomenal father even while he was travelling. And that really is what I've carried on. A lot of people ask what it takes to be successful, and it really takes people wanting to be connected to others and really loving the story and loving the people behind it. I think that's a part of what works for us, is we are one family, and instead of trying to be better than my father and my mother or whoever, I actually stand on their shoulders and hopefully represent a next generation that images the perfect imagery that they would want, and would make them proud.

Craig White:

Knowing you as little and as much as I do already, I think your family will be certainly proud of the leadership and the contribution and also the legacy that you're carrying on and creating, and as you say, taking to a next level. From my perspective, I don't know if it's the correct terminology, but I've got fantastic parents and the same values were impressed upon me. I always felt that you have to contribute, you have to be genuine, you have to work hard, and treat people as you wish to be treated, so to speak. You know that philosophy, do as you would be done by. For me that's been foundational in my beliefs and my environment. But I guess some people aren't, in a way, as lucky as us. They're not always born into a strong environment, but it's learning that actually you can choose to change your environment, as well.

John Rochon Jr:

There's no doubt about it, and I think it's about training yourself to be happy. I do believe that some people are genetically happier than others, but I believe that people have to work at it. It's not a rainbows and sunshine world that we move in, and it does take effort, just like the relationships will take effort, to be happy and to make others happy. I see it everywhere I go. I have enough happiness to go around the world, it's just who I am, I think it's a part of my DNA, and I'm happy to share it with whoever needs it, but that's my belief, the world has a chance of being the most peaceful place that we know of. The only way to get there is to have connectivity, where people are relentlessly happy and relentlessly cheering others on. I see it every day and that's why I can't stop. That's why I travel the world almost every day of the year.

Craig White:

John, I love that. You know, it's very rare nowadays, that people are showed appreciation, that people are told they're fantastic. You know, even just going out the way to hold the door open for someone. Something as little as that, a little act of compassion, I think really does make a difference. It's funny you mentioned the rainbows and the sun. My youngest, Alana, recently drew me a fantastic picture of all the colours in the rainbow. In fact, it was on a full sheet of paper and she's only four. And then, she also drew a little sun and a little rain cloud, because she said to me, "You can't have a rainbow without rain and sunshine." It's so true, and it's that contrast. We're always looking for the silver lining and the cloud of doubts, really, always looking for the sunshine past the rain.

You mentioned about you being a happy soul, and I've seen that, and I've felt that myself, and I've been in that environment, but recently I was with you in the UK and you were sharing a story to thousands of people, about how you made a choice to be happy. Do you know what? Through the adversity I guess you went from, can you maybe share that story with us and give people a little bit of an insight into maybe your challenges at an early age, but how you chose to be happy, and in your DNA you almost created that happiness.

John Rochon Jr:

You're right. You know, we talk about my family inspiration, but I think a lot of who we become is a learned reaction to the world that we live in, and when I was four and a half, moving towards five years old, it was Mother's Day weekend, Friday before, and I had a gift for my mother. She was there at the school to pick me up across the street, waved at me, I got so excited, as a five-year-old, or four-year-old would do, I promptly ran across the street and got struck by a car going 40 miles an hour. I bounced off, I think, seven or eight cars, broke every bone in my body, and when I say every bone, it was just pretty much every bone, and that experience of the ambulance to a few months later getting out of the hospital, changed my life forever.

It was a week into my hospital stay. I was told by a doctor that the chances of me walking again were very slim. My pelvis was completely crushed, destroyed, pulverized is the word they used, and they said, "You know if you never walk again you're going to have to learn how to take care of yourself." During that period of time, I also had to relearn how to speak. I did form a speech impediment at the time, I've obviously worked my way through that, but I really had to learn how to live again. And, a week into my stay in the hospital, after multiple surgeries, I was told I was going to get a hot bath. And I cannot tell you, after a week of pain and not having a bath but then all of a sudden having one, it was one of those tiny little moments where I realised at a young age, I'm going to be happy for the rest of my life. It can't get any worse than this, and it can't get any better than a hot bath.

So, at the beginning of that experience—the story needed a much longer story, but, to summarise it, I did learn how to walk again, I became a world-class soccer / football player and world-class baseball player. And it turned out that the accident that pulverised my hips and pelvis, actually turned out to be a good thing because I ran faster than any hawk on any team because my hips were not connected, and you know, just every experience like that in my life, when I get knocked down, that experience has taught me to get right back up and do better than I did the time before.

You know, we started this interview, this talk, this fun time with family, and what's interesting is, even when my baseball career was coming to an end, I was blessed by meeting my wife, we've been together almost 20 years, we have 2 wonderful children, and I was at the tail end of what I thought I was going to do for the rest of my life. I thought I was going to be a professional baseball player. I was well on my way, hit a road bump and it turned out to be the greatest blessing that has ever happened to me.

One step by one step, I've gone from a little kid dealing with some things that you should never have to deal with, watching other people in your hospital room pass away at a young age. I was in the hospice area of the hospital and so my new friends would leave me for good on certain days, but you learned to appreciate the new friends who would take that person's place the very next day. When you deal with that at such a young age, what else can get you down? Right? Yeah, life is tough, but you keep going.

Craig White:

It's great to hear you say that, because I think tough times don't last, we've all heard this before, you know I think it's what we focus on. Sometimes people focus on the depths of despair, and their focus will probably take them there, but I think when you're happy, when you're looking to contribute, when you're looking to influence happiness, it's about that philosophy of giving value without need of compensation. Doing it because you love it, and you can always hear in your voice that you love to share that happiness. As you've already said, you love travelling, you love sharing, you love connection with new people. From an early age, you were in a fabulous environment. As you said, your dad's your mentor, somebody you look up to, somebody you follow and look to make proud. I know your dad was instrumental in massive business growth for the family, and you're sort of taking that on and taking it to a new level.

For people that are looking to be entrepreneurs, for people that are already entrepreneurs or already know their business or looking to learn something new, what would you say would be your summary of your system to success. There must be some key areas of focus that you feel really make a difference. What you've learned, what was passed on to you, as well. What you've cultivated. What would they be, John?

John Rochon Jr:

Well, it's a long list, I have to pick my top few. I would say you really want to be able to embrace failure, understand and learn from it. Never make those mistakes again, but you have to make them. You have to like everything, you can learn from pain, and pain imprints memory, so without failure you're never really going to understand what it takes. But a daily regimen for my life—I barely sleep, I always claim it's because I sleep so well, but I only sleep four to six hours a night, I wake up every morning with a checklist, and I always write it down. I don't trust my memory, so I write it down and put a little box next to it and check it when it's done. It really is an attention to detail, the ability to finish projects is perfectly correlated to your ability to focus on the details necessary to complete the task, and in many cases tasks become irrelevant.

You can be halfway through and you can say, well, it doesn't seem like this one's really important. But out of practice and repetition you have to finish each project, because even if it ends up being one that is not as fruitful as others, you quickly find out that over time—this is an extremely important thing that I've learned, when you are a charismatic leader, not 100% of the time do you truly understand how many people are watching you and watching your work ethic and watching your attitude. And combination of work ethic and attitude are the two most contagious attributes of charismatic leadership. And it's one that is learned—people watch you. They want to see if you get angry, they want to see if you finish your projects, they want to see if you are everything that they see, and it's unbelievable, but people learn by your behaviours, so when you do everything to completion and some are more successful than others, that's just how life is. But if you are consistent and you stay on top of it, you complete each task with everything you've got, then what's going to happen is one day you're going to wake up, and look behind you, and you're going to have an army. You're going to have an army that will do whatever is needed to make this world a fantastic one.

Craig White:

It takes all of us to make any one of us successful, I guess, doesn't it? The power, the refined appreciation of the all of us.

John Rochon Jr:

There's no doubt. And you know what, just sitting here listening to you talk, everything you and I are talking about is how you and I became friends. Right? We came from two different places in the world, but we shared so much. Our beliefs, our love for people, our belief in love for the growth of others is a relentless thing, and I think that's what brought us together, our common goal of making the world a better place.

Craig White:

For sure, I think our collective mission to continue to do so as we look to develop business and foundations worldwide and influencing the many. You know, it's funny, I know you travel the world and you come from, obviously, the U.S., and you know a huge country. I was listening to something the other day and someone talked about how small the U.K. is, and it just dawned on me, the influence that's possible from my early stages of my life, going back to when I started working as an entrepreneur and started learning to contribute, and connect with people, and look to make a difference, look to leave every encounter with a positive vibe, and that kind of element of compassion.

It just dawned on me how big the world is, and sometimes peoples' thinking is smaller than what it should be, because you know what? We can change the world. Even with an act of compassion every day, compounded over time, following your leadership, my leadership, and other great people that are looking to influence people in a positive way, and look for peace and look for togetherness, look to create an extended family. You know, it's got to make a difference, John. It has to.

John Rochon Jr:

It is. And you see many times in—there's enough support, in life, even sovereign states much like the U.K. is dealing with now with your recent vote, you find out who your true friends are. And even competitors, like many of my good friends are my competitors, and I cheer them on as much as they cheer me on, but together we all make a huge difference. It is tangible. You can travel the world and see all of our work, hard at work. The villages in Africa and the well foundations that we're involved in. Or it's delivering clean water throughout the outskirts of China. We've seen that work. We talk about it only because we want everyone to become involved, but we're not the only ones, and that makes me extremely proud.

CRAIG WHITE:

So? you're involved with quite a few companies in different areas in different parts of the world, and from an entrepreneur I know you're leading them with passion and purpose, you know. I know recently a company was named after you, JRJR networks, and I just think that's fantastic, and it shows appreciation. But knowing the object of your contribution on another level as well looking to make a difference, for me that's something I want to get involved in and take to another level to get involved with contributions, to help in schooling of people who are underprivileged and under appreciated in many parts of the world.

JOHN ROCHON JR:

Call it reality, in that you and I can talk about the secrets of success, but that is reality. There are communities, there are countries around the world that desperately need our help. Yes, we make a significant amount of money, and I was always taught in my family and we teach in our companies that the only reason we make a lot of money is so we can give it all away. And we can really make a big difference in this world, and there's no better feeling than the reality. There are people out there that desperately need our help, and you never know. You absolutely never know—the more people you help that need it, they grow up. They become lawyers, they become future charismatic leaders, and it's amazing how they come back and try to help or get engaged with what I'm doing today. And a lot of them I've never even met, but they'll write letters, they'll say they joined one of my companies out of respect, and like I said earlier, it's an army, it's created in different ways.

CRAIG WHITE:

Yes, it's amazing. You're the second person I've ever heard mention that about earning money to give it away, and saying it with such sincerity, because I remember not so long ago—amazing how things come around so quickly. I can't remember who it was particularly but you're certainly the second person who said that and it's along the lines of what's the point of knowledge and money if you can't give it away, because that's what you do with them. That's fantastic. All this influence you're having around the world. One of the proudest opportunities you have to influence, I guess like your father and your mum have had with you, or you and your wife get to influence your three children to be their best in their quest. You know that must feel fantastic, John.

John Rochon Jr:

It is, and everything we talked about so far today, it applied to family. I have three kids, 14, 11 and 10 years old. They're so different, as many of them share that dynamic with our kids. One needs more in one category than the other. The one thing that I know that we deliver is a loving family atmosphere where hard work does pay off, you do not have to be perfect. The t-shirt that we wear at family reunion says, "The journey to be perfect took longer than I thought." That's a t-shirt we always wear because none of us are perfect and the ability to embrace that in each other and cheer each other on. I do think, you know, I'm a little biased, but I do think my little family is pretty special, and the ability to take them with us on our travels and see all of our hard work paying off, our foundation work paying off, is kind of what life is all about. It's why we're here.

Craig White:

True. John, I remember, actually, the first time you and me spoke in Birmingham, the U.K. I remember you telling me a story. It was about your eldest, your 14-year-old managed to somehow, with his friend, get on a flight to—was it to California? Was it South Florida?

JOHN ROCHON JR:

Actually, it was to where I am now. It was a year ago, about this time.

CRAIG WHITE:

I remember you telling me this, it's so difficult, there was that communication and they had monies to fly, and there was that element of you couldn't really be angry with them because you were proud they had the guts to do something like that. To jump on a plane, that's fantastic. Having that guts comes from having a gutsy family, a gutsy father, someone that's leading the way.

JOHN ROCHON JR:

Well, I appreciate that, and since this is recorded, my wife will be really mad at me, but you know, I was so proud, because he—everything I was taught, he was taught, to be self-sufficient, be able to take care of yourself. Not necessarily get on a plane and fly halfway across the U.S., however, he got there safely, got to where he needed to be. Oh my goodness, I hope he doesn't listen to this.

[laughter]

CRAIG WHITE:

It's just kind of fantastic, isn't it? He had the strength and character and guts to do that. John, I know you're a really busy guy and I think the guys are listening to this show and will stumble across our show in days to come I think are really going to enjoy listening to another really passionate guy that's passionate about contribution. One thing. What, for you as an individual, what is the heart of all you do? What is the passion? What is it that really keeps you up late, keeps you making your checklist? Keeps you contributing? I know that's probably a big question, but what is it?

John Rochon Jr:

Well, I would say those moments on the stage where someone has come from the very beginning, fought their way to success, and it's the first smile that I see when they come onto the stage, of how proud they are of their hard work. And I just feel like I played a tiny part in that. I'm kind of a junkie when it comes to that, not being on stage, but being up there with the true winners in life and the true people that actually make it happen. I don't know if I could ever replace that. Maybe with my kids someday graduating from high school or university, maybe having their own kids someday, but just the ability to watch people grow, into independent business owners, where they now control their futures. It's just a priceless moment.

Craig White:

I hear you, John, I really do. I think I'm—how old am I now? 38, 39, and do you know what? I grew up and I thought I was quite tough and strong and do you know what? It's that emotional connection that when you dream together, you work together, you play together, you achieve together. When you're seeing people, just as you're explaining, that smile, that sense of satisfaction of being proud of their achievement, I find myself welling up. I'm like what happened to this tough guy of the past? But it's emotional and emotions is where we truly connect with people.

John Rochon Jr:

Right. It's the proof that the soul exists.

Craig White:

Thank you, John, I'm really grateful you've joined us on the Passion to Succeed show today, and I'm sure the listeners will be looking to connect with you at JRJR to see what it is you're doing, seeing what your mission is, and I'm certainly pleased to have met you and to class you as a friend and I'll look forward to share a glass of wine on that beach with you someday. Have a great afternoon. Love to all of your family, and thank you very much for your time today. It's really appreciated.

John Rochon Jr:

Thank you so much. Anytime.

http://www.jrjrnetworks.com/

THE JRJR NETWORKS STORY

JRJR Networks is a unique portfolio of direct-to-consumer companies, led by an experienced management team, engaged in a long-term process of acquiring companies in this sector and maximizing returns for shareholders.

We define direct-to-consumer as any business selling products or services through a fully- commissioned, independent sales force, straight to customers via relationship-based selling rather than through retail stores, supported by the power of Internet support tools such as individualised e-commerce web sites.

Its chairman is John Rochon, a long-time pioneer in the direct-to-consumer sector. Mr. Rochon recognised that the industry was ripe for a dramatic new step. In September of 2012, Mr. Rochon launched his strategy of making JRJR Networks a platform for multiple direct-to-consumer companies, each of which would keep its own brand identity, leadership, compensation plan, product line and culture.

CHAPTER 4

Go For No 'What's your 'NO'tivation'

Show Notes:

Imagine never fearing failure or rejection again. Imagine feeling totally free to go for your goals while happily embracing whatever the outcome may be. Nothing holding you back. This can be you! In this podcast, Andrea is going to tell you exactly how she achieved this kind of freedom and how you can do the same!

In a world where everyone wants to hear 'yes', Andrea explains why you're statistically more likely to hear 'no', and more importantly why this outcome is something you should welcome and get excited about!

Using Andrea's simple formula will save you time, effort and energy, all while eliminating the unhelpful fear associated with rejection. Prepare to banish your limiting beliefs for good!

Craig White:

Welcome and hello again. I'm Craig White, and this podcast show is proudly brought to you by Passion to Succeed. I'm really excited today, really, really excited. I've got a fantastic lady joining us yet again. Andrea Waltz did a fabulous show with us a few years ago, now, and I'm really excited to have her back on the show. The feedback we got from a show that we published, it must be nearly three years ago, was just absolutely sensational. I know you guys are going to love connecting with Andrea as I am. I've got a little question, really, I guess to you to ponder and consider while we get started with this show. How do you take rejection? How does it make you feel? And what kind of impact does it have on your life?

You see, I'm excited today because the lady we've got on this show is the coauthor of a fabulous book, a book that I've recommended and shared with hundreds, thousands of people that I work with called Go for No! Yes, Is the Destination, No Is How You Get There. Along with her husband and business partner, Richard Fenton, Andrea has made it her mission to liberate people from fears, fears of failure, fears of rejection, and I believe they've opened and shared an entire new mindset about hearing the word no. Your failures are what make your story extraordinary. Today, I wish for you to discover the insights and mindsets of this amazing lady and to empower you to embrace and accept failure on your journey to succeed. So, Andrea, welcome to today's show.

Andrea Waltz:

Hey, Craig. It's great to be with you.

Craig White:

Fantastic, likewise. As I said, it's an absolute pleasure to have you back. The show we did last time when I had some amazing feedback and it's just really good to contribute and have you back again. Where in the world are you guys based? I know you're based in the States. Whereabouts, actually are you?

Andrea Waltz:

We've lived all over the United States, but right now we're based in Orlando, Florida. I know a lot of people in the UK are probably familiar with it, because it's the home of Disney World.

Craig White:

Yeah. My girls keep reminding me. They're four and eight now. They're getting to that age where I think it's going to be a year or two, I'm going to wait for the youngest to get a little bit older, and then we'll definitely be there. We're a world without borders, though.

Andrea Waltz:

Exactly.

Craig White:

What inspired yourself and Richard to coauthor and write the book, Go for No? What was the motivation behind it all?

Andrea Waltz:

We launched our company so long ago now. It's almost hard to believe, almost 20 years ago now. Our mission was to teach businesses, at that time, almost more corporations, our sales and management and customer service philosophies. We would do half-day workshops and full-day workshops. Of everything that we would teach, the one message that resonated with people the most, that people just loved, was this idea of "go for no". So, we went a couple of years doing our different trainings and working with companies. We would go in the back room sometimes at certain businesses and see posters and messages that say "go for no", and we said, okay, this really is a brand. It really is a great message, so we should really write a book about it. That is what started it, listening to our customers really tell us that that's what they loved. We decided, though, instead of writing your standard book, nothing wrong with instruction, but we really loved fiction writing. So, that's why we decided to put it in a fable format so that people could get a story, be entertained, but also get the important lessons which are in Go for No!

Craig White:

Totally. You know what's interesting and fascinates me, obviously, listening to you? Obviously, from a sales training environment and gaining that message of "go for no", to be instructional on that and to give people tips and advice, but to turn that into such a successful fable, for me, you've got to have some imagination, some focus, some real skills to go from just the philosophy of the "go for no". But really to get a phenomenal message across like you did in the book and throughout the story is really embracing that way forward as part of the journey.

Andrea Waltz:

Well, thank you. It is a challenge, but we know that stories resonate. In any business, in any industry, especially entrepreneurial endeavors, I think people love to hear stories of somebody who was struggling, since we all struggle, we've all failed, but somebody who got an interesting lesson was able to turn things around and become more successful. I think we were able to tap into that, and that's why at events, having people who can share their story and say, this is where I was, this is what I did, and now this is what has happened, is so powerful. It doesn't even have to be that it's our story. You can influence other people just by sharing those stories that you hear at events, which is so powerful.

Craig White:

Yeah. I remember learning something years ago, facts tell, stories sell, so to speak. For me, on my personal journey on personal development, and I guess for a lot of people, having a fable as powerful as the "Go for No story", it can almost be for some people a great entry level for them to realise that actually personal development can really be life-changing. I think sometimes when reading instructional books, I think the power does lie within a story, as you said, without a doubt. So, everyone loves the word yes. We all love to hear yes. We all love to smile and be pleased, to get the results that I guess we desire, which is more often than not when we get a yes. You've obviously done workshops and trainings and you coach people on an individual one-to-one basis as well. How do you coach people to adopt this mindset, this "Go for No" philosophy and gain the same love for the word no as we all have for the word yes? How do you coach that?

Andrea Waltz:

Right, right. It's not an easy task, Craig. It really isn't. One of our things that we teach people, first of all, is the fundamental philosophy which is, you have to hear more nos in order to hear more yeses. It's a philosophy that is based in statistics. If you want to be more successful, you have to be willing and wanting to fail, and convincing people of that can be kind of tricky, to teach people to go out and intentionally increase their failure rate, intentionally hear more nos. I'll give you a perfect example, and this is something that I've been sharing, it's such a good example for people to wrap their minds around, because we all have been taught and trained to live in that go for yes world, and this is one of the ways I show people the faulty way of their thinking. If you picture yourself having gone to, say, a networking event, and you meet 10 people. You have 10 nice conversations about your business and their business and you find out a little bit about them. When you go home, you think, well, I had those 10 conversations and let's say you got 10 business cards.

You got a business card for each person and you're all excited and you think, I'm going to reach out and contact each one of them. Well, what tends to happen in the go for yes world is, you look at those 10 cards and you start to maybe question and you start to make assumptions and you start to say, I'm looking at all of these 10 cards that I got, and I think that actually, these five, and you pull out five of them and you say, these five people, I think they would probably say no. They weren't as interested or excited in my business and in my products as I think they should be, so I'm just going to set those aside. Now, you have five cards left and you start thinking a little bit more and you say, out of these last five, three people were mildly enthusiastic. They seem kind of interested in my products and services. So, I'll set these aside and I'll maybe call these people. Then, you have two left and you say, okay, these people, we had great conversations. They seemed interested in my products. They even seemed interested in making some additional income on the side.

So, I'm definitely going to call these people. Now, what you end up doing, you maybe call those two people. You don't reach out to the three that you thought were maybes. You don't reach out to the five that you pretty much thought would tell you no. So, what you've done is, you've taken all that time and effort and energy and relationship building, and you basically got rid of 80% of the people. Now, you just limited it to these two people. So, really, that is operating in a very limiting mindset whereas go for no, we say, hey, reach out to all ten. Yes, some of them will tell you no, absolutely. It's probably statistically just that way, but we don't know who. Most of the time, we're always prejudging and deciding what we think somebody will do or say. Craig, I think we're probably wrong half the time.

Craig White:

Yeah. I guess that list is that assumption, isn't it, that is, I said when you play the numbers game. It's really putting the odds against your favour.

Andrea Waltz:

Yeah, exactly. We play all these games. We've taken all these great conversations and now we've just really limited our opportunities. When it comes to coaching people about "Go for No, I tell people all the time, hey, you don't know what somebody's going to decide and do, what kind of money they have to spend on things. So, to the extent that you limit yourself and say no to yourself instead of letting say no to you is how much you're going to hold yourself back from your own potential and your own possibilities for success. Now, that said, that's the easy part. If I can get somebody to embrace that, then the next thing we have to work on is some of the fear and some of the other things that can hold people back.

Craig White:

It's funny listening to you, because you're bringing things out in my mind that I've been living by, and you often don't really realise it. One of the philosophies in the book, talking about the guy, you just mentioned or touched on it briefly, is when people have that buying limit. It's when he's in the shop and he gets the sale. Forgive me for not getting the story 100% correct. He gets the sale and he finished off there, because he didn't keep asking the guy, because he stopped selling when he reached his own internal buying limit. It's that philosophy of our objections are a reflection of our own perception. Just listening to you then, you made me realise that since reading your book three, four years ago, I've lived by that philosophy to always make sure that I'm never limiting my opportunities through my own limitations. So, thank you. I've just realised.

Andrea Waltz:

Yeah. What's funny is, I'm glad you said that, because you don't notice it sometimes until it's pointed out to you, and I think it goes both ways. People who do it naturally like yourself, because you've just learned through reading personal development and behaving that certain way over and over again has become a habit. So, you're not aware of it until somebody points it out and you say, oh yeah, that's right. I do that well. So, it's good.

Craig White:

For some people, obviously, maybe there's a required expectation of nos. It's probably challenging for some people. Does it get easier? I'm throwing loads of questions at you, but I'm just passionate about getting this message across, because for some people, it could actually be a little bit demotivating when they're getting a lot of nos? How do people, from a coaching perspective get with a mindset that maybe it does get easier, and actually, this needs to be a motivating factor rather than a demotivating factor?

Andrea Waltz:

Right, absolutely, and it can be demotivating, especially at the beginning when you're learning and you're building your skills. It's kind of this way where, especially when somebody's new in a business and they're learning. They're not perfect at maybe delivering the message, sharing about a product or something. So, what happens is, they avoid hearing the word no and they're playing the whole game a little bit small. We teach them, go out and start hearing more nos, and that can be really demotivating until they learn more and have an opportunity to test and build those skills. It really requires that people have that belief in themselves and the belief in what they're doing to get themselves over that hump. Sometimes, it's a hump and sometimes, it's a big mountain, because if you're getting a lot of nos and you don't see the light at the tunnel and the yeses are not coming.

You have to see value in those nos, though, and understand that you're paying the price of what it takes to learn how to get better. That's a really important nuance, Craig. I don't want anybody to think, oh, you just hear no all the time and nothing changes and you never get better. That whole idea and the big part of it is, yes, you're going to hear nos a lot, especially in the beginning. Once you get more skilled, you may hear fewer nos, although I could make the case, actually, you could then start going after bigger nos with bigger prospects. You have to have that belief and that faith that it's going to get better, and see that value in what you're learning. For example, you go out and you set a no goal and you say, I'm going to try to collect 10 nos this week. I'm going to ask 10 people to take a look at my business or to consider purchasing a product, whatever.

You get those 10 nos. Instead of just saying, all right, I got the 10 nos and that was horrible and I'm not motivated, you have to say, all right, what did I learn? How did I approach this person and get that no? Let me try something different. Let me try approaching somebody in a slightly different way. So, that is valuing that process and learning and then saying, okay, I'm going to keep learning from my top leaders and keep getting better. Eventually, you get over that hump. I know it can be tough. It can be demotivating, and that's really where that belief in yourself and the belief in what you're doing has to come in.

Craig White:

Yeah. I think there's always going to be the ups and downs in life. It's what we focus on, I guess. For me, it's character building as well. I think people need to go through the nos to become stronger and almost to become, I don't know if it's the right way of looking at it, but maybe better for when the get the yeses. So, when they get a yes, they deal with it with more passion and more service orientated focus, because they're not just devaluing the yes. It's got more value because they've actually really worked for it. Tell us about your five levels of failure. Where do they come into to play with this "Go for No" philosophy?

Andrea Waltz:

Absolutely. The five levels of failure, starts with number one, which is the ability to fail. That is where we all start. We all have the ability to fail. Most people, though, don't want to fail. They don't want to hear the word no. They don't want to make mistakes. They want to come into their business and everything go perfectly, and that's just not realistic, but that is where everybody starts.

Craig White:

It would be lovely, though, wouldn't it?

Andrea Waltz:

Yeah, it would be nice. I had a great sales trainer tell me once, we don't get paid for the yeses. We get paid for all of the nos. If it were easy, everybody would do it, and then nobody would be well paid because it would be so easy. So, you get well paid because of a lot of the rejection. Level two is the willingness to fail. So, level two is to be willing to hear more nos in order to be more successful, in order to get those yeses. Level three's really interesting and that's the wanting-ness to fail, and going to bed at night and saying, I didn't hear one no today. Nobody told me no and saying, I want to hear those nos. If I'm not hearing enough nos, I'm not really building my business. I'm not building my character, to use what you were saying, which I totally agree with.

So, wanting-ness to fail, as odd as that sounds, is so important, because it really leads you to success. The next two levels are kind of interesting, and we always get some laughs when we share this on stage. The fourth level is failing bigger and failing faster. It's going after those big nos. In some businesses, they call this the chicken list. You have the people that you're scared of contacting. So, it's go after that big no. Be willing to fail, be wanting to do that, fail faster. In other words, get as many nos as you can and as fast as you can. Then, level five is failing exponentially. So, it's really failing as a team. If you can get a leader who understands "Go for No and can have the whole team start hearing more nos, it's amazing what that team can do under that person's leadership. That fifth level is a leadership thing.

Craig White:

It's a process as well, when you're talking about that wanting-ness to fail, almost getting up and thinking, I'm going to fail my way to the top. As you said, wanting the nos because you know you're moving forward. I know I'm sidetracking slightly, Andrea. you mentioned the chicken list and we talked about that earlier when you got the 10 business cards out and removed 80% of the effort you've put in. You don't make that call because you presume and make the assumption that they're not going to be interested. When really, the barrier is the fear of failure, the fear of maybe getting a no. I'm sure you've looked into this. Why are people scared of failure? What's the growing concern?

Andrea Waltz:

You're so right. We have dug deep into this, this idea of why people don't like to have those nos. I think a lot of it just comes down to how we're all taught and raised. Some things are cultural. You have some groups, some countries, where you really have people who don't like the word no and don't want to fail at all, and it's really seen not as a badge of honour, but seen as an embarrassment and not something for you to be proud of. If you say, I've started a new business and somebody says, well, how is it going? And you say, well, I've talked to 100 people and 97 of them have told me no, you tell that to most people and they'd say, oh, my heavens. You're terrible, you should give up now. Of course, Silicon Valley, California, where they have the Apple headquarters and they're innovative and they're always trying new technologies, failure is seen as a positive there because it's all about how creative, how innovative, how many things they can try? I think a lot of times, it's just that background.

As kids, we start off so tenacious, so willing to be persistent and we don't have any problem with failing or looking foolish in front of our friends. Then, we hit teenage years and it's like, oh, gosh. What do people think of me? How are people perceiving me? Then, we hit adulthood and we say, okay, I'll start a business but I better succeed at it, and I better succeed in six weeks or this thing doesn't work. I saw the funniest meme on, I think it was Twitter or Facebook or something. It says, I just started a business a week ago, I'm still not a millionaire. This thing's a scam. It's like, okay. Not so much. You have to be patient. You have to take a while. One of the things that we teach is, give yourself permission to fail. Be that kid again, and don't expect the perfection, just like if you were teaching your son or daughter to ride a bike or when they're learning to tie their shoes. You don't expect perfection the first time. You know it's going to take them time after time, try after try. So, why would you expect yourself, especially when you're starting out new, to just pick everything up and be perfect at it? But I think that's what we do.

Craig White:

Yeah. I think having kids myself and looking to impress upon them this attitude of they can achieve anything, just to have the passion and the willingness to try and to fail and to get up and keep on going. Many conversations with my eldest, certainly over the 12 months as she goes into new arenas, stepping out of her comfort zone. I guess it's really powerful to have this kind of mindset and this philosophy that we share. For those maybe that haven't had that negative conditioning, I guess, what you're talking about, that final level of exponentially failing and having a leader or getting into an environment where you've got somebody that can lead you into that mindset. Or even, obviously, like yourself as a coach or having somebody as a coach to coach you and to really embrace that failure-success formula.

Andrea Waltz:

Right, exactly.

Craig White:

Moving on then. If you were coaching me, how would you coach, or maybe guide me practically to really embrace and understand this failure-success formula? Are there certain rules that you would look to follow for me? Or look to guide me down?

Andrea Waltz:

Yeah. That's a really tough one, and one of the things, that is different for everybody. We share the model that we share in the book. I really impress upon people not to just gloss over that model. The model is where you're in the middle, failure is on one end and success is on the other end. It's like we see these two things as choices. Oh, should I be successful or should I fail? It's one or the other. Really, the model, and we outline it visually, graphically in the book, which is you're on one side. The failure, rejection, hearing the word no is in the middle, and the success is on the other side. It takes some people some time to embrace that because I don't do a lot of one-on-one coaching, but I do guide people.

We have a Go for No challenge Facebook group that has over 1,000 members, and I'm constantly reminding people, you guys are always focusing on the result, and I'm just telling you to go out and execute a behaviour, which is go out and make a call or go out and message somebody on Facebook, whatever your method is, but you have to take that action and focus on the action rather than the result. That, I think, is a big way to help someone embrace that failure-success formula so that they're not always saying okay I'll go out and do it, but all I want is the yes. It's, let's focus on the behaviour and get you good at that, and then you will see that those nos and that failure becomes easier to deal with when you encounter it.

Craig White:

Brilliant! You mentioned behaviours and getting people to go out there and work in that behaviour model of that understanding the process. Having read the book, when you're talking about the visual model, I can see it in my mind's eye, which is just fantastic. I wonder, understanding a little bit about habits and habitudes and people's behaviour patterns that are maybe ingrained in them and they're developing out through guidance from your book and maybe through this Facebook group, etc., and other mediums. How do we stop people falling back into old patterns of life and maybe adopting that go for no philosophy for a period of time? Creating a behaviour but then falling back into, I really need a yes?

Andrea Waltz:

Oh, what a subject. Yes. If I had the recipe for this, I would be a multibillionaire, because that is the thing, isn't it? It's falling back into our old patterns, and I had a really interesting conversation when I was interviewing someone actually, I'm sure we'll probably talk about it in a minute, this next project that we're doing. He was telling me how so many people will come and they will say, tell me about your daily habits. I want to do what you do. What do you do in the morning? What are all the steps in your daily process? I want to model all of these things. Or, it'll be something like, how do I do this? How do I do that? This guy said, it's not about the how-to as much, and it's not about, well, what are my habits? He said, I can teach that all day long, and I teach and I teach, and I tell people, and then they don't do it. So, it really comes down to two things.

It comes down to reprogramming your mindset. In our case, it's reprogramming how you think about failure and rejection. Then, living that, and it's a constant reminder. It's constantly trying to not fall back into your old patterns. Then, secondarily, Craig, it's the vision. It's really having that vision of what you want, and I think people sometimes get lost because what happens is, they learn a new skill. They learn some skills, they learn a new mindset, but they're not focused on their vision and what they're trying to achieve. So, what happens is, they get off-track really easily. What I've seen is that the people that are really focused on their vision are able to stay in that "Go for No mindset for a much longer period of time and use it, and continue to use it.

I think sometimes, you need it more early on, and then the more skills you get, the more successful you will be, it just becomes natural and it becomes a habit. Like you were saying, I don't worry about what somebody is going to spend. I just ask. I just go for it. These things become natural, but in the beginning, they don't because people who lose track, lose sight of their vision. The mindset becomes so important. The vision becomes so important with any of these behaviours, whether it's "Go for No or any successful behaviour that you learned from any top leader in any company. It's, what am I trying to achieve?

Craig White:

Yeah. It's all about the motivation. I've heard you guys talk about the motivation. I'm so grateful to have obviously had some time with you again, and I'm sure the listeners of our show are really grateful to have you back, and I know, you guys are both really passionate about this "Go for No message. The book is fabulous, and I highly recommend it. If there's any of you that haven't come across the "Go for No philosophy or even this book before, then get onto Goforno.com, get onto Amazon, just get yourself a copy. You did the "Go for No video as well, which I thought was absolutely fantastic. Is that a year, or two years old now, the Go for No video? Because time now flies, doesn't it?

Andrea Waltz:

Oh, it so flies. Yeah, it's been a few years, actually. Our partner in the UK is Knowledge is King, and they have books and CDs as well. So, for those people on your show who are listening in the UK. I get a lot of people writing to us saying where can I get this in the UK easily, where I don't have to pay a gazillion dollars for shipping? That's our UK partner. The video, which was so much fun to make, it's been a few years now. We're working on new "Go for No things, but I always tell people, come to "Go for No. We've got tons of blog posts and videos and things for people to get motivated over.

Craig White:

Fantastic. Obviously, the book is very much the beginning, and so's the video as part of your "Go for No adventure. What are you guys up to now? I know you love to write fictional books and stories, which is something that you guys are very passionate about. Where to next with this Go for No adventure?

Andrea Waltz:

We're doing a Go for No book just specifically for network marketing, and that should be out first part of next year. We also did something fun, a motivational fable. Very American, though, about some American business icons called The Diamond Line, and we put that out this year. We also have a fun one called The Fear Factory, which is an audio book on Amazon. That one is all about a fable just like Go for No about a guy who learns how to embrace and overcome his fears. Where does fear come from? The Fear Factory is a place that manufactures and sells fear to the public. It's a really weird, crazy fable, but it's a lot of fun.

Craig White:

I have no idea how I haven't come across that. I will be checking that out when we finish this show. Hey, Andrea, I'm very grateful for yours and Richard's time and contribution to our show yet again. It's an absolute pleasure to have you onboard. Thank you very much. I hope you guys have a fantastic day today. I know it's relatively early morning for you. I really appreciate your passion about this Go For No adventure and this Go For No message. I'm sure the listeners will be as grateful as I am. So, thanks again, Andrea.

Andrea Waltz:

Absolutely. Thanks, Craig.

Andrea Waltz is the co-author of Go for No! Yes is the Destination, No is How You Get There. After hitting #1 on Amazon's "Sales" List in 2010, it has remained in the top 20 of all books on 'Selling' ever since. Along with her partner Richard Fenton, their mission is to liberate people from fears of failure and rejection, sharing an entire new mindset about hearing the word NO. Visit: www.GoforNo.com to learn more!

"Do you want to achieve success? If your answer is 'yes', then you need to get more no's. This book will show you why and how."
– Darren Hardy, Publisher, SUCCESS magazine
GO
FOR
NO!
YES is the destination
NO is how you get there
RICHARDFENTON & ANDREAWALTZ

CHAPTER 5

The Greatest Networker In The World

John Milton Fog's book titled "The Greatest Networker in the World" was published over 20 years ago. To mark the occasion John discusses the misunderstanding when it comes to network marketing business models.

In terms of business, John believes networking in the ultimate freedom. In this business, you can structure your approach, your daily methods of operation and your goals. All of it is totally up to you.

In this podcast John also share stories of his new book titled "The Greatest Network Cures in the world", the subtitle is twenty-one ordinary people who became millionaires in network marketing and the true stories of how they did it

John has been inspiring others for more than 25 years, so don't miss this amazing opportunity to soak up his knowledge.

Craig White:

Hi, everyone. It's an absolute pleasure today to have one of my mentors and inspirations. I'm mega excited about the guest we've got chatting with us today. In fact, you could possibly say it's my original mentor. Some years ago, back in 2001, the first book I was lucky enough to be handed to me by a good friend of mine called Robbie was The Greatest Networker in the World written by John Milton Fogg and it's John that's joining us today. He's been involved with the network marketing business now for well over 20 years. Sorry if that gives away your age, John, but I believe you've probably written one of the most well-known and influential network marketing books in the world, certainly in my life and the people that I'm consistently connected with. It's high on my recommendation list. So, an absolute pleasure to have you with us, John. How are you today? What's happening over in America?

John Milton Fogg:

I'm wonderful. It's distressingly chilly. It's April's 11th and we have weather that's behaving more like winter. So, it's time to break out the fleece jackets and put away the shorts. A week ago, it was 85 degrees Fahrenheit and shorts and a t-shirt and now it's freezing. It's very strange here. It's wonderful, the diversity. Tony Robbins would be happy.

Craig White:

Indeed, he would. It sounds very familiar to what we're experiencing over here in the UK at the moment. One week we've got beautiful glorious sunshine and the next week I've got friends up North that are building snowmen in their back gardens. But it's great to be in Europe. I've just disappeared off to Spain for a few days, got a little bit of sun, chilled out on top of a mountain, I suppose you can always get away, get on a flight and get off somewhere quickly, can't you, with this amazing business that we're involved in and the freedom that it offers. John, you've obviously been involved in the industry for 20 years. Was The Greatest Networker in the World the first book you wrote?

John Milton Fogg:

No. The old term for it is ghost writer. It's not a term I like because it's fairly disparaging to the person who's listed as the author but I've written books with John Kalench and other people before I wrote The Greatest Networker.

Craig White:

Oh, okay, fantastic. John Kalench wrote some fabulous books. Being the Best You Can jumps out straightaway for me. This book, The Greatest Networker in the World, I know it's a fable. I'm sure you were inspired by relationships and your involvement within the industry and I'm not sure how much of this, if there's any truth to any of the story from your life experiences but when I read it I just got the business, I understood the power of this industry truly I think for the first time although I'd been involved in the business for a few months. But this book really sent me on a connection with understanding the business and also reconnecting with my dreams but also on a journey of personal development. So, a massive heartfelt thank-you from me but where did you get your inspiration from this book? Where did it all start for you?

John Milton Fogg:

Oh, that's a great question that I'm really not certain how to answer, Craig. Up until the time that I woke up at oh dark thirty in the morning, made coffee, and jumped on the computer, I had a mental block that I could write my own book and that I could also write something that was fictional. Now, I heard an interesting radio broadcast the other day about a man who's written a book about writing books and one of the things he discovered was that so many of the authors that he was able to speak to, obviously, he couldn't speak to Dickens and Shakespeare and others, but the contemporary authors that he spoke to, many of their characters did not come out of thin air. They were based on people in their lives and they were massaged around to fit into the story that the writer, the author was doing. He made an example of Mario Puzo's Godfather and that in fact, that character was not based on Puzo's total imagination nor was it based on a Mafia don. It was based on his mother and The Greatest Networker in the World is like that. Just about every story, every scenario in there is based on a true character, a true scene, an event, something like that but I grabbed these different things, Craig, from different places in my life and stuck them together and wove a story out of that yarn if you will.

Craig White:

Wow.

John Milton Fogg:

And yarn, all puns intended.

Craig White:

Brilliant. So, what is it that you love about our business? I'm passionate about the industry and how it influences everybody and allows people to, I believe, connect with what's true to themselves and gives them the freedom but what do you love about our business? What is it that you're really passionate about because you're still really focused on providing great information for people involved in the industry? What are you passionate about so much in this business?

John Milton Fogg:

That list is more endless than this call can be.

Craig White:
I imagine so.

John Milton Fogg:
Off the top of my head, some things that jump out at me more than others, one is this is the only business model I'm aware of where you can do it the way you choose to do it. Now, that flies in the face of things like duplicatable systems, but it's a bottom-line truth. If you want to do this business and simply turn people on to great products that you've benefitted from, you can do that. If you want to do this business as a slick sales pro who for the last 20 years has been selling ice to Eskimos, you can do that. If you want to do this business throw them up against the wall and see who sticks, bam, bam, bam, dialing for dollars, you can do that. If you want to do this business as a spiritual experience, you can do that. If you want to run your business like an accountant, like a carpenter, like the CEO of a multinational corporation, like a small business, like an artist, like a restaurateur, any way you want to do this business, you can. Bottom line is does it work, does that work for you or not?

But any approach you want to use and I think in terms of business, that's the ultimate freedom and I don't know anything else where that's true. If you're a small business person, I mean, there are policies and there are procedures of course and there is morality and there are ethics. All of these things are so but they're so in life. In this business, you can structure your approach, your daily methods of operation, your goals, all of it. All of it is totally up to you. You can choose to be absolutely in love with the people in your business and you will not bring anyone in that you're not in love with and you can choose, right or wrong is not the issue. You can choose to just bring people in, sign them up, and never talk to them again. Any of that will work, I'm sorry, not necessarily will work but is allowed. It's permitted. It's even encouraged and I just think that is the most extraordinary thing about this business. It's one of the things that really puts it on the leading edge of free enterprise.

It's an extraordinarily flexible embracive business model, we don't care about your past successes, your failures. We don't care what your religion is, what your age is, what your sex is, your nationality. We don't care if you had an education or not, we don't care about any of that. Everyone is allowed in and everyone is given the same opportunity to succeed. What they make of it, that's their deal and that's another thing I love about it. This business allows you to discover qualities you didn't know you had. It allows you to aspire to values and virtues and skills you don't have now and to develop them here. Personal growth and development as a professional and as a human being are paramount in this business. I think they're required. I know very few people who become tremendously successful in network marketing who are idiots or jerks. I mean I just don't know them. I know they exist and law of attraction, I don't hang out with them but in this business, we have a number of axioms and clichés and they got to be those things, Craig, because of their truth if you will and this business, your business in network marketing will grow as fast and as big and as deep as you do as a human being and growth in this business is a requirement.

If you don't, you won't attract people to your business, you won't bring people in, it will not thrive, and probably won't survive because every time you click up in this business to another level and another level and another level, you have now new demands made upon you as a human being that you've got to develop and grow. Most people, most of us don't come into this business as -- there's an expression with people who train horses and it's called a made horse. A made horse is a horse that is comfortable with a saddle, that understands the commands that come from reins and the rider's knees, etc. That's a made horse. You don't come into network marketing as a made horse. You come into network marketing more often than not as a clean slate and if you come in with a whole bunch of stuff already on your slate, chances are pretty good that you're going to have to get out your eraser.

CRAIG WHITE:

Yep, it's amazing, isn't it really? Because listening to you sharing that inspiration I find is literally everyone that I've ever chatted to and read about and associated with that's been successful in this industry often looks back and one of the key parts of their journey has been this development of these skills, this aspiration to create new values. Obviously, Jim Rohn always used to talk about it's the becoming and listening to you then, it reminds me of the environment that I think sometimes we can take for granted, John, where we forget how empowering it is and I think often from my own personal experiences, the dreams I had as a child faded away over the years through the social conditioning of falling into the corporate job world environment, dog-eat-dog, being paid, what somebody else felt I was worth, your dreams start to fade away and then I think sometimes we can forget this empowering environment and this association that we have in this business of connecting with positive, like-minded, aspirational people, people that have walked the path, taken the steps to succeed, and are willing and that's one of the things I love. They're willing to spend the time with you, very much like you in this original book that I read, The Greatest Networker in the World, willing to build a relationship and spend time with people to help them reconnect with what as you said discovering the qualities that they already have and I think sometimes we forget that environment and actually it's probably one of the most empowering things I find about the business and actually the life that we have. Would you agree?

JOHN MILTON FOGG:

Yes, sir. There are so many other things, Craig. I know that I've dealt with more the soft side. On the hard side, bottom-line numbers side, I don't know what it's like in the UK right now. I'll bet a nickel it's not a whole lot different than it is here in the States or colonies as you may choose to call them or us but right now, the world of work is a mess and it's a mess because it's going through an evolutionary jump. What we knew as ways you could make a living in the past, many of them are gone. Many of them have totally disappeared.

I firmly believe that the answer for a tremendous number of people is network marketing. They really don't have a choice in another way to earn a living because we allow both part-time and full-time participation. This is the best hedge against the kinds of things that are going on in the job market, in the world of work today of anything I know. I think everybody should have a network marketing enterprise in their portfolio, multiple streams of income, whatever you want to call it. Also, if you have the desire, I've just written a book called The Greatest Networkers in the World and the subtitle is Twenty-one Ordinary People Who Became Millionaires in Network Marketing and the True Stories of How They Did It. One of the points of the book, Craig, is to prove beyond a shadow of a doubt that if you'd really like to make a great living in terms of money and all the rest, some of what we've spoken about before, the fulfillment, the satisfaction, the creativity, the lifestyle, all of that, I don't know where the heck else you can do that except in network marketing. I mean I am a very successful author. I've written two books that have sold a million copies. I should be rolling over rich because of my success, my reputation, the accomplishments I've made in the business of writing books and from books, I'm not rich.

Well, if I've had that success and I'm not rich and I'm not living the life, how can the normal, not super successful, blessed in this area or that human being, what the heck are they going to do? Well, in network marketing, they can do it. It's going to require certain skills, certain disciplines, and hard work, no kidding. It's going to require that and more but it's possible and I don't know where else that's possible. Where else are you going to do that? Working for somebody else? Working your way up a corporate ladder? Opening your own business? How many Richard Branson's are there in this world? Not very many. So, network marketing is this most equal of equal opportunities on the planet where anybody, no kidding, anybody. You look at the top echelons of all the network marketing companies and you will see people who absolutely positively when they started would never be there, never, not a chance in Hades and yet there they are, million-dollar income earners, multi-million dollar annual income earners. How did they do that? They did that because we've got such an utterly inspired business model that allows anyone to come in here and in American -- I don't know what you would say in cricket -- but an American, hit it out of the park, hit a home run, win the championship. You can do that in this business. I don't know anything else around where you can.

Craig White:

The business model, obviously, I'm in an agreement 100%, the model is second to none. There is the cliché of ordinary people achieving extraordinary lifestyles and I think your book, the follow-on, because obviously the fable of your original book and then going into 21 real life stories, it's very inspiring because you've got 21 people there that have gone from rags to riches and they've all joined the business from their own reasons but again with this business model, they've created phenomenal success and the opportunity is there for everyone and what better time in this current economic decline, the social environment that they're in at the moment, I think the business is just going to see a new point of growth, a new lease of life worldwide, any business, every industry or in this industry even. I've got a passion for coaching and leadership and if I go back to -- I call it your original book, forgive me -- The Greatest Networker in the World, the fable, the story, you had a chapter in there -- forgive me, I'm not sure what the title of the chapter was -- but it was about is it the softball league where the kids were being coached and that's really when I understood, when they were talking about coaching kids and the fun and the learning, the growth, the recognition, the development, that winning mentality, I understood coaching and from there, it's very much where I've stemmed an attitude and a philosophy not to, I know you said earlier if you wanted to, you can just sign people in and never speak to them again.

We don't teach that. It's possible but actually the way to do it is to actually build relationships and coach people and lead people. So, I'm very passionate about that but for people to literally take this business model, I know it's hard work as you've highlighted but for people to get hold of this business model, there are reasons why people succeed and there are reasons why others won't succeed. I know again it's a long list, John, and we haven't got all day to really share all of them but what would you say would be the core areas of focus or the core attributes to look to unleash from within? What points would you feel people should focus on to really take advantage of the business model we've got because it's there but unless people do certain things, they're never going to unlock the keys, are they?

JOHN MILTON FOGG:

Well, a couple of things have come out of The Greatest Networkers in the World book and one of them which sounds really stupid on the surface except if you dig into it or allow it to swirl around you a little bit, you'll get it and that's don't quit. One of the stories in that book is a guy named Jordan Adler. Currently, Jordan makes over $2 million a year with his company here in the United States and Jordan's first ten years in this business, he was with 11 companies and, Craig, he did not sponsor a single distributor, not one in ten years, in 11 companies. Now, every time he ran into trouble, it was the product that didn't work, the comp plan that didn't work, the up-line that wasn't there, the training that didn't work. He just quit and he quit and he figured something was wrong and he quit and he quit and he quit and he finally realised that the one constant in all of these failures was him. He quit and he had an opportunity where he went to his very first out of town meeting as the up-line leader and he came from Arizona, hot desert Arizona and he landed in Boston, Massachusetts in the middle of a snowstorm. He spent two and a half hours driving to the place where his meeting was and nobody was home, the house was dark, he stood out in the snow in days before cell phones and in the middle of a blizzard and an outdoor phone station, not even a phone booth, he tried to call and left me messages and it was just a disaster. He had everything he needed to quit one more time, to say that's it, I'm done with this, this is BS, I'm out of here.

But this time, he told himself I'm going to stay the course. This is not going to stop me. It's the chapter title of his chapter in the book called Quick Quitting and he stuck with it and he stayed and in that company, he made a million dollars and more and then he moved on to his next company. That company did go out of business. It was a company called Excel, it was in telephone services here in the States and now the man is on top of the world. That's one of the major messages. Another one is the message of a mentor. Every single one of these people had a mentor or more often than not, mentors plural who took them under their wing, who guided them, who showed them, who directed them, who supported them, truly a sponsor, a sponsor in the real meaning of the word which is someone who takes responsibility for the success of the person that they bring into the business and there are many other lessons from the book, personal and professional growth which we've talked about, learning how to listen, developing skills, daily methods of operation, building people not building your business or building your business by building people.

All of these things if you can -- I know this is self-serving but in the UK, Barry Phillips, Knowledge is King, is offering this book and selling them. It's a great collection of true stories. Unlike The Greatest Networker which was fiction, these are all real and it's such a wonderful cross section of the different kinds of people, people who were born poor in poverty, people from broken homes, Lynn Allen Johnson who didn't get involved in network marketing until she was 50-years old, had lived her adult life on food stamps and welfare here in the States who became a member of her company's million dollar club. Just amazing, the discipline, the ability to stay the course, stick with it, learn, constantly learn, develop, and grow and every one of these people is focused on people, on contribution. That's the juice in the jazz for them. I'm reading a book for the second time by Dr Wayne Dyer called Excuses Be Gone. He's got a great line in that book, Craig, which I truly treasure and it's, "If you want to get to the heart of how to be a big success in network marketing, this is it, want what you want for yourself even more for other people."

CRAIG WHITE:

Wow.

JOHN MILTON FOGG:

And network marketing, we pay you to do that. In corporate America when you support the people underneath you so to speak, you make them competitors. If you're a real estate agent and you teach one of your agents everything you know, pretty soon they're going to leave you, move down the street, open up shop, and compete with you. In network marketing, that's not so. We turned it upside down. We've turned the pyramid upside down.

CRAIG WHITE:

Oh, yes, and that's exciting. I love this philosophy of it falls back to helping people get what they want. I think it was Ziegler that I think may have said it in one of his books. If you help enough people get what they want, in turn you'll have everything you want but it is about that contribution. I suppose one of the things in this book of the 21 real-life millionaires in our industry, they've all got the same message of they've come from adversity, diversity but if they can do it, anyone can do it and that's really the message that I suppose you're sharing in this Podcast. But you say it's book one, are there more books to come, John? Is that a vision for the future?

John Milton Fogg:

Yes, I'm working on book two. I got a great new idea for a book three. It's a lot of work, Craig. I wrote The Greatest Networker in the World in three weeks.

Craig White:

Wow.

John Milton Fogg:

This takes me six months. It's the hardest writing work I've ever done. So, book three is not going to be those people who are making a million a year who are already millionaires. It's going to be those six-figure income earners who are destined to become millionaires, the hungry people, the business builders, the people who are out there rock-and-rolling, and book four will be all on Napoleon Hill, the greatest networkers' laws of success where I'm going to take these things we discussed like mentoring, don't quit, skills and I'm going to highlight those and illustrate them by the true stories of each of these people.

Craig White:

That's fantastic. I think you're certainly going to be leaving a legacy for the business of today and in the future which is just sensational. I know one of the things and I'm conscious of time, John, but one of the messages you've got across to me through the books, through your website is relationships are very much the key to success in our business. Any information, any tips that you can give any of our listeners on how they can transform their skills in the area of being a great networker and building relationships? I think Tony Robbins says the quality of our life is within the quality of our relationships and that's very much what our business is all about. It's not like a corporate business where you don't mix business with pleasure. On the contrary, with our business it's all about friendships, it's all about relationships, it's all about having fun, it's all about mixing pleasure and business so that I suppose a team that dream together, work together, play together, stay together. What's your thoughts on relationships and for people to develop skills or unleash what they already have within them?

JOHN MILTON FOGG:

This business is shipping and receiving, relation shipping, moving into friend shipping, moving into partner shipping and developing your group, your team through leader shipping. When you do all that shipping well, you receive the rich rewards of this business. One of those is a check but more importantly, it's the people that you meet, that you work with, that become friends and partners for a lifetime. Do you have the ability on your website, Craig, to give somebody a free PDF article?

CRAIG WHITE:

Yeah, I can do that. I can certainly do that. Yeah, definitely.

JOHN MILTON FOGG:

Okay. I've got to run as you know but later on today, I'm going to email you an article called The Four Cornerstones of Get Rich Slow. Now, I know there are a lot of people who say get rich slow?

Hey, I'm here to get rich fast. Well, guess what? Take your time, go slow. It's the fastest way of all and that details a number of elements of The Greatest Networkers' philosophy and I'm happy to share that and have you share that with your people. So, later on this afternoon when I get back here, I'll send that over to you and you can distribute it as you see fit.

Craig White:

Thank you, John, I'll certainly do that. I really appreciate your time. For those of you that haven't read these books, I've read them both and I'm inspired from the fable, the fictional book through to the real-life stories and I know the journey's part of becoming, it's part of fun, and I just wish everybody every success and to connect with John you can obviously in the UK here get the books from Barry at Knowledge is King but also you can get onto The Great Networker in the World, the GreatestNetworker.com website and connect that way. There's an abundance of information on there. John, thank you for connecting with us today, I really appreciate your time. Enjoy your winter weather over there in Virginia and I look forward to connecting with you again soon.

John Milton Fogg:

Craig White, thank you.

JOHN MILTON **FOGG**

Since the late '80s I've been working in Network Marketing and personal growth & professional development.

Author/co-author/editor of more than two-dozen well-known and best-selling books, including 'The Greatest Networker in the World'... which, having sold more than a million copies, is among the highest-ever selling Network Marketing books.

Founder/co-founder of several US Network Marketing magazines... including Upline, Network Marketing Lifestyles, Networking Times, and The Network Marketing Magazine.

Coach and mentor to more-than-I-can-count individual Network Marketers.

I live with my family (and laptop!) in Virginia, USA.

www.johnmiltonfogg.com

CHAPTER

6 Motivation From A Tortured Mind

Motivation and inspiration – both necessary for successful work, but not always available when we need them. Michael, 2x author and personal growth mentor, is someone who understands this struggle entirely.

Desperate to write a book but trapped in a work schedule with no free time, he was determined to create a formula that would make achieving his goals possible. Through setting simple goals and targets and working to his own deadlines, Michael completed the impossible and produced a successful book all while managing his other responsibilities.

In this podcast, Michael reveals that the foundation of motivation lies solely with your 'why' and how you can use this to kick start your success right now!

Craig White:

Welcome, and hello again. I'm Craig White and as always, this podcast show is proudly brought to you by Passion to Succeed. I want to know today guys, where does your motivation come from? What is it that unleashes your motivation and where does it reside? Because on today's show, we have an amazing guy, a great friend of mine and a mentor, Mr. Michael Khatkar. Now, Michael has had such a positive influence, a massively positive influence on my life over the last 15 years while we've partnered together and achieving things from challenge to travel, from leadership to pure inspiration. What's interesting and what's fascinating for me is Michael really does have a charismatic and uplifting influence on thousands upon thousands of people throughout the world today.

He is now a two-time successful author of firstly, Motivation from a Tortured Mind and more recently, Tortured Love. You know, I have yet to personally devour Tortured Love yet from my experience Motivation from a Tortured Mind is one of the most powerful books I've ever read, and it really does capture Michael's core values of compassion, integrity and a desire to have a positive influence on other people. So, I'm really proud and excited to welcome to our show today, Mr. Michael Khatkar.

Michael Khatkar:

Oh, fantastic to be here, Craig. Such a privilege to be able to speak to you and speak to everybody else. Really appreciate this opportunity and as you quite rightly said, we've known each-other for many years. But in return, you've motivated and inspired me along the way and for many years you've mentored me. So, it has been a very symbiotic relationship we have and it's a very powerful one where two people mentor each-other and influence each-other positively. It's one of the greatest relationships you can have. So, thank you for the invitation; I really appreciate it.

CRAIG WHITE:

Oh likewise, Michael. For me, the quality of our life does lie within the quality of our relationships and our relationship not only influences us but, I like to feel, creates an environment to influence others, the environment that we find ourselves in is important to our success, would you agree?

MICHAEL KHATKAR:

Totally, 100%. Not only do we have that symbiotic relationship between each-other which is just amazing, and so few of those exist that if you find them and stick to them, it probably does influence the environment around you. The power and the passion that we can create from the relationship we have, it's absolutely outstanding and you know as well as I do, we have proven that time and time again, and we will continue to do that as the relationship nurtures and grows. I absolutely agree with that.

CRAIG WHITE:

Michael; I know you're a really busy guy and leading thousands of people and travelling the world and really, looking for more opportunities to develop and grow. Dare I ask, where in the world are you today? Are you in the UK? Are you travelling?

MICHAEL KHATKAR:

No; I'm in the UK today. Travelling is done for this month. We're only halfway through the month but there's a lot more travel on the cards and as you quite rightly say, everything I do is based around people but today, firmly situated in the UK which I might add, is the greatest country in the world, if you don't mind me saying so.

Craig White:

Well mate, you share a passion of mine, very patriotic. I heard something recently; I'm not sure where, but something had come into my environment, I was looking at obviously, the size of the world. I think it was really on the back of what's happened with the Brexit recently, people were talking about, we're probably only the third biggest economy in the world I believe if I'm correct there. And yet actually, we're such a small island and I think sometimes we can always forget how small we are. I look at what people achieve in the UK; entrepreneurs, business owners, and people that are looking to be passionate about success, I guess in all different walks of life.

I look at what they achieve in the UK and I thought to myself when I heard that, God, we're such a small island yet such a powerful nation of people that can influence the world. Think about the growth worldwide that people may be able to have when they think about the size of the world, and it impacted me to think, actually, we're so strong and so powerful and have such a large contribution but from such a small island, it's amazing, really.

Michael Khatkar:

Totally agree with you, Craig. I mean, I'm very patriotic about our country. I mean, you're absolutely right; we have a track record and a history of massive, massive achievement. You can go back as far as you want in history and our country has always been at the helm of everything that's great in the world and no matter where we are today with whatever has happened with Brexit and whatever does happen, we will still be amazing one way or another. We are a country of survivors. This country's track record in achievement is unbelievable. I'm incredibly patriotic about this country and, through all the travels that I've done throughout the world, I will still say that this is where home is. Not only is this where home is, but I can proudly say that it is the greatest country in the world, and it truly is.

Craig White:

You know what, I agree – I'm no politician and I'm passionate about connecting with the world. I think we have a history of leadership. As you said, as long as we go back, we have a real strong history of leadership and of achievers and I think we need our leaders to come together now. And, we've got an opportunity to connect with the rest of the world and we are a small island, but this is a world without borders nowadays. I'm glad you're based in the UK because we've got a great line. One of the reasons I wanted to bring Michael to our show today is, he's without doubt, certainly one of the most passionate and transformational people I know and I feel we can delve into his mind a little bit today, maybe some of his philosophies of how he continues to be one of the most passionate people based in being passionate to succeed that I've known for the last 15 years.

But firstly Michael, what I want to do and obviously, knowing you as I do and having read your book, I know a little bit about your story and where you come from. But, tell us a little bit about your books. What was the passion – you had this reason why and all through your book, Motivation from a Tortured Mind, you talk about your song and how someone's song is influential in their actions. What's your song? Why did you become an author?

Michael Khatkar:

Well, having studied English and psychology, I was always aware that everyone and I mean absolutely everyone has a book inside them; a book that would influence people, that can inspire people and motivate people. Everybody has a story that will affect somebody else. Then, having worked in personal development for over 25 years now, it was personal development added to the fact that I know everybody has a book inside them, that allowed me to set the goal to write because I thought to myself, hold on; I sleep five hours a night. I'm busy 24 hours a day, seven days a week doing something. When and where am I going to squeeze in a book? And then I thought, hold it a minute; personal development teaches us to set goals and to have deadlines.

So, I decided, 1,000 words every single week without fail for 57 weeks, and that's exactly what I did. Come rain or shine, come night or day, I got 1,000 words in every single week for a solid 57 weeks irrespective of where I was in the world or what I was doing. Hence came the first book. That first book is a personal journey but outlined to inspire others with every day happenings. Yes, there are some happenings in there that are very unique to me but each chapter in that book has some form of inspiration where people can look upon it and think, I can relate to that, I can work with that, and I can grow with that.

That was the motivation behind the book, the fact that everybody has a book inside them; the fact that setting the goal to write, yes I could do that because I know anything is achievable, including writing a book, even if you have no time to write it. And, a basic story that has inspiration in every chapter to try and influence people throughout their own lives, that really was it, Craig. I'll tell you most of all it was knowing that if you set a goal to do something that seems impossible at first, it will get done. So, you have to believe in it, you have to break it down, and then you have to fix your deadline. As I said, my deadline, come rain or shine, night or day, was 1,000 words a week without fail. I did that solidly for 57 weeks, and there was the first book and I can honestly say, I'm as busy as you are, Craig. We are busy 24 hours a day. But, when you want to do something and you want to do it badly enough, then you will get it done.

Craig White:

This is what you mean when, in the book, you talk about your song and how finding it gives you your purpose, your reason why which, clearly, you've done it. It's amazing; I was thinking only today when I was in the gym this morning, the personal development journey that we've been on, and you're almost confirming what I was thinking today – well, you are 100%, actually. I was thinking about how self-made millionaires, from things I've learned in the past; how literally, they find their song, as you would call it. Their reason why they achieve their goals and obviously, you've set that goal, you've chunked it down, you formulated a plan and then as you said, you worked on it day in, day out to hit your goal. That's what achievers do!!

Michael Khatkar:

Absolutely agree. Having your own song, simply defined, is your reason why. A lot of people never find their actual reason why. I know, Craig, you know, and every entrepreneur in this world knows that your reason why is your golden key to the kingdom. When you have your reason why, you can open any door in the world because that reason why pushes you through; it pulls you through; it takes you where you want to be, no matter come rain or shine, night or day. You will get to that destination because that is your song. Your song is the reason why. The hardest and most profitable exercise you will ever do is work out your reason why. If you can work out why you're doing and what you're doing, why do you want and what you want? If you can work that out, you will have the golden key to the kingdom which will open any door for you, and that is your song.

Craig White:

So, from your song perspective, what are your intentions now? You've wrote your second book, Tortured Love, and this is more of a novel. Tell me a little bit about this book.

Michael Khatkar:

Yes. Tortured Love is a novel and it's again, a novel based on life, death and hope; three areas that we all witness at some point in our lives. We all witness life; we all witness death, but, we all must have an element of hope. The story is based around that. I'm currently writing my third book which is a romantic novel called Make My World Complete Again; a very different slant because I've learned that you can do anything you want if you put your mind to it. So, writing became a passion even though I would have been the first person in the queue to say, I haven't got time to write and I can now tell you, Craig, there's no such thing as not having time. When you want to do something bad enough, you will find the time.

But, my passion really, beyond writing, is simple in one word. My passion is people because I have learned that – and we'll talk about more about this later; but if you support and build people you can achieve anything in the world. You support and you build people. Help people realise their reasons why, and you will build an empire in anything you want to do. I've worked in industries that only involve working with people and that is what I enjoy the most: writing books and working with people.

Craig White:

That's interesting, that your intentions and your commitment to write this third book. Obviously, it's clear that, when you move, you create motion which unleashes emotion. And, you've got yourself. You've set that goal, you've got your first book under your belt. And, success is a habit and you've implemented the habit of fulfilling your song and making it influence, and clearly your third book is bringing out the old romantic in you, I gather.

Michael Khatkar:

It is, indeed. It's a collection of poetry and general romantic happenings with the usual Michael Khatkars within them.

Craig White:

You're – talking of twists – again, I need to devour Tortured Love. But, Motivation from a Tortured Mind, I mentioned it earlier, and it's one of the most challenging and inspiring books that I've ever read. What I mean by that is, Michael, it takes you on this journey and on occasion, I say, hang on a minute, where are we going with this? You're almost taking you into these depths of the unknown and then, all of a sudden, he hits you with this point, this poignant point that really hits you and makes you stand up and go, yes, I need to develop my song and yes, I need to understand. One of your messages in the book, you talk about the importance of, people concede, they struggle, or fight. And, I guess too many people concede rather than fighting for what's right.

Michael Khatkar:

Absolutely, Craig; people – what I mean by concede is that they will give in to whatever is thrown at them. So, when they have something negative thrown at them, something that they didn't want, something that they didn't appreciate, they just accept it and take it. That's what I call concede, and so many people, for whatever reason – it's not a criticism of these people; it's that so many people will just give in at the first hurdle, or the first thing that hits them; they will just give up rather than accept whatever's coming their way. Then, you get sets of people who struggle, and the reason they struggle is because they don't have a plan to get out of the situation they're in, but they just do day-to-day routine things to try and get out of the situation they find themselves in.

You know as well as I do Craig, that if you want something extraordinary, if you want something out of the ordinary, then you have to put an extraordinary effort in because if you put an ordinary effort in and if you put everyday effort in or, as you would say, Craig, if you don't put sweat equity in, you'll only get mediocre. You will only get that, so the only way to go forward and to achieve those huge things that you dream of is to fight for them; is to work over and above everything else; is to go that extra mile because as you know, Craig, there is no competition in that extra mile.

It's all there, available for you so if you want more, you can't just concede and accept what's coming your way. You've just got to say, no, this is not the way it's going to be. You can't just carry on, struggling doing everyday routine, because every-day routine will get you everyday results. You literally have to fight day and night for what you want, and you know what Craig, every single time, and you're a great testament to this, that fight is always worth it because you will get what 95% of people conceded for and struggled for. But, you will get it. You will be the 5%.

Craig White: You know what, I completely agree Michael. I think that passion to fight is almost the fight for the right to win. And, I think too many people focus sometimes on the outcome whereas -- I think that focus of having a great day, working hard as you said, fighting day and night for what's right for you, for your song and for your plan. I think, if people can focus on that, the outcome is irrelevant because at the end of the day, it's what we say to ourselves that counts and if we can look in the mirror at the end of every day and say, I've won; I've left my rubber on the tarmac; I've left my sweat in the game because I've won regardless of the outcome because I've delivered my contribution, my focus and my level of activity.

Michael Khatkar:

Absolutely.

Craig White:

I'm sure you agree; people more often than not might not get what they want, but they'll get what they expect. They'll get what they focus on and I think too many people, need to understand that life is about ups and downs. We're going to have challenges; we're going to have ordeals; we're going to have elation; we're going to have happiness, and the ups and downs of life – well, they're a part of the cycle of nature; from the way, we breathe, from the night and day, the way the sun moves the world – the oceans, etc. Everything has a positive and a negative; there's always clarity through contrast and I think if people can focus on what they want – for example, if they focus on the depths of despair, the ups and downs of life will probably take them there. Yet, if they focus on elation, achievement, success and maybe, removing themselves and having an ambition greater than themselves, maybe an ambition for people which is what you're really passionate about, then the ups and downs of life would take them there, too.

Michael Khatkar:

Absolutely. Craig, when I think about you and what you've achieved, for me, one sentence always sums it up. You were willing to do the things that other people found easy not to do. You did all that extra to get to where you are and you've had a phenomenal life and career so far and I still believe it's only beginning, because you did over and above what anybody else did. You did all the things that people found easy not to do, and that's got you where you are. That sums you up in one sentence because you did that and you did it with pride, and you did it with ambition, and you did it with my favourite word, gusto.

Craig White:

Well let's look at that because I have the complete same vibe and feelings towards yourself because I think the influence you have, the way you impact and uplift people, your passion for people first is why I believe you continue to succeed; you continue to influence thousands of people on a daily basis, and not many people have that leadership role, and it's a role of responsibility; it's a role of leadership and in a way, you're a prime example of a leader of one, is a leader of many; if you can't lead one, you can't lead any. You've learnt yourself to chase your song, to become a successful author on two occasions, writing two great books and on to your third already. I'm sure that will continue onto your fourth and your fifth because not only can you influence people in your environment, but I guess your books enable you to influence many more people worldwide.

If people can grasp the concepts, I really do think they can change their life because how we change is how we succeed and you're a real prime example of that entrepreneurial spirit; that ambition to be passionate about people. So, you talked about people earlier. You talked about your passion for people. Where does that come from? Is it something that you've developed over years? Because I know you've studied people; I know you've studied many areas in life, from people to success to, obviously, literature. But where does your passion for people originate?

Michael Khatkar:

Well, various areas. Just in-depth in various facets of psychology. But, it was during my very early career, and I remember a manager saying to me, and it was the only valuable thing this man said. He said, no matter what you do in life, no matter what job you do, what career you follow, what company you work for, no matter what organisation you run, always identify great people, support them and build them. Always do that throughout your life; identify, support and build. Do you know what, Craig? He didn't even tell me why that was such a good idea; I learned why that was such a good idea. He just said, always find people that you can support and build.

In years gone by, then I learned why that was so important because, if you can nurture and identify and support and build people, no matter what company you're in, no matter what organisation you run, no matter what self-employed situation you're in, you will always grow as a result of that, and that brings us to Zig Ziglar's most famous quote; if enough people get what they want, you'll get everything you want. So, always focus on identifying, supporting and building people. It's something I learned very early in my career, even at the point where I didn't even understand the reasons why you had to do that, but now I do because, if you can help people get somewhere, you will get anywhere you want. Focus on people; focus on building them because so many people in this world do need support. Do not forget that people need to be supported.

There is greatness in everybody, but not everybody ever locates that greatness because the rest of the world goes around telling people they're not good enough; they're not great enough; they can't achieve it. If you can go along and identify that in people, you can tell them they're great enough. You can support them to be brilliant. You can continue to build them until they reach their goals; then, you have achieved one of the greatest ambitions any man should have, any person should have, and that is to build, support and identify people for growth. As I said, I learned that very early-on.

Craig White:

I am so pleased that you had the faith to listen and understand it as you went along for the experience. I guess the one thing that you're unable to give us is experience. However, your words of wisdom, for me, this is something that you are great at; you're great at finding out what it is that can impact people. You're great at uplifting people, finding out what their strengths are and reminding them, and I agree; people throughout the world are not told how great they are often enough. How often are people appreciated? How often do we feel grateful about others? One of the things, I've started to implement in my life, and I know it's something you do too and it certainly inspired me over the years, watching you and seeing the impact you have on others is, that philosophy of having a positive influence. I'm not sure where it came from but we all know the cliché of, if you've got nothing nice to say, avoid saying anything.

For me, it's about leaving every encounter, leaving every impression or opportunity with a good vibe, a good feeling. Even if it's going out of your way just to hold the door open for somebody, or if it's going out of the way just to say to somebody that they look fantastic today because I think people are not surrounded in that positive bubble enough which, a lot of people laugh at me because they're like, Craig, you live in your positive bubble. I love my positive bubble because it just doesn't penetrate. But, one of the things I think you are fantastic at, and certainly I've taken from you over the years is having that positive influence on people and making sure people are aware of that because it's not told often enough.

Michael Khatkar:

Thank you, Craig. Thank you, appreciate that.

Craig White:

So, when we look at highly passionate people, yourself included, how – what – I guess there are many traits of passionate people, and there are many habits. How do you stay so energetic, so uplifting, so positive? I'm sure you have your times where you have your own time, where you can chill out with a lovely bottle of wine, read a book, write a book. When I see you and when people hear you and the people who are listening to the show now hear you, you have an energy in your voice, and you have an impactful way of influencing people. How do you stay on-course? How do you stay passionate about people, regardless of the outcome?

Michael Khatkar:

Okay, Craig. I mean, on a very personal level, number one, it is to understand that reason why -- I would say, it's paramount in absolutely everything you do and everything you tackle, and every single day. So, number one, understand your reason why. This is not a frequent number one. It is the basis of everything you will achieve. Understand your personal reason why because that will be the golden key to the kingdom; that's number one.

Number two, fully understand and accept, we have two dates; the date we are born and the date, unfortunately when we die. But do you know what? In-between that is a short dash of time. Two dates and a dash of time; that's all we have. If you don't understand that your time is limited, then you won't make the most of it. So, understand we have a small dash of time and in that dash of time, you're either going to concede, struggle, or fight for everything you deserve. So? for me, I understand that facet every single day, that I had a date where I'm born; the date when I go, I don't know when that is, but in-between is a very short dash of time. So, I have to make the most of every single moment, and that does keep me uplifted.

Thirdly, for me personally, it's all about self-competition. I've never competed with anybody else. Never, ever, have I ever competed with anybody. It's all about self-competition; being better for myself. Being better than I was yesterday; being better than I was last year; being better than I was five years ago, with the promise that tomorrow, I'll do even better than today. That self-competitive edge gives you exactly that: it gives you the edge, but it's competition with yourself. You're going to make yourself better. I don't care about how anybody else is doing it except the people I'm supporting, of course. I care about them, but I don't compete with people, I don't compete with companies; I only compete with myself to make myself better.

So, one, understand your reason why, and the golden key to the kingdom – that will open more doors than you can ever imagine. Number two, accept the two dates and a dash of time, and that dash of time is just what it is. It's just a dash and you've got to make the most of it. You either concede, you struggle or you fight for the time that you're give. Number three, self-competitiveness. Compete against yourself. I will regularly go to bed thinking, today wasn't good enough. Tomorrow will be better. I regularly do that, and if you can compete with yourself you will continue to grow.

Now, if I was able to add a fourth, it would be to consistently do what I've already said, and that is to support people to greatness. Support as many people as you possibly can to greatness. Identify, support and build. Those four things are my personal keys to success and I stick by them every living day.

Craig White:

Thank you, Michael, I'm buzzing listening to that, what a great overview of your passions and your purpose, and your song to influence. That philosophy of being self-competitive; I love it because too many people, compete with others when it's about focusing on our game, what's important to us and, as you rightfully said, being better today than we were yesterday; being better today than we were in the past. For me, you are certainly one of the best of the best, my friend, and I'm really appreciative of your time today. I know you are busy making a difference, influencing, planning and goal achieving, and leading the way for thousands of people throughout the world today.

Thanks very much for your time; a great finish to a show. Four cracking points that, I believe, if you guys can listen to Michael, learn from Michael and follow his lead, you can have a really exciting future. It's remembering, how we change is how we succeed. This is obviously a fantastic show. We're talking to passionate people and we've had the passionate Michael Khatkar today. I want to thank you for joining us, I appreciate your time, and I'm sure, maybe we'll have Michael on again when he unleashes a romantic, passionate novel on us, god help us.

But, I look forward to that and Michael, again, thanks very much. Hope you guys have really enjoyed today's show. And, remember them four key points: why, dash, self-competitive, and making a difference in other people's lives, and your life is most likely to change for the better forever. I wish you all the best, and have a passionate day.

Michael Khatkar:

Thanks a lot, Craig. Bye.

Fasciated by the incredible power and fortitude of the human psyche, throughout the entirely of my life and career, I've studied people in one way or another from the analysis and hypothesis of Human Psychology & Behaviour to the indisputable, tangible lives of real people. Through this intrinsic, perennial learning I've carved a successful career in people orientated industries and continue to comprehend the fundamental ingredients and perception of success & failure.

My personal journey frequently riddled with provocation, controversy and often acute subjectivity has only just begun destinations are rarely reached with curiosity and imagination harmoniously, opening new doors and bulldozing conventional, humdrum walls.

michael-khatkar.com

CHAPTER 7

Is It Your Time To Shine?

Are you genuinely "Happy?" Are we putting milestones before happiness? Are we programmed to think that a dream job, a nice home, a family, or even a relationship will make us happy?

What is preventing you from true happiness?

In today's society, we seem to focus on material objects to make us happy, we rely on others for happiness, even our careers. What goals are we setting ourselves to achieve happiness?

Alexandra uncovers the mistakes we are creating that prevent us from true happiness. We choose what we do and who we are. Clear those obstacles in your pursuit of happiness, using Alexandra's three simple steps to bring out your inner diamond, eliminating all the negative myths.

PREPARE TO LOVE YOURSELF AGAIN !!

CRAIG WHITE:

Hi, everybody. Joining me today we have an amazing lady. She is and has been an extremely successful entrepreneur for the last couple of decades, and is actually considered the leading happiness coach in the U.K. She has a wealth of knowledge and experience, and really, the experience is working on X-Factor, being the life coach of Leona Lewis, we all know the success that developed from there, working with Olympic athletes, celebrities and many business professionals across the U.K. And one of Alex's core focuses and passions is women in business. She's the best-selling author. I'm really proud to be talking with her today. She's a best-selling author, as I said, of a book called The Happiness System for Women, and today, she's living true to her purpose, and I think when you're living true to what matters to you, you just have a fantastic life. It's an absolute pleasure to have you joining us today, Alex, and I really appreciate you giving up some of your time to chat with us and share some of your wealth of information and inspiration to the women listening to this podcast show. How are you?

ALEXANDRA WATSON:

I'm great, I'm delighted to be here. Thank you so much for asking me.

CRAIG WHITE:

It's a pleasure. Guys, I've talked with Alex a couple of times. I've been lucky enough to see Alex share some of her wisdom from the stage over the last couple of years, and she always looks dynamite and fantastic on stage, but you have a great message not just to women—I know your focus is women in business and that's where your passion is.

ALEXANDRA WATSON:

Good to hear.

Craig White:

How did you become a happiness coach? Where did it all start for you? You've had quite an adventure.

Alexandra Watson:

I have. I came 'round the houses, I suppose, because there's no direct route that I know of to become a happiness coach, necessarily, or there wasn't back in the day when I started, because I started off in life, as it were, professionally, as a marketing and PR person. I threw myself down that route passionately to a point where I became very successful. I started my own marketing and PR business, and then, suddenly, it hit me one day that I wasn't happy, and I wasn't fulfilled. That really worried me, because I'd worked so hard at becoming successful in a very competitive industry. I did actually love working with my clients, but really, it was just one pinnacle moment I remember. I was sat in a board room with one of my clients and I was actually bored. Bored in a board room. Not a good place to be, and I thought, "Crikey, is this all there is? Is this all there is for me?" And that thought, really petrified me.

Anyway, that thought never left me, that fear never left me, and I kept talking to my friends and family about it, and they said, you know, "Well, carry on, this happens. Don't worry, it will pass." The feeling didn't pass, it kept nagging at me that I should be doing something else, I should be doing something else, but I wasn't sure what. Then, one day, just out of the blue, as these things happen, serendipitously, somebody said to me, "Well, you'd make a great life coach." Now, Craig, bearing in mind this was about 15, 16 years ago, in this country, and if you can set your mind back that far, really, life coaching was not as well-known as it is today. I said, "That sounds great. Does that mean I work in a swimming pool?" I had no idea what a life coach was. As if by magic, my friend actually rummaged in her handbag and pulled out a leaflet, can you believe, all about life coaching. She handed it to me and went, "Here. You'd make a great life coach, do this."

So, I studied the leaflet and I went and found more information about it. And I just thought, yes, this sounds just up my alley, this is what I want to do. I trained for it, I did all the courses and got my certification, and everything like that, and very quickly I left my marketing and PR business, which people thought was insane. They asked me if I was crazy? You have all these clients and this successful business, but you're leaving it for this business that nobody knows what it is?" And I kind of said, "Yes. Call me brave or call me stupid, either way, I'm doing it." And I did it, and I haven't looked back since, because when I started initially with life coaching, I very quickly got it. It was just like second nature to me, and I loved it incredibly, and got passionate about it immediately, and could see, for the first time in my life, a very long, clear future with this.

I started my own practice, did very well and loved it, and then I thought, "Right, what's next?" because I am a bit like that, kind of go so far and then I go, "Right, what's next?" And what I found next was writing the book, The Happiness System for Women, because what I found was two things. Firstly, that I couldn't coach everybody I wanted to in the sense that I didn't have enough days or hours in the day to coach the people I wanted to coach, or the people that wanted to be coached by me. Second thing was, I found that at that time, I was sort of saying the same stuff to people over and over again, and it was very much about the will to be happy. So, I thought, if I wrote it down, then I could give a book to people I haven't got time to coach, so really help people en masse. So, that's what I felt I wanted to do.

How I got to write the book, really, was studying happiness. So, I went back to ancient texts, you know, Marcus Aurelius and all the old philosophers, right the way through history into modern philosophy, and pulled out what I could see was a systemic approach to happiness, that it was a step-by-step method. Because up until that point, people sort of found happiness to be quite a mystery, and they were, "I don't know how to be happy," and people were doing all the wrong things, like trying to buy happiness through shoes, clothes, houses, holidays, you know, or trying to find happiness in somebody else, like a boyfriend, husband, wife, girlfriend, etc., and making all these mistakes. And I thought, "I want to give people an absolute map to have happiness that is very, very straightforward." And that's when I became a happiness coach. I focused on happiness because that's what people want more than anything else in the world, even above and beyond their health. So, I focused on happiness, and that's where it all started from. Then the book came out, and from the book, that's when the X-Factor found me, and it sort of started from there.

Craig White:

Exciting, really. Do you think most people reach a similar point in life, where they question where they are in life, they question their happiness?

Alexandra Watson:

Back when it happened with me, sort of 16 years ago, it was a generation thing, in the sense that the generation before, and possibly before that, had the mid-life crisis at about 45, yes? Our generation had the 35-year-old crisis, and the generation now behind us are having an even younger mid-life, so-called crisis, I think because we stay younger longer these days, that people are starting to question it. The main thing I found, when I was coaching back in those days, coaching a heck of a lot of people who had, say, become a lawyer, or another big profession like that, because they thought they had to, or they thought they should. And actually, they didn't want to at all. And that kind of thing happened with me, in a funny way. I thought, "Well, this is marketing, I quite like that, I'm good at it, so I'll go and do it." But it actually wasn't my passion, and hence the big career change, and it happens for so many people, you're quite right.

Craig White:

I think it takes courage, and obviously, you made that decision, 15, 16 years ago, and a lot of people would have said, "Hey, you're crazy," but actually I think that's quite courageous.

Alexandra Watson:

Thanks.

Craig White:

Well, I think it is. Just listening to you, there are a lot of people who reach these points in their life, so I think that's common, probably across the world, but certainly in the U.K. where people are falling into what they feel is the right thing, or they're following somebody else's goal for them rather than being true to themselves. And they're probably always going to get to this point, and I'm sure you've coached many people in making these decisions and having that courage to take the right steps in line with what's really true to them.

Alexandra Watson:

I put it this way, though, Craig. You probably understand this completely, is that if you've got a decision like that to make, or you've got that kind of nagging feeling in yourself that you're not in the right profession or you're not doing really what you want to do, but you don't feel you're ready to move forward yet and change that. Well, let me suggest this. What if, five years down the line, you're still in the same place? You're still having the same feelings that you're having now. Or ten years down the line, it's not happened yet, and it probably looks like it never will. Can you imagine those feelings?

CRAIG WHITE:

Scary, isn't it?

ALEXANDRA WATSON:

Imagine how you will feel, it petrifies you, to think that things will never change. Because we put things off, we procrastinate because of fear of the unknown, and we know that it's going to take a huge leap of faith, faith in ourselves and faith when we jump, the universe somehow will catch us and support us. And in fact, it always does. But it's actually taking that breath and going, "Ok, I'm doing this." And when you do, very, very rarely, if ever, do you regret it.

CRAIG WHITE:

That's nice. That's great.

ALEXANDRA WATSON:

If you don't do it, you will regret it.

CRAIG WHITE:

You talk about your love for coaching people. You obviously still do, and have that wider influence now, because of the power of your book, and I know you do some fantastic seminars as well. What is it you loved and love about coaching people? What aspects of it do you really enjoy?

ALEXANDRA WATSON:

Reminding people of who they actually are, because people come to me in all different states, if you will. Some are stuck. Some people can't slow down, you know, too much going on in their lives. So, however they show up with me, really what I'm doing with people, no matter what their circumstance, is reminding them of who they are. And, reminding them that they are a powerful creative being, and not this fearful, self-doubting, playing small creature. That's just an illusion.

Craig White:

With this book that you've written, it's obviously allowed you to reach that wider audience, and the system for happiness, which I know your core focus is women entrepreneurs and women in business, take us through the principles that are in place to empower people. I know there's a lot of things you focus on in increasing people's happiness levels and their confidence. What's the core aspect of the book, and as to the ladies that are listening to us today, maybe they've not come across you yet. Not where have you been for the last 15 years, but if they've not come across you and been lucky enough to meet you, or seen some of your work and been inspired, what can they expect from the book? Because I highly recommend that they get a copy.

Alexandra Watson:

Well, bless you. I'm not actually omnipresent yet, but I'm working on it. If you haven't heard of me before, it's fine. It's not your fault, it's my fault. The actual core message of the book, and what I actually tell my gorgeous women entrepreneurs that I work with, and when they own a business, because we are very emotional creatures. And that's perfect. A lot of people see that as a weakness, being emotional, but actually it's an incredible strength. And it's to really understand that whatever work we do, or choose to do, should be, in order for us to be successful and happy and fulfilled and confident, is for it to be an authentic expression of who we are. So, if what you do for a living is an authentic expression of who you are, then you are going to be successful. You need the strategies in place, obviously, for business models, etc., and that's what I teach, as well.

But, coming from the core of who you are, it has to be authentic. If you are trying to be somebody you're not, that is where life becomes exhausting and frustrating and unfulfilling. When you are actually being your true self and playing large and not hiding away, and shining—I call a lot of the stuff I do Time to Shine. Shine from inwardly outward, so people can really get the gift that you've been on this planet to give. We all have unique gifts, we all have something to contribute uniquely to this world, and when you can tune in with that and connect with that and bring that forward into your life every day and have it as a vocation, then that is the ideal scenario.

Craig White:

I completely agree with you. I've learned and grown a passion over the years. I think everybody has that inner power, that specialist inside them that's just waiting for maybe, the right environment, or somebody to believe in them, or for them to reach a point in life where they say, hang on a minute, this isn't me, and they have the courage like you've had to maybe unleash what's inside them. But it's always been there, but maybe sometimes society hinders that, or prevents people from really living what's true to them. Would you mind taking us through that philosophy of what you mean by that?

Alexandra Watson:

Of course, yes, I do, this is what comes from Time to Shine because I believe that we all have the ability to shine. We were born with the ability to shine from within, with this beautiful purity and power and strength, just like a diamond. There's nothing tougher on this planet than a diamond, naturally occurring. So, I think that when you allow yourself to shine, and this, in a diamond, can get buried over time, when people happen to us that aren't always positive in our lives, situations happen to us that aren't always positive in our lives.

Then, if we don't have a balanced guidance through it, we doubt ourselves, and we hide away. I teach people how to dig up, if you will, unbury this diamond and let it shine again, naturally, from within. When you do that, you can connect with all of your innate, inner resources like confidence and wisdom and nurturing and power and all those types of things that we already have within us, and reconnect you to that, so that you actually feel that you're living the life that you should be living.

Craig White:

You have, on your website, AlexandraWatson.com, which, albeit a man, I have enjoyed scrolling around and having a nose, on there you talk about easy ways for people to increase their happiness levels. For those listening, for instance, what steps can you advise people to say, "Hey, go and make a difference in your happiness levels, right now, today."

Alexandra Watson:

Easy. I love this bit. Are you ready? First thing you do is decide what happiness is for you. You personally. I know that sounds simple, but the reason I say it is because, though peer pressure, parents, society and influence can tell us, and definitely in the newspapers, and TV and all the media, can tell us what happiness should be, should look like. But, absolutely, happiness for you has got to be a personal thing. So, what makes you happy may not necessarily make somebody else happy, even your best friend, or your sister, or your brother or your mother. It's a very personal thing, and you've got to just sit down and decide what makes you happy. And then, go and pursue whatever that is.

Now a lot of people think, if I have more shoes or am more successful that will matter. I can tell you that that doesn't necessarily make somebody happy. It's a very personal thing. So, find out what happiness is for you and ignore what people are telling you will make you happy. It's never anything on the outside. That's a hint. All right? It's never anything on the outside. Maybe some outdoor pursuits make you feel uplifted and boost your energy, and you can connect with nature that way, but happiness really is an internal journey.

The next thing to do is to get rid of what you have been buying into as far as happiness is concerned, which are things like—I've heard this one before, can you believe, Craig? This is frightening when I hear this. People say, I'm too old to be happy. Okay, if you say so. Just be careful what rules you're putting around yourself when it comes to happiness. What you're saying, "Well, this has to happen first before I'm happy." Or "I will be happy when this happens." That is putting rules before happiness and you're not living in the moment, because you decide to be.

Then, the next step would be for you to clear the pathway for happiness, which means that you have to get rid of the obstacles in your way, which, once you've cleared the myths and the lies about happiness, which is all the material stuff and all the nonsense I've just mentioned, and really understand that you have to get rid of negative beliefs about who you are. When you sort of exercise negative beliefs about yourself, that frees you up to accept who you are.

And then, when you get to loving yourself, we actually want to love ourselves unconditionally. That's the pathway to true happiness, because when you start to like yourself and then perhaps love yourself, and not in a narcissistic way but in a true, loving, nurturing way, and understanding and kindness, then you become unstoppable, which means that life can throw whatever it wants to at you. Any kind of hideousness, God forbid, but it can, and you will feel happy no matter what. Yes, you will feel sad at certain points because there will be things that happen that make you feel sad, but you bounce back. And you don't actually lose that inner core of happiness. Once you get to that stage, then you become unstoppable, and you really are a truly happy person—not faking it, but you are really, truly happy.

Craig White:

So, it's three really simple steps that people can start to work on. Would you say one of the issues is that people don't spend the time on these three core steps deciding what happiness really is internally, getting rid of the rubbish, the negative, the myths that you're talking about so you really learn and love oneself. I like that philosophy that you can only truly love others when you love yourself first.

Alexandra Watson:

Yes. Yes, absolutely.

Craig White:

You've talked before about having deadlines to work within, so we get things done. Would you say an idea for people would be to say, "Hey, look at this daily, or maybe set time aside daily or weekly or somewhere in your life, in your schedule, to actually focus on these three core elements of happiness."

Alexandra Watson:

Yes. I mean, we can sum up these three in one particular, very ancient philosophy, which you find in lots of different religious and nonreligious philosophy-type scripts, which is "Know thyself." It is really about self-awareness, and knowing who you are and what you want. You can't say it more simply than that. When you know yourself, I mean, really know yourself, not think, "I'm this quiet or shy person who's not ready and fearful of this and I can't do that." That's not true. Those are the negative beliefs. When you actually know who, you are, like I said, this powerful, creative human being, that's who you really are—when you know that for sure, then that's it. You've got it cracked. And I think that there are other things as well.

The reason I made a sort of happiness system, if you like, a step by step, is you've got to go down those three roads first, before you can start doing things like affirmations, or start, like you say, to have decent relationships that are going to last without hang-ups and whatnot. Things have got to happen in a chronological order. That's what use to make me chuckle sometimes, when I saw people say, "To be happy, go and kiss a puppy or watch a sunset. That'll make you happy. Sit for five minutes and read your favourite magazine." Well, I know for sure that doesn't float everybody's boat, you know, that if you actually ask a woman to sit down for five minutes and read a magazine, the first thing she's going to feel is guilty.

Craig White:

Okay.

Alexandra Watson:

All right? She's going to feel guilty that "I'm not doing something, I'm not looking after my children, or I'm taking this time off for myself." So, you've got to actually got to get to that place where you allow yourself the nurturing time off, if you will, the selfful time. So, you can sit down with five minutes or more with your favourite magazine and be okay with that, and not feel guilty about it. Women are complicated creatures, but it's a beautiful complicated way we are, and so, having a systematic approach to happiness makes sure that you lock-in the real aspects and characteristics of what inner happiness is before you touch the outside and have other people's influences involved.

Craig White:

I really love that, and I really, truly understand the power of spending time with oneself to really connect with what's true. Obviously, as you mentioned at the beginning, you're living true to your powers. One of the things I love and I feel I've noticed about you, you're not just sharing this information, it's how you live. I have a lot of respect for that because there's a lot of fabulous information out there that comes from all areas. We can consume inspiration from many areas, but it's just great to see somebody who walks the talk. These philosophies are things that you actually live by, and you can tell that, you can hear it.

Alexandra Watson:

I do.

Craig White:

I know I'm really kind of chatting to get as much information out of you as possible. You mentioned something there, and just to gain a little clarity for people, you mentioned things have to happen in a chronological order. What do you mean?

Alexandra Watson:

Well, thank you for asking that because it's a really good point that I can't emphasise enough, which means that a lot of people say the way they know to be happy is to have gratitude, for example, to be grateful for what you have. And I get that, and yes, it's right, but you've got to approach gratitude in a certain way after you've done a few things first, because, quite frankly, it's very difficult to have truly authentic gratitude when you, for example, are resentful of somebody in your life. You have this holding a resentment for somebody.

So, to put the chronological idea into this point, you would have to therefore go through forgiveness before you could have gratitude. Truly. You would have to get rid of those resentments and absolutely go through the pathway of true forgiveness, of forgiving people and forgiving yourself for certain things, or whatever it is, before you can have gratitude. Otherwise, it's fake. It truly is. I feel like I'm the little boy in the fairy tale The Emperor's New Clothes. I mean, hello, the emperor's naked—that doesn't work. I'm kind of a whistle blower for the fake information you get about how to be happy, because I'm passionate about people understanding it and taking the mystery out of happiness for people. So, if you're trying to be happy through gratitude, fantastic, however, you've got to get rid of all your anxieties and resentments before gratitude can actually work.

Craig White:

So, in a way, I suppose, let go of the past in a way.

Alexandra Watson:

You have to let go of the past because it's nothing to do with you, really. I mean, you can have the argument, which is true, that you wouldn't be who you are today if it wasn't for the past, but you're in the moment. We're living in the moment, and I'm a planner, don't get me wrong—I love projecting myself into the future and planning ahead, that's great. But, I'm very aware of the here and now, my choices that I make in the here and now, because my choices are another thing. One way to true happiness is to make really good, powerful choices. But again, you can't make powerful choices or you'll be limited in the powerful choices you can make, if you have negative beliefs about yourself.

So, something's got to happen first in order for you to make powerful choices, in order for you to have gratitude, and what I mean is, it's got to be a step by step process, and that's what I developed.

Craig White:

Yes, I completely understand what you mean now. And I can see how you can take that to different aspects of life to get the philosophy of the chronological order.

Alexandra Watson:

Yes, you've got to have the chronological order, otherwise, it doesn't do what it says on the tin. You know, you've got to have it in the step by step process, you've got to have it in the way, "first things first", as the great Stephen Covey says. And it's true. You've got to have the first thing first. If you want to be happy, the first thing is, "What is happiness for me?" Second thing, let's get rid of all the crazy ideas about what happiness actually was, and then for women, that can be a man coming along to save them, or very recently in the last generation is my work's going to save me. So, it's not about that, you need to get actually inside, get internal and do what I call the internal work. The internal work consists of going through all these things and clearing the way of all your negativity and resentments and things like all that. But also, it's about filling up the vessel again, and that's with positivity and loving yourself and allowing and being open rather than closed. And even if you do have fears, and we all have fears on different levels, it's being able to make the choices around your fears, not because of your fears. Listening to your intuitive self, trusting yourself, all of these incredibly important things to, because if we live our life based on fear, then we are going to live a very mediocre life, unfortunately. Because that's all we'll ever allow ourselves to do. But when we come from our intuitive self and our soulful voice or our gut feeling, if you will, then we have a more powerful, courageous and vibrant life.

Craig White:

I think we're here where we have this life to live abundantly, don't we, and have the becoming and have the feelings and enjoy what life is meant to be.

Alexandra Watson:

Yes.

Craig White:

I love how you talk about being emotionally driven as well, and how women are very emotional. But I think we are all emotionally driven. We're not intellectually driven, are we? It's the emotions of that incredible strength that I think we all carry.

Alexandra Watson:

It's all about the awareness I was talking about, as well as aware of your emotions, because emotions are feedback. So, when you're feeling really, really good about something you're doing, your emotions are high, your adrenaline's high, your endorphins are high, your serotonin's high, so you're going to feel great and empowered and sort of motivated. And so, you listen to that. You follow that. You keep going for that feeling. And as soon as something feels down or low energy or not so great or icky in some way you can't quite put your finger on, you stop doing it. I understand the philosophy behind it, is that you push through. Keep going, push through this. I think it's a little bit crazy. I think you should actually forget about your weaknesses or something you don't like, and move towards what you want to do and what you do like and what you're good at.

Craig White:

100% agree with that focus, and I'm all on the power that we carry.

Alexandra Watson:

Yes, let's do it the easy way, not the hard way.

Craig White:

I completely agree with that. So, another kind of real core aspect, I believe, is confidence.

Alexandra Watson:

Yes.

Craig White:

Sometimes people lack confidence, maybe because of their social environment, it may be necessary to their beliefs and the negative baggage that they carry, but you also have some simple secrets that you share with people on your website to create confidence. And I know we'll give people your website so they can go and check it out for themselves, maybe get some more info, get a few peeks at you. But what can we share with people about creating that instant confidence and releasing that inner strength that we're talking about?

Alexandra Watson:

Of course. Just to let you know that there's a lovely freebie on the website, too, that they can just go and get. So, just go and have a look at that. It's an audio of me telling you how to be unstoppable in happiness and confidence. That's a perfect preview for them to go and get, my gift to them. But yes, what are the core secrets to it? Confidence is a really interesting one, actually, because it is something you can actually fake. Hands up, who's faked being confident? Hello!

Craig White:

It's an attitude, isn't it?

Alexandra Watson:

Practice it. I've seen very well-known people of stage and screen fake it. Absolutely fake their confidence. And people that would surprise you, that you would think are super confident, and because of their demeanor and whatever, because it's something you can fake. Hurrah! You know, that said, I'm all for faking confidence, in the sense, you know, "fake it 'til you make it", but don't fake anything else, only confidence. Because confidence is one of those things like a muscle. We've already got the muscle within us, but sometimes it's something we've not used quite often, therefore it's a big flabby muscle, so we need to work it out. In order to work out that muscle and get it stronger, and to be more of a part of what we do on a daily basis is to imagine yourself feeling confident.

This is what I call mental rehearsal or a visualization, if you will. That is just to remember a time that you felt really confident, and we've all had those times. Even if it was just a tiny moment at one point in your life where you felt really good about yourself and felt confident and relaxed and happy. You want to get back to that memory and work on that memory. Use that memory. Make it a bigger memory, longer, really act into it, revisit it with more power, colour, and remind your body of what that felt like. And do that often, to remind yourself.

Now, that's one way to do it. And there's other ways to do it, which we do naturally without even thinking about it. It's a subconscious thing we do, and that is, for example, if you've got an interview, or an important meeting, for example, that you go to, we always dress up, right? We put on clothes that make us look smart, or make us look more capable, more confident. That's the great thing. You can put on clothes to make you feel better, so use that, too. Go in your wardrobe. What makes you feel good, what makes you feel better and more confident? Wear that stuff. Because I know you feel different going around in your trackie bottoms than you do in your best power suit, right? There's a difference in energy, a shift in us is made when we put on different clothes. So, use that too. It's a very simple thing to do. But do it.

I've got a pair of shoes that I wear on stage. I don't know whether you noticed them, Craig.

Craig White:

I did. You can't miss them

Alexandra Watson:

I love these shoes. I get loads of confidence in these shoes, they're absolutely fabulous, and I love them to death. And they're really high heels, and I don't usually wear high heels a lot, but they're really high, these beautiful satin, purple shoes, and I put them on, and bam! Instantly I'm in that super-confident mode. You can train yourself to do that. It's very, very simple. We can train ourselves to be in any state, but in confidence, yes, you can do this, this is the easiest one to do. So, find a piece of clothing, whatever it is, when you put it on think "Yes, I feel confident" and then, you can just wean yourself off the piece of clothing, but keep that feeling.

We do it as babies and we can do that now. We can emulate how we want to feel by just recalling a feeling we've had before and then making it ever-present, and focus on it more. And that's how you create it within you.

Craig White:

I love that. It reminds me, I've got a friend who's a magician, and he's quite shy off the stage, but as soon as he puts that magician's hat on, he's a performer, and that confidence is unleashed. I'll share a quick story. I remember being in Rome, and we're going back some years, beautiful city.

Alexandra Watson:

I love Rome.

Craig White:

I was staying in the Cavalieri Hilton Hotel, beautiful hotel, probably one of the most spectacular hotels I've stayed in. Bad habit at the time, Alex, I smoked at the time, and I remember walking down the shops for some cigarettes. I'd had a party with my friends the night before and I wasn't feeling at my best, and I probably wasn't looking at my best, either. But what I noticed, as I walked to the shop, was all these Italians, the locals, were dressed, looking sensational. They looked fantastic just to go to the shop to get the morning's paper and a packet of cigarettes. And I could see that they walked strong, they walked confidently. And here's me not looking so great, not feeling so fabulous, kind of dragging my feet a little bit. And it really made a strong impression on me, about exactly what you're saying, dressing for success and how that actually makes you feel great from within as well.

Alexandra Watson:

It sure does, and what could be easier? Very easy thing to do. So, why not do it? Actually, just talking about that a little further, I've got this story. I don't know whether you've heard this one, about Beyonce, just coming off your lovely story about your magician. When Beyonce, goes on stage and she does those amazing performances, she says, "It's not me that's doing them." She says she has an alter ego that she calls Sasha Fierce, and she turns into Sasha Fierce when she's on stage, and then she's Beyonce off stage. I think that's fascinating, that she creates an alter ego, and I know a lot of other performers do a similar type of thing, is that they create an alter ego that they become when they perform.

We all perform in life anyway, for one level or another. I don't actually have stage lightings and cameras, but we all have a performance whether it's at work, or at home, or whatever it is. I think that's a fun thing to do. You can create your project to work on, or you've got a big event to go to, or a big meeting or an important interview or something like that, and create this super persona of your bigger, shinier self, and step into it. And walk around in it, and use it. You can always come out of it again, later, but see how it feels.

Craig White:

That's exciting. I'm sat here with a smile on my face.

Alexandra Watson:

I'd love to know what yours looks like, Craig.

Craig White:

Okay, a little bit brilliant. Well, it's been a pleasure talking to you. I think I can see and understand why you're a mentor to so many women in business and entrepreneurs. I mean, you must have your mentors. Who are your mentors, Alex, if you don't mind me asking?

Alexandra Watson:

No, not at all. I've had so many over the years, and I've had some amazing ones. I always have tried to go to the best I can find, because that saves you time, energy and money. Right? I've had a lot of people come to me because they've chosen mentors that didn't that for them. So, I've always made sure I've chosen really fantastic mentors and one of the first mentors I had was Mark Victor Hansen, and Robert Allen. They were two of the probably still, I'm not sure how they rate with J. K. Rowling, but some of the book best-selling, Robert Allen did The One Minute Millionaire and all of that. So, those guys taught me an incredible amount, and I was with them for three years. And then Jack Canfield himself, the author of Chicken Soup for the Soul. There's been Marianne Williamson, of course from Return to Love.

Yes, Dr. John Gray, Men are from Mars, Women are from Venus. He gave me a lovely testimony on my book, too, which was very kind of him. And more recently I've sort of been looking towards people who are more business orientated in a sense, because I'm really fascinated with business, you know? I think it's such an incredibly interesting thing to do, is to have your own business. It's incredibly challenging, but so fascinating and so fulfilling. So, more business people.

I've been reading like crazy, all the different biographies of well-known and very successful business owners. I just can't stop learning, really. I want to learn as much as I can. And I definitely tell other people to do the same, never stop learning. Always keep learning, and get mentors whenever you need to. Mentors do many things for you, but the main thing they do is to give you a quantum leap in life, and they can jump you from where you are now to years ahead. And that's why I've always used them myself, and I always will.

Craig White:

I think it's a shining example of the importance of continuous and never-ending improvement. That philosophy of the more we learn, the more we become, and the more we can do.

Alexandra Watson:

I think it's a passion. Indeed, it's a passion to learn more. One of the reasons we're on this earth I think is not only to give our gifts and fully express who we are, but actually—I know we have unlimited potential, but to really stretch the boundaries of our potential and see how far we can go, and what we can become, who we can become. Because I've always said, you know, in this country I think there's a slight wobble when it comes to money. Other countries, especially the United States, quite happy about making money, that's the American dream. But over here we're far more reserved about making money.

My point is really about money, what if entrepreneurs come to me and say, "I love to do what I do. I don't need to get paid for it. I'd happily do it for free." Whereas that's wonderful, and I love working with the heart centered entrepreneurs who work in those types of industries, the service industries where they're just helping people, but at the same time, you've got to understand that money's not a bad thing. Money's a good thing, because what actually is, the more successful you become, and therefore the more money you get, it's actually stretching you and challenging you to be a bigger version and a better version of yourself. So, I don't see money or becoming wealthy as a bad thing, I see it as a very good thing. Because it's who you have to become in order to be successful, really that is personal development itself.

People always say to me, "Well, I'm happy to give away what I do." And I say, "That's not serving the world if you do. Whatever you do has to be an exchange of energies. So, what have you helped somebody do, they really should give you an exchange of energy back." Now back in the day that was bartering, right? We used to barter a bag of rice for a bag of peas. Now it's money. The commodity we use is money. Therefore, be happy about that. Be happy that you are going to be paid well for what you do, for what you do is of great value. I think that's what I teach a lot of the women that I work with that have their own businesses, so encourage them to move towards being the best version of themselves, to play big, and to shine fully. I think that's the most important thing.

Craig White:

Alex, it's been an absolute pleasure speaking with you today and I'm positive, women in business listeners have loved today. Hopefully they'll connect to you and look upon you as an inspiring mentor. And I'm sure those men of the world that are connecting with their feminine side like myself—I like to believe.

Alexandra Watson:

Yes, we love you too.

Craig White:

We hope you've enjoyed the show. Alex, thank you very much.

Now's YOUR time to break free of what's holding you back so you can leap to your next level and become more successful.

Be all You Can Be within a short space of time – say goodbye to lack of confidence, procrastination and fear and instead feel good about who you are and where you're heading with more clarity, focus and energy.

Your success is waiting for you, so what are YOU waiting for? Take this opportunity to make a firm step towards your future because it IS bright and shiny!

Alexandra's expertise helps people like you create a 'Successful Mind' one which creates wealth in all areas of your life whilst abandoning doubt and limitations. You become happier, more fulfilled than ever before and very, very masterful at success – and right now, you're closer than you think!

99% of the time you're very close to making that breakthrough to success but something (and its often invisible to you) is holding you back. Knowing HOW to change that (and never look back) is what we promise - ONLY if you agree that it's YOUR time!

Being all you can be is your life's journey. It is what many of us set out to do but now there is a way to achieve this faster than ever before...

...Alexandra will show you HOW to ACCELERATE SUCCESS!

About Alex

Hundreds of people have created successful and prosperous lives through Alexandra's guidance and mentoring. You too can leap to your next level by accessing her teachings and support.

Founder of The Success Experience a never-done-before combination of training, coaching, education, support and entertainment in one great club - that's free to join!

Testimonials

"Happiness is about knowing who you are and what you want in life. Alexandra takes you on a vibrant and exciting journey to the center of your soul"

Dr John Gray - Best Selling author of 'Men Are From Mars, Women Are From Venus'

"Alexandra's wisdom helps you 'pick up the mirror' take charge of life and ultimately gain the happiness you so richly deserve."

Susan Jeffers - Best Selling author of 'Feel The Fear and Do It Anyway

http://alexandrawatson.com/

CHAPTER

8 Prosperity Through Passion

Do you know who you are, what you stand for and who you can be? What is the better version of you and what does that look like? Do you embrace your life experiences as your blueprint.

True prosperity is not about being better than anyone else it's about being better than what you used to be. Striving to be the same on the inside and on the outside emotionally, spiritually, financially and physically. Living a life of purpose.

Imagine feeling totally free, without judgement to go for your goals while happily embracing whatever the outcome may be.

In this podcast, Dillon will share his 8 pathways to your personal powers formula. Prepare to banish your limiting beliefs for good

1) Mental Power

2) Physical Power

3) Spiritual Power

4) Emotional Power

5) Vocational Power

6) Financial Power

7) Social Power

8) Charitable Power

CRAIG WHITE:

Welcome and hello, again, I'm Craig White and this podcast show is proudly brought to you by the Passion to Succeed. I'm absolutely buzzing for today's show. We've got a fabulous guy who's become a great friend of mine over the recent years. Dillon has been on the show with us before and I'm happy to have him back on today's show because what Dillon's going to talk to us about is about prosperity through passion, through purpose and through profit. This guy really is on a mission to contribute.

I've got a question for you. What does living on purpose mean for you? What does giving value without need of compensation mean to you? What do you do because you love it from within? Look, guys, this guy Dillon has become, and I believe, one of the most rounded people I know. He's an expert and professional personal development speaker. He's a full-time Forex trader, property investor, and a guy who's on a mission to create a community of high performers. What inspires me most is the work Dillon has done in Rwanda, where he is on a mission to invest £10m over the next ten years to fund young, innovative businesses. Do you know what? He's already started on that mission, and I find that really, really inspirational.

So, Dillon, welcome to today's show, it's absolutely great to have you onboard. I want to get straight into the show. What I want to talk about is, and I believe you very much have the blueprint for success. You know, you've contributed over the last few years, you've created a seven-figure business, and for a minute, I just want to talk about you. What has enabled you to make all the difference? What has enabled you to start to achieve some of the success that you deserve, maybe you crave? What were the changes you made, and I'm aware that success isn't all about money? But what's enabled you to consistently make money?

DILLON DHANECHA:

I always had the gut instinct that actually what allowed me to make money consistently was everything else that I'd got right in my life, so I'd optimised my life in my mental, spiritual, physical, emotional pathways. I had started really leading from the heart, really coming from a place of service, and I had just got a grip, a real control, over my money mechanics. And all of that together then meant that I could pick up any system. I could look at a property system and make money from that. I could jump onto the markets and make money from that. I could get into digital marketing and make money from that. I could speak on stage and make money from that.

And it's not that I was a genius at the techniques, it was just that I had the right state management, and the right infrastructure systems and blueprints in my life, which meant that the widget, the system itself, really didn't matter. There weren't any confidence issues, there wasn't any fear other than the natural anxiety about learning a new system, there was an addiction to education and learning new things, and there was an optimised life, into which that could be slotted in. That's really where the whole proper model for limitless living came out of. It says, look, most people will start with making money, and the thought process goes, "if I make enough money to pay my bills, then I can figure out what I really love doing and do that, because my bills have been dealt with, and once I'm doing what I love, then I can be happy."

But we've flipped that on its head and said actually what we've found through over a decade of my own application, and over two and a half thousand students in the last three years that are the Prosper Trials, and previous to that, in the Make Money Trading the Markets business, I've found that actually, the people who focus on the front end, say let's get life in order first, let's really simplify, systemise and scale life, so the mental pathway, the physical pathway, the spiritual pathway, those three pathways I call vital energy.

If you've got your mental pathway in check and you're taking on new information, you're conscious of what new information and new messages you're taking in, you are applying the learning from kind of getting things wrong, so you actually get the opportunity to turn bad judgement calls into good judgement calls by leveraging the experience that comes from them, if you move more, say you focus on your physical strength, focus on your physical endurance, focus on your physical flexibility, and then you add onto that a level of spiritual connectedness so you just decode the world around you in a way that's conducive to success, that's kind of vital energy.

The supplement to that is your emotional pathway, so how do you live the laws of love? In terms of optimising life, if you can get your mental, physical, spiritual and emotional pathways really fine-tuned, they're your inner, your inward-looking powers, then your outward-looking powers, so that's your vocational pathway, how you serve others, that's your financial pathway, what you do with the money that you make from serving others, your social pathway, how you develop inspiring networks, and your charitable pathway, how you sow seeds of prosperity for others. If you get your inward-looking pathways right, then your outward-looking pathways, they just sort themselves out. Yes, there's work to do, yes, there's systems and blueprints to put in place to get them to work, but they're much easier. I think a lot of people focus on the outer powers, the outer pathways, before they focus on the inner powers and the inner pathways.

Craig White:

Totally. One of the things I've noticed with yourself, that is since we met at the gym—for those of you that have listened to our previous podcast show, you know that we met at the gym and I think connected through that almost kindred affiliation. I think we were talking about Dr. Wayne Dyer at the time, and I think we just got into a really great conversation. You've become a great friend of mine over the years, which is just great, and an inspiration in many ways. Just listening to you now, it's getting me thinking, me focusing on how to change, how to grow, how to become more in order to give more. You know, how we change is how we succeed.

But one of the things I've always noticed, being in the same environment as you, often when we kind of bump into each other over at the gym, you have this childlike wonder of kind of happiness and contribution to everybody. In the gym, you're always friendly, you're always warm, you're always positive, but you also have this childlike wonder to listen and to grow. I guess what you're saying is by getting your inside right is what's going to enable you to contribute more on the outside.

So, how does someone go down that route? What would you try to guide people to really start to get their insides right? What's the key things that you do, you've done, you've maybe done in the past that you're reconnecting with? I know we were talking about tracking earlier, before the call, with regards to your swimming. So, I guess there's lots of points to focus there, and blueprints to get inside, right?

Dillon Dhanecha:

There really is. First of all, I'm totally humbled and honoured by that. To be an inspiration to anybody is remarkable, let alone to people that I've known for years and years, and like you say, we just have this beautiful relationship ever since we were talking about Dyer, and The Power of Intention, and some of his other work. So, totally humbled, and I'm honoured by that kind of description of our relationship, and I'm absolutely with you there.

The other thing I smiled at when you said, is this: childlike wonderment. And I call it kind of an inquisitiveness, a curiosity, a desire to actually find out more. You know where that comes from? That comes from looking back at a time in my life where—I never had it really bad. My parents came to the country as refugees, so on and so forth, but I never really felt that--we grew up in a massive council estate in the late '70s, but I never felt like the son of refugees. I never felt like we had the financial difficulties that my parents obviously had. This is not a sob story, and I think there are many, many people probably listening this who had it far harder than I ever had it, but I still managed to waste my time at school.

Now, I got good grades and I got my GCSEs and my A levels. I did fail my first year at uni but I still managed to come out with a 2:1 at the end of it. A lot of that was just being really petrified by having to go home to my mom and dad and tell them I failed, so there was a fear factor there, definitely, but I look back at that time and see a young boy who constantly and consistently lived life for his friends and more than that, approval from the people around him. It was this desire to get people's approval that really stopped me learning everything I could have learned in all those phenomenal years at school, phenomenal years at university. I remember all through that time, now looking back, that I was just living for other people, Craig.

I was living for their approval, I was living for the significance that I got in certain situations, you know, spending money that I didn't have, not paying attention in class, and that went on to university to almost being kind of the big character on the outside, but being a very small, shy, lacking in confidence guy on the inside. There was just never any congruence between the inner me and the outer me. Because I was living for other people's approval, of course I never really followed my heart in those days. I had a real desire to learn more about science, for example, but at secondary school—I went to a comprehensive school, massive comprehensive school, it was not the done thing to be into science. Therefore, I kind of made it my mission to sabotage my success in science. And that didn't work because I still continued to—I wouldn't necessarily say get bullied although there was a bit of that, but it was more around, when you're not congruent, people see that you're not congruent.

Human beings resonate with congruence. If you know that somebody is a bit of a moron and he himself knows he's a bit of a moron, you're probably likely to share a drink with him at lunchtime, or in the evening, and have a laugh with him, because it's totally congruent. But if you've got somebody that pretends to be something and they're not, because you can't read them, you don't really want to spend any time with them. It's not the "he's a great guy" or "he's not a great guy", it's just that, is he congruent or not? And we resonate with congruence. And actually, if you look at some of the big personalities at the moment in U.S. and U.K. politics, it's interesting that the polls for, I wouldn't necessarily say likeability but I'm going to use that word, the polls for likability actually show we like the congruent guys better than we like the people who portray themselves to be good guys. Does that make sense?

Craig White:

Yes. Totally.

Dillon Dhanecha:

So, congruence is what really drove me to say look, I want to live a life where I am the same on the outside as I am on the inside. I remember there was a moment in time when I started learning in the sociology organisation, I did a module on the sociology of organisations, and in that module, we talked about front stage and backstage, and how, when you are at work, you play the front stage character in a theatre, and when you are at home, you play the backstage character in the theatre. This is all about understanding employees. This would have been in the late '90s I was studying this. I remember at that time, thinking why does there have to be a front stage and a backstage at all, and can you not turn around and just set light to the frickin' curtain until there is no front stage and backstage.

It took me another ten years to really live that principle. What changed for me was that desire to not waste any more time living life for somebody else. I know that that's a real cliché. When people used to tell me, "Live for yourself, not for other people," I thought it was absolute nonsense. I didn't realise I was living for other people. But it was a desire to say, "I've got dreams, I've got ambitions, I've got intentions, there's things I really, really like." I'm looking back at the last ten years feeling like they were slightly wasteful years, and I think as people who are spiritually connected and have studied personal development material, I think we now look back at those years and see them very much as learning years and that's why.

But at the time I didn't. I was at rock bottom, spiritually, financially and emotionally, physically totally destroyed. I'd tried to make money in jobs and on the markets and as a consultant, that hadn't worked, I couldn't ever keep hold of any of that money. I was spending way more than I should have done. I was giving away more than I should have done, like this guilt-ridden giving. I then gave all that up, went out to Rwanda to volunteer for UNECO, for the United Nations Economic Commission for Africa, and I volunteered my consultant services there. I ended up giving away every last penny there, and getting into more debt, just to support individuals who I thought needed more money than me.

Anyway, none of that worked, because I came back totally penniless, had to hitch a ride, funnily enough, from Kigali back to Nairobi, which is a trek and a half, because all I had left was my plane ticket, and I was at that stage too proud to call my dad. We'd left on beautiful terms. I love my parents to pieces, but he did tell me "You can't help the poor by being poor. I'm not telling you what to do, but just bear that in mind." I was too proud to say, "Dad you were right. Can you pay for my journey back home? I can't afford the entire flight." I hitched a lift on one of the container lorries of the coffee plantation that I'd been helping out there, and I just said, "Look, I need to get to Kenya, I need to get on a flight back to London. I've got my return ticket from Nairobi Airport, but I haven't got any money at all to fly from Kigali to Nairobi." And just that trip alone was fascinating. We saw container lorries that had been looted on the back roads it was a daunting trip, but a trip where I really got the opportunity to think about what I was doing and why I was doing it, and who was I doing it for.

I didn't have any of the tools and the blueprints and the systems then, but something said you've got to stop living for other people. You've got to stop living for significance and excitement and start living for giving and growing in parallel with each other. Giving and growing, they have this symbiotic relationship. You can't do one without the other. And you have to start living love and be love. I wasn't that articulate with myself obviously, being as low as I was. That level of articulation just wasn't in my capacity at the time, you know, I was beating myself up and proclaiming how much time I'd wasted and so forth, but I was definitely having a word with myself.

Craig White:

Wow, it sounds like one hell of an adventure. An eye-opener, I guess. So, what's at the heart of your success now? Obviously, fast forward into today. You've created a lot of top value products that have obviously been distributed into the market, that people have gained much from. I was speaking to a lady at the gym recently, and I could see in her whole mannerisms, body language, even in her eyes, because the eyes never lie. And I know she's focused on one of your courses at the moment and enjoying it and it's uplifting her, and it's almost her time with herself, like that hour of power she's giving herself every day. An hour of power with Dillon.

Dillon Dhanecha:

[laughing]

Craig White:

So, what is at the heart of your success now? Where we are today. I know in the past we've just gone on and discussed Prosperity Fruit, Passion, Purpose and Profit. What's your focus, and not necessarily how people can connect with you because we'll talk about that later, but how can we influence people to delve into what's important to them and unleash that passion that they have inside?

Dillon Dhanecha:

Penny is a great example of why I do what I do, and also a great example of what anybody can do to turn their life around. Penny is completing the Overwhelmed to Overdrive program, it's one of our flagship audio programs. It's one of the audio programs that I am blown away by—I just would never have thought that I had the capacity to create a program that has touched so many lives in such a deep way. So, in that sense, that's such a cliché to say, "I live for the service." But I truly, truly do live for the service and the difference that our products make to people's lives. When you see Penny and every single session she completes, it's like another breakthrough, another "Aha" moment, another distinction of life, and she, in her heart, feels lighter. In her eyes, she's sparkling again. It's like she's found this kind of passion for life again. Not that she'd lost, but she maybe hadn't connected with for a while. That's why I do what I do. That's at the very heart of what I do.

When I sit down to map out another quarter in our business, or another decade in the business, and now we've just put together 100-year plan for the business, you know, what is the impact of the Prosper School for Limitless Living in 100 years. How is this, what we're doing today going to be the ripple in 100 years-time. Whenever I sit down to create those plans, it's about saying, "How do we want to impact people's lives? How can I change an individual's life, and by doing so, have them be the ripple in the pond of their life? How, when Penny goes from overwhelmed to overdrive, how is she now the ripple in the pond for her family? And how are they going to be the ripple in the pond for their friends and family?"

That's as true and we've got three streams of development, if you like, three laboratories of experimentation. One is kind of where we engineer consciousness, the other is where we engineer enterprise, and the third is where we engineer wealth. When I create products in any of those schools, if you like, in those laboratories, we're always thinking, how do we impact lives by what we're doing, not just today, but tomorrow and the next day and the next day and the next decade, and so on. That's at the very heart. I truly believe that service is the new selling. I don't think we need to sell anything. We haven't built this seven-figure education building in less than three years by selling. We've built it through servicing. And I use the royal "we". Of course, now, we've got the team of individuals and I've got a great group of collaborators together. It's all come through service.

So, where does that even come from? How do you go from a place where you're absolutely distraught and you've got no money, I was £100,000 in debt, couldn't even afford to catch my flight back home? How do you move from a place where you're that low, to a place where you're just on cloud 9 every single minute of every single day? You do it by falling in love with yourself, and you do it by saying, "I can't give what I don't have. So, I've got to get strong in order to give strong."

How do I do that? Well, first of all, I have to accept where I'm starting from and where I'm starting from is right here, right this minute, just here is where I start from. I can't start from anywhere else. What's done is done, and what's yet to be done is yet to be done, so I'm here, in the present moment. My journey is a reflection of the decisions that I've made so far, and they're neither good nor bad, so I'm not going to view those decisions with any sense of judgements, but I am going to view them with a sense of asking myself a simple question. Did they work for me, or not? Did those decisions work for me, or did they not? Did living for the approval of other people, whether it's my friends, whether it's my family, whether it's people I don't even know, did that work for me? No, it didn't. And so, what can I do differently?

It's this kind of reflection on life and on our life experience, but without any judgement. That is ridiculously hard to do, because we are all conditioned to either pat ourselves on the back or kick ourselves in the ass. That's the reality. We've got to stop doing either of those. It's not about congratulating ourselves on the great decisions and kicking our backsides for the bad, but it's saying, what are the decisions that brought me here, did they work for me or did they not, and what can I do differently? And how can I love myself throughout that process, because loving myself and filling myself up with love, living the laws of love, embodying love, being love every minute of every day, is what's going to get me through.

My job here is, in essence to develop my consciousness, develop my intuition to spot and act upon the coincidences that kind of come across my eyes and my heart every single day. I can only do that from a position of love. If I'm hating on myself, my eyes are not going to be open. I'm going to be moving through my days in a really low state of vibration. Some of this stuff gets a bit "woo-woo", but I firmly believe that the results are rooted in the woo-woo, they really are. It's about, first and foremost, falling in love with myself, it's about falling in love with who I am, what I stand for, what I stand against, so if we try to guide other people, it's about that. Fall in love with who you are, fall in love with what you stand for, what you stand against, if you don't know what you stand for and what you stand against, fall in love with not knowing and that's fine because that's a journey of discovery. Fall in love with your journey, the good bits and the bad bits, the light bits and the dark bits. Fall in love with everything you have been, everything you are right now, and everything you ever will be, because that's all you have. Once you fall in love with that, you really start to love the experience of life.

There's this concept of white light. White light is made up of all the different colours of the rainbow. My dad used to work at a company that produced commercial printers, and he used to bring these prisms home, which they used in the machines. I loved the prisms. You shine sunshine through them and the light comes out the other end like the rainbow. I didn't really know what that meant. I started thinking about this concept while I was in Australia. We spent three months in Australia, January, February and March, this year.

I was thinking about this concept of light and dark, yin and yang, and I was thinking about white light, and if you want to shine a bright, white light, then what we have to do is to embrace all the colours of the rainbow. Now we might not like all the colours of the rainbow, i.e. the different experiences in life, but we just have to love them all and experience them for the learning that they give us. Love them for the learning that they give us. You can only do that, again, from a place that says, "I love everything about me right now. There's nothing I do not like about me, because that's me, and that's all I have." I might think I need to get down to the gym a little bit more, I might think I need to swim a bit faster, I might think I need to work a bit harder or work a bit less or spend more time with my family or less time with my family or pay my partner more attention or pay my partner less attention. There's all these things I think I might need to do, but that shouldn't stop me loving who I am, because that's all I have.

Craig White:

I used that philosophy in being your best, I guess it always sets down our beliefs which, you know, literally that are not necessarily true, it's just us going into the state of mind of them being so. It's that vibe or philosophy of being as best as the best but no better than the rest.

Dillon Dhanecha:

Absolutely. We have a phrase at our school, which is, "True prosperity is not about being better than anybody else. It is about being better than you used to be." If you can focus just on being a little bit better than you were yesterday, and probably not quite as good as you're going to be tomorrow, you make progress, and all that's needed to be happy in life is this sense that you're making progress. You're moving forward. If you have that and if you feel that, you never look back and think you wasted time because you have this sense that you're making progress.

True prosperity's not about being better than anybody else. It is about being better than you used to be. Quite often, you might compare yourself to somebody else on the outside, but it's not about comparing yourself to somebody on the outside, it's about saying, "Who am I right now, and who could I be on steroids? What is the better version of me, what does that look like? And how do I get there?" And that way, you become totally consumed in your own journey of development and expansion. And then it stops being about the outside world and it just is about you and your journey. I'm here today, I want to get to there tomorrow, I'm going to try my hardest to get there. I'm going to work my hardest to get there. I'm going to be and do everything I need to be to get there.

But actually, I'm not really that bothered about getting there at all. I just want to embrace the experience of moving towards that. It's this balance between setting goals and detaching from the outcome. The balance between the be and the do is very, very important in this. That rests upon your ability to stop comparing yourself to other people, to stop criticising your performance in the context of what you think you should have done, or what other people think you should have done, and to stop complaining about the world around you. There are the three deadly sins, criticism, comparison, and complaint, and if you can get rid of those from your life, that's a great start to falling back in love with yourself.

Craig White:

I just love the share, the philosophies, and the way you word things, because to me, and talking to the thousands of people that I do, and the many that I coach, it's about, as you said, removing the need for an outcome. It's about enjoying the process. One of the things I've learned over my years of personal development from yourself and many other people, it is about enjoying the journey. It's about loving what you do, doing it with passion, doing it to your very best ability, and as you said, that may not be as great as you may be tomorrow, but doing it with the best tools that you've got today. At the end of each day, regardless of the outcome, if people can remove that need for results, that need for compensation, if they can give the value, give the passion, give the activity and enjoy doing so.

And I know you're talking here about how to impact people's lives, because I think as a world, as a nation, as a community of people, if people could learn and live by that one philosophy, of making a positive impact on people's lives, doing something. You know, that value of contribution, that need that we have to make a difference—and I think everybody has that, they probably just don't realise, or they've not had somebody believe them, or their social conditioning or their environment hasn't enabled them to believe in themselves. This is why we do what we do.

If we can connect with people that never had this environment, you know, I think in a way, both yourself and me, we're lucky to have the parents we have. Strong parents, believe in us. Maybe the trials and tribulations that they may have had in the early years, but having that strong environment around us. Some people don't have that, Dillon, and I guess this is why we do what we do to impact the people. Your vision of the ripple effect has just blown me away today, because I've always believed in that, but your vision of 100 years' ripple effect. Sometimes I think a gesture of good will has a ripple effect. Even going out of the way just to hold the door open for somebody, is the base of having the right attitude to make a difference to people, and if more people even start small, and over time they grew their contribution, the ripple effect, just by making somebody smile, is going to have an impact on them making somebody else smile that day. I guess sometimes people don't realise how big an impact we can really have with a relatively small contribution. It's insane. I love it.

Dillon Dhanecha:

I absolutely agree. That has to then come from a place where you feel that you are valuable enough to contribute to the lives of other people. And you're quite right that this desire to contribute, this desire to collaborate rather than compete is within everybody. It is what the human civilisation is really founded upon, and was built by. If you look at some of the ancient civilisations 15,000 years ago in Turkey, when they honour these ruins, these ancient—more than ancient, ruins, they found no evidence of walls, they found no evidence of mass graves, and they found no evidence of weaponry. Which says to me that that was a place without war and scarcity, it says that that was a place that they didn't need to be protected by weaponry, it was a place there wasn't any mass killing.

So, what was it then? It was a place of collaboration. It was a place of community. It was a place of giving and growing together, and it's only really when you look at what we consider ancient history to be—so, at school, we considered ancient history to be 5,000 years ago, and it was the ancient Egyptians. Of course, there are many, many stories of war and infighting and killing and taking on leadership and so on, and so forth, in the Egyptian stories. But back a little further than that, and the human civilisation was all about collaboration. And I think that there has been a tendency towards competition which has permeated the mindset of a lot of people of the society of a lot of individuals, and organisations and communities and countries, that is not conducive to our long-term success and our long-term survival, even.

And we have an opportunity as individuals, building organisations today and creating families, today, and sharing messages with hundreds of thousands of people every year, we have an opportunity to shift or to play a part in the shift of human consciousness from the "I" and the competitive to the "we" and the collaborative. And if we're able to do that, just for one person, by holding the door open, and they're having a bad day but you held the door open for them, and all of a sudden you restore that individual's faith in humanity just for that split second, or we're able to do that on a much larger scale by taking people through structured programs of development, as you're doing through this podcast, then I think we really start to have the level of the ripple effect that I believe we can have, I believe everybody can have. Everybody is the pebble in the water of their own pond. But that has to come from a place where you feel valid enough to make a difference to the lives of other people. In order to get to that place, we come right back to falling in love with who you are, what you stand for, what you stand against, even if that's nothing, and embracing every part of your life experience as the blueprint of your life journey.

So, how do you do that practically? How do you get from a place where you might be rock bottom, and you're trying to create this new life for yourself? And remember, the life comes before the enterprise which comes before the wealth, so you've got to get life fine-tuned. So, how do you do that? Well, a great place to start is to just take the eight pathways we call the personal powers. The first personal power is your mental power. That's how you harness your brain magic. The second personal power is your physical power. That's how you sculpt your energy center. Your third personal power is your spiritual power. That's how you decode your world view. Your fourth personal power is your emotional power. That's how you live the laws of love. Remember those four are your inward-looking powers.

The remaining four—your vocational power, that's how you deliver your ultimate purpose in life. Your sixth personal power is your financial power, so how you leverage money mechanics. Your seventh is your social power, how you create inspiring networks, and your eighth is your charitable power, how you sow seeds of prosperity.

If you take those eight, mental, physical, spiritual, emotional, vocational, financial, social, charitable, and you just spend five minutes a day on each of those, just five minutes, nothing more and nothing less, set yourself the goal of spending five minutes developing each of those personal powers. So, what might that look like?

Your mental power, that might be listening to just five minutes of one of your podcasts. Your physical power might be just five minutes of jogging on the spot, bouncing on a trampoline, running around the garden, doing a few stretches, whatever that is. In your spiritual power, that might be a five-minute meditation, just sitting in silence for five minutes. In your emotional power, living the laws of love, that might be five minutes spent writing a love letter to that special person in your life, and if you have no special person in your life, write yourself.

In your vocational pathway, five minutes spent on understanding what your skills are. And we do a whole program on identifying what your purpose is, what your absolute skills are. In your financial pathway, five minutes on just, maybe even a daily balance sheet. That's a great place to start, what did you spend today, what did you bring in today? Some money tracking in your financial pathway, five minutes. In your social pathway, maybe joining a group on Facebook that is full of kindred spirits, and if you're already part of a group, maybe five minutes a day on supporting members in that group. So, we have a private members' community, and I encourage everybody in that community to support and be supported. So maybe five minutes a day on supporting people within your group, within your circle, in your space, Craig, supporting other people in the network marketing space.

And in your charitable pathway, if you can do nothing else, if you can't buy someone a sandwich or a coffee, then five minutes sat talking to that guy outside the tube station, that guy outside Starbucks, that guy sheltering in the rain because it's chucking it down. Five minutes. And if you do that every day, that's forty minutes of your time spent developing your eight personal powers, and it starts from there. And it's so small that it feels insignificant.

But what's easy to do is also easy not to do, so it has to be a conscious effort, a conscious drive. Five minutes a day spent on each of your eight powers is less than an hour. You can have it done before your family is even awake. It's that kind of task. And it starts from there. And you'll get addicted then. Because then it turns into six minutes of a podcast. Then it turns into six minutes of bouncing on a trampoline. Six minutes of meditation. Six minutes on a love letter. Six minutes considering what your skills are, etc., etc., etc. Does that help to get it a little more practical?

Craig White:

I think so, and I think for people to associate with that and literally look at the eight powers, both inward and outward, that you're discussing, I think that makes perfect sense to people. Then everybody can make the choice to give some time to themselves. We've discussed in the past, one of the biggest things is people spend too much time, like you said, trying to please other people, rather than actually giving themselves some quality time to develop from the inside and then, obviously, on the outside. Practically, I think that's fabulous. I think people can go away and start to work on these eight powers that they possess, and develop them to become better tomorrow than they were today.

Dillon Dhanecha:

Absolutely. If you want, if there's any material that you want to add to your show notes, or—I don't know how you work the podcast, I don't know whether you have show notes or not, but we can definitely put some material up there, even if it's just a list of the eight powers. Whatever. You let me know.

Craig White:

The show is obviously got out through iTunes and Stitcher and Sound Cloud, so that's great. We do have the website, Passionto-Succeed.com, where people can access the show notes, so that's certainly something we can do, Dillon. You mentioned the first of August, and you've got this launch of the Prosper School, which I know you're really excited and passionate about this contribution. How can people connect with that? They're listening through iTunes. What is the simplest and quickest way for people to connect with what's going on with you?

Dillon Dhanecha:

If I can do a shameless plug, that's fabulous, Craig, thank you. We're launching on the first of August. It is www.Prosper.school. That's www.Prosper.school. It is the Prosper School of Limitless Living. I'm super excited about this massive launch that we're doing. We've got a brilliant team behind it, and great content being pumped out, and a great opportunity for people to engineer limitless life, limitless enterprise, and limitless wealth, and do it from a place where you are right now. It doesn't matter where you are, but you've got an entry point to the different areas of the school. We work with people that have already got six, seven, and nearly—one person, nearly an eight-figure business, but we also work with people who are right at the beginning of that journey. So, people who are even struggling to breathe, even struggling to stay afloat, we've got entry points at that level as well. Www.Prosper.school.

Craig White:

That's fantastic and I'm so inquisitive to get connected with that on the first of August, and really appreciative for your time today. I know you're a busy guy and I'm sure the listeners on Passion to Succeed have enjoyed listening to you again, my friend. I bid you a fantastic day. Thanks again for joining us, and guys, I really do hope you've enjoyed today's show as much as I have. Look forward to connecting with you soon. Dillon, you're a star, mate! Thanks a lot.

Dillon Dhanecha:

Thank you, Craig. Take care. Bye-bye.

Dillon Dhanecha. Fails fast. Falls hard. Finds solutions. Committed to supporting entrepreneurs navigate the process of turning Ideas to Income. Dedicated to bridging humanity's biggest equality gaps with his collective of 10,000 conscious-capitalists; created, launched and scaled in the Legacy Makers Incubator.

https://www.facebook.com/pg/legacyincubator

CHAPTER

9 Modelling for Success

What would you do if you and your husband were both made redundant in the same week? Despite this set back Jackie is testimony that with the right mindset, attitude and work ethic you can model yourself to be a success.

Discover how Jackie with no confidence learnt how to unleash her entrepreneurial spirit by breaking the mould and surrounding herself with positive and likeminded individuals who inspired her journey of personal development.

Jackie's aim is to deliver a practical, relevant message that can make an immediate impact on people's professional and personal lives.

Craig White:

Hi everybody, hope you're well. Joining me today, we have an amazing lady. Somebody I've been lucky enough to know and associate with for many years now, in fact, my whole life. I often joke in our circle of friends and within our family that I've been dragged into this business when I was brought up. But actually, I'm quite proud to be talking to my mum today, Jackie White. I know my mum and dad have brought me up very well. They taught me some great philosophies and some great attitudes throughout my life. I do joke that I've been dragged up with my mum's Scouse background and my dad from Hammersmith. But jokes aside, I'm very proud to have had the upbringing that I've had. I really wanted to chat with my mum today as I know she's had a massive, massively positive influence on my life and hundreds, even thousands of people across a 40-year span.

To stay at the top of your game and to inspire, empower and coach thousands of people to succeed and to make their life better, to really make a difference in a short period of time is great, but to consistently do it for over 40 years, I just felt it would be great to speak to my mum today and find out where they are, get an idea of where this all started and some of the philosophies that they've lived by, and that maybe my mum can share with you. So, it's great to have you on the call, mum. I really appreciate you giving some of your time up for your son, so actually you probably should because I am your son. How are you today? Have you had a great day?

Jackie White:

Yeah, I've had a fantastic day, thanks. It's Sunday, I've seen the grandchildren and I've been out to lunch. I've contacted some people in the business, I've sent some emails, I've been very excited about some positive results of success that people have achieved, and had a really great day. Every day's a good day.

CRAIG WHITE:

You see guys, this is the kind of attitude I've been brought up with. So, what's life like for you now, mum? I obviously see yourself and dad often and see the life you have, but for the people who may not be aware, what's life like for you nowadays?

JACKIE WHITE:

Well, our life is sort of like a picture postcard life now, really. If you would have asked me this 15, 20 years ago, I'd have said we had a great lifestyle. We had a lot of freedom, and that's the most important thing to me. We had the nice cars and we had a nice little home. A small home, but a very nice home, and we had one or two holidays a year, and we just enjoyed ourselves. We weren't in great debt. We just did quite well out of life, really.

CRAIG WHITE:

I remember growing up as a kid, and I've been lucky enough to see some of the wonderful places around the world. But, I also remember how much you and dad worked in the roles that you had. It wasn't something that was just given to you, that lifestyle. It was something you had created, even though I know it all changed, didn't it?

JACKIE WHITE:

Yes, it did. I've been very fortunate to work from home. I've done that for a long time, but about 14 years ago, we were both made redundant in the same week. Now, that was a bit of a shock, really. However, we started a business from home with not a massive outlay. We didn't have to borrow any money to do it. We learned something new and since then, our life has just changed. Not from the very start, we really put some time into it in the beginning. We really learned what to do and we put together a fantastic system, and we have built a huge, huge business that gives an unbelievable royalty income right now.

At our stage in life people say to us, why don't you retire? I think, why ask that question? Why would I ever want to retire? We have just the most wonderful lifestyle, we're free to do what we want, we choose to work or not to work, and there's a difference when you've got a choice. We are kept very young in our whole outlook because we mix with a lot of young people, and we have about eight or nine actual holidays a year. We've got a beautiful home, a home I never dreamt I'd ever have. We draft the calls we want to draft, we mix with really positive people with lots and lots of energy who have big dreams themselves, and that's a clue to keeping on-top, to keeping happy. We've also got the most beautiful farm. A villa on nine acres of land on a mountain in Spain, and that's what we call our retreat. We love going there, but we're in-touch with our business whilst we're there.

Many people from our business also enjoy that because I think we've just been so fortunate through our lives. We've met good people, we've associated with the right people, we've learned from the right people and taken good advice, and worked hard. I just feel we are so fortunate, and other people who are coming along with us, working hard with a good work ethic, having good dreams, we want to share that with them, too. It's a place that we really, quite frankly, share together. Our lifestyle right now is absolutely fantastic. Lots more to do, lots of places to see, lots of parts of the world we haven't been yet, and lots of things to achieve in our business.

Craig White:

You could say that you very much live the dream and that you've created a vehicle. So, what is a royalty income? What exactly is it, and how have you created it?

Jackie White:

A royalty income is an income where you're paid for the work that you have done probably years ago. We're building that royalty income even bigger, quite frankly. It's sort of like somebody who writes a book or writes a song, you could say like The Beatles. They wrote their songs many, many years ago. They worked long and hard. They worked around the clock, they travelled a lot and in-between, they sat down and they wrote songs. They are paid royalties on all of those songs now, so they're getting paid for a lot of hard work that they did many, many years ago. Those Beatles that are still with us are still working. They might be very rich, but they are still working. Why is that? Because their passion is about what they do. Well, we're exactly the same. We work very hard. We built our income. We built that royalty income. We will be paid a royalty on the business that we've built that will continue to grow. We still want to be a part of it, but we will be paid that income until the day we die.

What a wonderful way to earn a living. You would wonder why anyone would want to work for a boss. That's such a fantastic way. We are so fortunate that we do it. We are so fortunate that we found out about it, and that's what a royalty income is. We're going to continue to work because we're passionate about what we do, too.

Craig White:

Good use of The Beatles, there seeing as obviously, you come from the Northwest. You've obviously built that royalty income, but you talk about the freedom that that gives you and obviously, why would people work for a boss? But, I know from knowing you that you worked in the corporate world for 20, 25, 30 years. Albeit, working from home. What was it that you were doing and how did that set you up? I know you gained a lot of experience and knowledge from that business where you began working for somebody else, albeit working from home and gaining the skills that you adopted from your family.

I know you always talk about how granddad had a massive influence from his attitude of being an entrepreneur when you were younger, and obviously, that's influenced me when I was younger as well because it's given me that entrepreneurial spirit. You mentioned associations, and that power of association is important with our social environment. But, very important with our upbringing. For those of us who have got kids, it's really important that our attitudes are at the right level and were grateful, we have gratitude and we have a positive mindset, maybe an entrepreneurial mindset because that's then passed on to our children. Would you agree?

Jackie White:

I agree wholeheartedly, and obviously, a lot of my attitude, same with my sister and my brother, was given to us by our parents. My dad particularly, always wanted us to do more than our best. He always used to say, if you do your very, very best at everything, no one can ask for more. Always do your very, very best. And, make sure that the very best is a little bit more than other people do. That was one of the philosophies we were always brought up. We were always brought up to work hard and we got that work ethic I'm sure, from my parents. My dad was in business and had various businesses. A lot of it has got to do with that, but I don't want anyone to think – because this is important – there are a lot of people who haven't been fortunate to have that upbringing. I do believe that if you're in your 30s or 40s and you didn't have a good upbringing, you've probably been out of the influence of your parents for 20 years or so. So, you don't have to look back and think I wasn't lucky. You just have to read the right books. Surround yourself with the right positive attitude, the right positive people. Learn from people, and you can have the lifestyle you want.

I believe anyone can, and as far as where did it start, I worked in an office. I hated office politics. I hated going into work, wondering what mood other people were going to be in because I always wanted to be in a happy-go-lucky mood. I always wanted to have fun. I haven't actually worked in an office or normal place of work since I was 20 years old because I just couldn't stand it. When I left work, and started to have my children -- I had my children quite young -- I always worked from home, and I started to work from home for many, many years. I loved the freedom of working for myself. I also had the discipline, and this is something from my parents, to put that workload in and plan to put the work in to get what I wanted. I just knew that was a fantastic opportunity.

As time went on, I was always learning and working for myself. And then, in the 80s when I was working from home with a party plan company they promoted me onto the staff. I'm still doing the same job, still working from home, still growing a business, still growing and teaching people. But, I was on the staff for a while and that's when I got made redundant. So, that was quite some time. But, most of my time, even though I was on the staff, was spent building businesses. The only way, and the best way I can see to build a business is through the power of people. I think building people -- there's a little thing that, if you want prosperity for a year, grow flowers. If you want prosperity for ten years, grow trees. If you want prosperity for a lifetime, grow people.

I have to say that there is nothing more rewarding than helping people to find themselves, helping people to find what's within them and to find the talent that everybody's got. But, some people never can recognise it. That's important to me. That's why I feel fortunate to have met the people I've met in my lifetime that have had a great influence on me. There is something called the power of association. I never knew what that was until recent years, but I am so happy that I've been associating with the right people. Because I could never mix with negative people. I've always had to get away from them. That was a natural thing. It's something I've never been taught to do, I just had to get away from the maliciousness of the world.

I've always surrounded myself with people who were encouraging. With people who were inspirational. With people who I wanted to grow to be like. Because I've grown myself to be like somebody good, then I found somebody else to grow to be as good as them. You're always striving to improve yourself all the time. That's not a difficult thing to do. Anyone can do that. It's who your mentors are, who you associate with, who you would really like to emulate, who you'd really like to be like. We can all find people like that.

Craig White:

While you're talking about mentoring -- and I know the story. It's one of many stories you've told me about where it all started for you and the fun you've had building businesses from an early age when you got involved in party planning. It was self-employed then, wasn't it? You then developed into actually working for the company and running that sales team across the UK and Europe. When you first started in party plan, I remember you talking to me about how you had to make certain changes and mentor and model yourself. What was it you did? Why did you do it, and how did it empower you back then? And, how can people take that same principle into succeeding in their quest today?

Jackie White:

I'm glad you asked me that because whilst I had a lot of determination and whilst I had a very positive attitude, I was strong. I was a strong person. I was also extremely shy. I won't go into how shy I was, but I'll just say one thing. If I was getting a bus and I walked to a bus stop, I'd scan everyone waiting in the bus stop very quickly. If there was anyone standing at that bus stop that came into my dad's shop or lived on the estate, or somebody I would know by sight, if I had to say hello to them, I would not stand at that bus stop. I'd smile and I'd walk on. I'd acknowledge them just with a smile, and I would walk a mile to the next bus stop. Now, why was that? Because, if I acknowledge them I might have to speak to them, and I would be worried about, what can I say next?

So, I just wouldn't put myself in that situation. I'd walk a mile to another bus stop, and I'd scan that bus stop and do exactly the same thing. There's many a time I've walked all the way home because I saw somebody at the next bus stop. But also, if I got on the bus I would always go upstairs. If there were only four or five people on the whole bus, rather than sit in an empty seat by a window, in case somebody who ever got on the bus and vaguely knew me sat by me and wanted to speak to me, I would sit next to somebody already sitting on the bus. Somebody I didn't know, who was a stranger, and there was no way that stranger would start to talk to me. That is real shyness. That was real shyness and what I was like.

So, when I started party plan, I was more frightened to say no than I was to start Party Plan. I was nervous. I was hopeless at it. But, I started to go to meetings and started to get a tiny bit of success, and the guy that sponsored me really coached and guided and mentored me, and tried to mould me, and give me confidence. Little bits of success gave me confidence. Going to meetings, I saw a girl called June Middleton. Now, June Middleton had a fabulous personality and everywhere you saw her, there was a crowd of people around. She was always making people laugh, she was always smiling and she always knew what to say to people. I thought I'd love to be like her, so I would watch her.

When she demonstrated in the front of the meeting she was a wonderful demonstrator. She just made people want what she had, want what she was offering. I just wanted to be like that, so I would write what she said in shorthand, and when I went home on the bus I'd read it like a parrot. Then, when I got home I would sit in-front of the mirror and I would say these words that June had used. I would try to look like her and use her mannerisms. Well, I did this for a long, long time. I changed my hairstyle. She used to smoke, so I started to smoke. That was the only reason I started to smoke. I was 23 before I actually smoked, but I had to have the same image as June.

Over the years, I spoke so much like her that years later, we had a beauty salon together. We became very good friends and if anyone rung, either her husband or my husband, they couldn't tell our voices on the telephone apart. The only person who knew our voices apart was my dad. Even her husband would ring up and say, hi love, and he would start talking to me and it wasn't June, it was me. So, I had a lot of fun with that, actually. But at the end of the day, I emulated her so much. We walked alike, we talked alike and when we had our salon, people thought we were sisters.

Our mannerisms were the same, but do you know what? I felt really good. In other words, I lost the Jackie Dawson that I was at that time and I moved – it's like being an actor or an actress. When you step into someone else's part, you become very confident, and I'd stepped my life, the shy girl stepped into June Middleton's part. So, to do with business I'm very, very confident. I'm still June Middleton today, but put me in a different environment and I'll go shy for a couple of hours until I sort it out.

Craig White:

So, you very much modelled yourself for success really, like many people can. They can find mentors in life, people that have attitudes or skill sets to really gain confidence in that area of life, I suppose. Be it business or building relationships or communicating in a crowd or on a one-to-one basis, because I suppose everybody has different challenges in life. But, they can model themselves on a mentor, and from the association, can gain confidence in any area to succeed.

Jackie White:

Yeah, and you know what's important – I just have to say this – every single one of us who's a parent, we will care who our children mix with. We will find it very, very important who influences our children. So, why aren't we like that ourselves as adults? Is it not just as important who influences us? Should we not make sure we have a good influence in our life, in our mindset, in the way we look at things? Should we not make sure we are influenced by the right people? Because many people are influenced by what they see on the television. They are influenced by the miserable attitudes of a lot of people, or what it says in the newspapers. Why be influenced by that? It not only affects our own lives or your life. It would affect the lives of your children and your grandchildren. So, why can't people just be influenced by the best of things, to have the best of life? There's so much abundance in the world today and we can all have a part of that.

It's a very abundant world, but when people think it's not abundant they close themselves off to the great things in life instead of opening themselves up and being influenced by the right influences. By the books you read. By what you listen to. Even by the songs, the words of songs. Make sure they're happy words. Make sure they're good words, because it all goes in and what goes in, stays in.

Craig White:

There's very much that philosophy of – I'm not sure where I read it, but it's very much become one of my beliefs really. Our beliefs are the birthplace of excellence, and what we believe to be true, will it to go in the state of mind of being so. We live our life by our beliefs, don't we? I think the crazy thing is that our beliefs are actually built by an outside influence, and generally unless we take control and start consciously influencing ourselves through that power of association, through mentoring as well as influencing ourselves through inspiration. I think you said to me not so long to me, about making sure we influence ourselves through inspiration but also through that choice of personal development, what we read, what we're listening to, who we talk to, who we hang out with, so to speak. It's having that impact on our internal beliefs, which is what we live our life by. So, it's so very important for people to get that right.

Jackie White:

I think whatever influences us is our expectations in our life. And, our expectations are our limitations. So, if we're influenced by people who have a ceiling on what they feel they can achieve then already, we're not expecting to have much of a life, much excitement, much fun, much adventure. If you don't expect to have those good things, you just don't have them. It's something that I think is very, very sad. I think people don't have a lot of variety in their life, and variety is the whole spice of life. I just know from going to a job every day when I went to work, driving along the same road every day, going around the same roundabout, stopping at the same traffic lights, passing the same buildings, parking in the same carpark, going into the same office, sitting at the same desk with the same people, week in, day in, month in, month out, year in year out.

How do people exist like that? There is no variety in their life. If they're working in a place where there are stinking thinking people, that also has a bad influence on people's lives. People have to do these jobs, I realise that. But, that's not for me. I like to surround myself not only with positive people, but sometimes with people who, in the beginning, going into business on their own is a little bit scary. The people who genuinely want to do something about their life, there is nothing more rewarding than helping that person along. Helping that person to see there is something greater they can achieve. They can think a little bit bigger, they can dare to dream, and they can learn how to work and plan to work to get those things in life.

I really believe variety is the spice of life, and when I see people, or I overhear people's conversations, I can tell by their attitude, by their tonality when they speak, whether they have a life of fantastic variety, or whether it's a humdrum life, going to the same place every day, driving the same route every day, having the same income every month. They can't live above it. They can't dream and if they do dream a little bit, they get into debt because they're not in control of their income. That's because they are controlled by their company.

A lot of people have to have a job, but there are many people who can break that mold, get out of their job, be their own boss and learn. Whatever is inside of them, someone can help it come out if you would just mix with the right people. As long as you've got a good work ethic, you're willing to learn, you can make a plan and take advice and follow a plan with discipline, anyone can be free, whoever they are. Once you're free, you can work towards financial freedom and to have the life of your dreams. I really wish that more people would wake up and dream.

Craig White:

I think people are starting to realise now, there seems to be a shift that it's not about a job for life anymore. That philosophy of working for somebody all their life, I think there has been a shift and people are maybe looking for an opportunity rather than a job nowadays, but still maybe have that fear, that those sorts of things are for other people. I suppose we all go through that in the beginning, that stepping out of our comfort zone to be our own boss. What you're saying is, anybody can do it because there are always guidelines. There are always points of interest, points of focus where other people have laid the road and taken those steps before us. I'm a firm believer that anything in life can be achieved because generally, everything we look to achieve that's maybe goal-oriented, generally most things have already been achieved by somebody else. So, there's a way forward. There's a map from A to B.

People have just got to be willing and, as you said, right at the beginning get passionate about their life and passionate about their future. Passionate around what's important to them. I know that you and dad do very much live the dream, and having that mountain villa, that nine acres of farmland, that farm has been a dream of yours since when you very first got together and you met out in Majorca. To have that come true when over time, maybe that disappeared but it's been re-ignited through taking charge of your own life, running your own business and, as you said, working and supporting, coaching and empowering and inspiring other people to succeed, too.

Jackie White:

I agree with you, and I do feel that it is very scary in the beginning. But, if many people could realise you can be in business for yourself but you won't be by yourself, if you join the right thing, if you start the right way, if you get the right backing, the right support, it hasn't got to cost you much money to get into business, and you can get into a business working from home. You won't be by yourself, you'll have lots of advice on every single aspect of the business, everything you can possibly do. I just want to liken this to say, it's the Olympic year this year. We're going to see a lot of athletes, and maybe they started out quite young, going to little clubs and somebody saw them and saw that they might have had a talent inside them.

Well, I think everyone's got some talent inside them, and no athlete, no gold medal winner, no one has ever succeeded massively without a coach. Without somebody behind them, somebody coaching them, mentoring them, driving them. Now, that's all the athletes we're going to see at the Olympics so why can't every single person have someone behind them and achieve some of the dreams they want in life? If they can just break out of that mould, find the person who's going to mentor them, find the right thing to do, start in business for yourself with the right people, then I'm certain that many, many people could break free and have the freedom, the freedom in life that we were all destined to have.

We can be free, we just need the guidance sometimes and if it's scary, we can bite the bullet. There will be someone behind us.

As long as you've got work ethic, there will be somebody behind you, always to guide you and I think that's very, very important. Everyone can improve their lifestyle, everyone can improve their income and everyone can improve what they're doing to get to the dreams. Some people call it work. I call it the process. The process to success, it's the process to your dreams and if you work at something that you enjoy doing, and you can enjoy anything when you get quite good at it, and you get good with a mentor, then you can be passionate about what you do and you never work another day in your life. You will never feel that you work, so it's not work. It's a process that you're going through to live the life that you dream about, and we can all go through the process.

Craig White:

To have more, people really have got to focus on that process and becoming more. But, what key principles should people have in-place? To get from A to B what do they need to know? What would they need to implement? What would they need to learn? How would they need to act? What key principles, if I was to say to you, on the spot now, give us your top five key principles to make a difference in your life, where does it start for people? What do they need to do first? Maybe not necessarily regarding what they're going to do, but how they need to be, is what I'm talking about. What do they have to have in-place to be determined to do things that other people wouldn't ordinarily do, to escape from drowning in a sea of mediocrity where people are watching the rubbish on TV because it makes them feel so much better about their existence, their mediocrity, because worse things are happening to other people.

That's the negative impact that the news has. Sometimes people think, well my life's better than that. But, is it what they really dreamt of? Is it what they're worth? Or, is it what they want? Probably not. Some people dream of wealth and health and freedom, but have got more chance of being killed by an ironing board than they have of winning the national lottery. For people to take control of their own life, for people to take and own their future, what top five key principles would people need to get in-place of how they would need to be and act?

Jackie White:

Number one, they have to have the desire. They have to have the desire that they want to change how they are. They want to change the way they're living. They want to change how their future looks. People have to have a desire to do that first and foremost. Then, they have to have a bit of a fire in their belly and be prepared to learn something new. To create new skills, just to learn something different. Obviously, people would have to have a work ethic to put time in and to be able to plan that time, and to make some changes to personally develop, to want to develop. All this encompasses, really, desire. If anyone desires a different lifestyle everything else can be brought together. There is nothing in our business that we can't do. There are no skills that cannot be acquired by anyone, whoever they are. There is nothing difficult about anything.

As long as people have first of all, got that desire, everything else, everything from within, the power that is within so many people can be brought out. Anyone who wants to make the change, who's willing to learn something new, who's willing to practice, who's willing to plan, or has a goal or has a dream, can make the change. Anyone who really wants to, those are the only attributes you need. Everything else, everything else can be created. Everything else can be taught. Slowly but surely, people can evolve, and I believe the whole human race has evolved to where it is today, and each individual person has evolved by the influences that they surround themselves with. Anyone else can change those influences and evolve into whatever and whomever they want to be. So, it's the desire, the fire in your belly, and the passion to do something different. If you haven't got anything else but those things, you can learn everything else. A little bit of belief, that's all you need to have.

Craig White:

So, that desire and belief, just to really change the subject to something really random. I know not so long ago, 2-3 years ago, you had a collapsed lung. And, you defied what the doctors presumed and you went onto a Caribbean cruise. They thought that you had pneumonia and a collapsed lung, but actually you would never have known. Being around you, you were as healthy and as happy and as vibrant as everybody else. When you went back to the hospital for the check-up on this lung, for them to do something about it they were amazed because your lung was no longer collapsed. What was your response to the doctor? What was it that you said to him when they were shocked that your lung was no longer collapsed, that it was back to how it should be?

Jackie White:

Well, when I went back to the hospital after having the CAT scan and I went to see the specialist, I was told that I had acute pneumonia and that I should have been hospitalised. I was quite shocked. I didn't know I had acute pneumonia and I said, oh, I thought I felt really terrible. I said, I did have a day in bed. She was quite amazed that I'd just had a day in bed. If there's ever something wrong with me, even if you're in pain with something, if you lie in bed you're still in pain. You may as well get up and do something and be in pain. Going to bed isn't always the answer. Fill your life every day with something, but not lying in bed unless it's the flu and you can't get up. But, I had pneumonia and I didn't know I had it. Sometimes I think the unknown is better.

When I was told that I had the collapsed lung, I panicked for a couple of days and didn't know how to react. I was on the floor for a couple of days, I have to say. One morning, I got up and I thought, hang on a minute. This is my body. I've had it longer than anyone else. I know it better than the doctor. I've only been going to this doctor for three years. The person at the hospital who's done this scan, they don't even know me. I know my own body, so I'm not having this. I'm going to do something about it. Thanks to the influence, and there's that influence again, of Dr. Wayne Dwyer and Dr. Deepak Chopra whom I've never met, but I've read their books and listened to their CDs, I decided I was going to blow my lung up.

Now, many people might laugh at this, but I imagined, with all the strength I've got in my mind – our mind's a very powerful thing – I imagined that my lung was a yellow balloon, and I would breathe deep. I have to say, I also started yoga classes to learn yoga. I would breathe very deeply wherever I was. Every couple of hours I would breathe very deeply and imagine – if I could close my eyes, I did. If I had to have my eyes open because there were other people about, I would sort of trancelike myself. And, I would imagine I was blowing this balloon up. The imagination went, and years ago, old movies when you saw an operation, the people under the anaesthetic would be breathing into this flat inner tube of a football, and thus the inner tube would expand slightly and you knew the person was breathing.

Well, I imagined this yellow balloon was like that, and as I breathed really, really deeply long and hard, I just imagined that yellow balloon was just blowing up a little bit, blowing up and inflating a little bit. And, I did this every few hours. I didn't tell anyone I was doing it, I just did it. I was determined I was going to do something with my own lung. It's my body. I've only got one, I should look after it. So, when I went back to the hospital and I saw the lady, the specialist doctor and she told me I'd had acute pneumonia and I told her I'd felt really badly and I'd had a day in bed, she said that I should have been hospitalised, and it will take eight months to get over this pneumonia that I currently had. I said, well that's fine, I'll get over that. But, can you just tell me about my lung, my collapsed lung? She said, well this is what's amazing, it's not collapsed. It's no longer collapsed. This is quite amazing.

I told her what I did, and I really thought she'd poo poo it but I was amazed that she didn't. She said, that is quite amazing. So, I told her to listen to Deepak Chopra's tapes. He's a doctor, and she just smiled so whether she did, I'll never know. But, she did encourage me and I found that wonderful. I had to go back a second time because I had to have another X-ray, and when I went back a second time, sadly I saw another doctor. I told him about my lung because I thought he'd be pleased to hear, and he looked at me as if I'd gone mad, I'd gone crazy. I thought, how can he do that? On one X-ray, my lung had collapsed. On this X-ray, it's not collapsed. How can he dispute that I'd blown my lung up? Because lungs don't blow themselves up apparently. I don't know, I'm not a doctor. But, if you've got the desire and you got one body – I'm not saying I could do everything, but I'm going to learn a little bit about this moving forwards. I just feel that we are in control of our lives.

Craig White:

That's right. That story just popped into my mind, and to me it just really sends home the power of desire, our internal beliefs, and the power of our mind. I think if people can really understand that life's meant to be abundant and we can, be and do anything we want as long as it's for the greater good of one and all, I think we can have anything we want in life and achieve anything because of the desire you've mentioned, those belief systems and the power of our own minds and our own beliefs, what can compel and propel people forward to achieve all they want.

Jackie White:

Yes and one thing we haven't mentioned really much is having fun and having adventure. I think having fun on a daily basis because when you surround yourself with fun people, you're working your business and you're growing your business but people are fun. And yet, we get disappointments and we all learn to recover in no time at all and move on, because we're moving on to the bigger picture to our bigger dreams, and we're all together. So, I just think that's wonderful. We have a lot of fun. We also have a lot of adventures, and this one little thing I think is very, very sad. We live in the most wonderful world. There are the most beautiful places in this world. I must say, I haven't seen them all. The most wonderful experiences, many of them I've seen, many I haven't seen yet.

We can read about it. Why watch it on the television. Why be a spectator in life? Why not experience it yourself? Why not go to these places? We live in the most wonderful world, and many people never, ever get to see it. How sad that is. We are only here once. Let's make the most of it. Let's do it all. Let's have it all. Let's enjoy it all. We can do that, we just have to have that desire and we just have to make that change in our lives and have someone to guide us. It's as simple as that.

Craig White:

Well, it's been great talking to you, mum. I know I'm lucky enough to chat to you often. Probably not as long as this because I am your son, although I am one of them fun influences in your life, I know. But, it's been a pleasure. I'm sure guys, for those of you listening and enjoying this podcast, you can see why I wanted to chat with my mum because I think she just carries a lot of power, great attitude and very inspiring. I hope you can really take away some information from what we've been chatting about today, to make a difference in your life, your Olympic year, as my mum said. Mum, if people want to connect with you, where can they find you and how could they follow you?

Jackie White:

They could just go onto the website and leave me their details. It's PeterAndJackie.com. Look forward to it.

Craig White:

Yeah, so that's your website and then obviously, you're on Facebook as well, aren't you? Jackie White, so people can connect with you and send you messages, etc. if they want to know more about this inspirational woman they're speaking to today. Mum, thank you very much. Guys, I hope you've really enjoyed the podcast. Enjoy, share it. I think the greatest possession we carry in life is the possession we have to share. So, share anyway and I look forward to speaking to you all soon. Thanks again, mum.

WEBSITE:

www.peterandjackiewhite.com

Book Coming Soon

CHAPTER

10

THE 6 KEY PRINCIPLES OF S.U.M.O

Imagine losing our job due to poor health, failing medicals which meant you could not work? Paying off a mortgage with £180 benefit money after a successful career.

Discover how Paul McGee, one of the UK's leading speakers on the subject of change, workplace relationships and motivation, proactively changed his life. How listening to a tape helped him find his purpose and passion for Personal Development.

In a world where we are influenced by society and conditions. Paul believes that leadership should begin with you and you should take responsibility. Write down very clear goals, your vision and purpose and what you want to achieve in your life and consistently review them and adapt them to your lives. A small change can make a huge difference.

Using Paul's shared philosophy and inspirational approach in his 6x key principles of SUMO (Shut Up, Move On), adapt your mindset into more positive thinking.

Paul has spoken for over 900 organisations in 36 countries to date, and from Todmorden to Tehran and from Bradford to Brisbane, Paul's messages have resonated with a global audience.

Craig White:

Hi, everyone. It's Craig here again. Thanks for joining us today. I'm extremely happy, actually, to be chatting with the S.U.M.O. guy today. Some of you may know him as the S.U.M.O. guy. Many may know him as Paul McGee. Aside from being a Mancunian, Paul has got a lot of great things going for him. We won't hold that against him, that's for sure. He's the managing director of PMA, an international training and educational company, a bestselling author, and an internationally sought after speaker, recently travelling across to the wonderful island of Mauritius. Someone I've been very lucky enough to share the stage with and importantly be inspired by through his powerful presentations and a couple of his books, although I aware of a new book that's recently hit the book stands, which I'm excited find out a little bit more about. How's things with you today, Paul? How's life up in the Northwest?

Paul McGee:

Aside from being insulted that I'm a Mancunian, Craig, which I just have to shut up and move on about, I'm doing great, and it's really good to be talking to you. So, it's great to be involved now through social media.

Craig White:

Yeah. Fantastic. I know we've obviously been lucky enough to have you at a couple of our events, which has been fantastic. There have been a lot of people within the organisation that have heard you speak. There's a lot of people that are actually plugged in from all around the world actually don't work with us as well, which is great. Tell us a little bit about your story, Paul. I'd love to share some strategies and tools with people and ideas that everyone can maybe take away from today and put into action. Where do you come from? You've got quite an inspiring story, really.

Paul McGee:

Some people may say that. I often say your life happens and you take what happens, sometimes, for granted. Many years ago, working as a so-called high flying graduate management trainee with Unilever, prestigious organisation, prestigious graduate program to be on. I know all the trappings of that, the kudus, the passion, everything. Then, I lost my job for ill health; myalgic encephalomyelitis, yuppie flu or chronic fatigue syndrome, whatever you want to call it. I went from all the kudos and status as an undergraduate and trainee to then a £35 a week invalidity benefit and had a mortgage based on a salary I no longer had, no mortgage protection. We took in lodgers in order to keep the house. And anybody that knows this illness, knows that it's particularly misunderstood, and there was a suggestion that it could be all in my mind. I had to go see a psychiatrist. Very, very challenging, but in the midst of all that, someone gave me a tape on personal development. It was by a guy who's still going today called Richard Denny.

He quoted something along the lines of, within every adversity is a seed of equal or greater opportunity. It really did trigger a passion for me for personal development, and that was the support of family and friends. Maybe I just did get lucky. I don't know why I recovered in the way I did compared to some other people. That's very much the part of my history, Craig. The challenge I had, though, with the illness was that even after two and a half years of not working that maybe I could do some work, nobody would hire me because I couldn't pass a medical. So, I hired myself. As I like to say, in all humility, I was absolutely awesome in the interview. I answered all the questions really well, and was successfully appointed by myself. That was in March 1991. So, been in business now 21 years. That's a little bit of the background.

Craig White:

Obviously, I know you share a passion for personal development, and obviously, it comes back from that first cassette tape that obviously you picked up. I know you said you've obviously had a lot of support from family and friends, etc. Maybe my thoughts and beliefs, but you've really pulled yourself through, through that positive mental attitude, from having the right areas of focus. Would you agree with that?

Paul McGee:

Yeah. I think it's got to start with yourself. I have a little phrase, leadership begins with me. You have to take personal responsibility back. That's an absolute given, because actually there can be lots of people that do want to support you and that you fail to plug into that, you fail to tap into that, or you fail to utilise what support is available. You're right. friends and family do play a part, absolutely. I want to credit people for that, but you're right. I have to say that go look at yourself and I guess if I hadn't taken responsibility, then I don't know what kind of place I'd be in now.

Craig White:

For sure, and I think of a lot of people in not just the UK, worldwide, could understand that little quote that obviously has made a massive impact on your regarding with every adversity there's an equal seed of an equal opportunity or greater opportunity. I think people can really look for the sunshine behind the rain, which is often harder to do than not, really, but it's having the passion to do so, I suppose.

Paul McGee:

Some of this stuff, let's be honest, it can sound a little bit cheesy and twee, but you know I'm living evidence, I'm living proof that this stuff is actually very, very powerful and can change people's lives. I've been fortunate, really, not just to be able to use this stuff on myself, but I've spoken in 45 countries. No matter what the culture, the context is, the stuff that I talk about and the stuff that you and everyone talks about is incredibly powerful and invaluable. It really is. You've got to apply it, you've got to use it. Zig Ziglar said something along the lines of, motivation is a bit like having a wash. You've got to do it more than once to get the full benefit. You've got to keep on working at this. I've been in business 21 years, but I've had a crazy morning, still working hard. Business schedule this afternoon, travelling down to London. Lots of stuff's happening. I'm just going to keep on keeping on, but over time stuff really does add up and it makes the difference.

Craig White:

I was going to say, you must love now being able to really, from your own experiences—one of the things I love about some of the information that I've learnt from you over the years is the strategies to actually put it into action, because obviously, that's the key, isn't it? You must love really knowing that you're making a difference, whether it's in the UK or in obviously the countries that you've been blessed enough to be able to speak in.

Paul McGee:

Yeah, and it is a privilege. What we've now developed is, we've got S.U.M.O. for schools, both primary and secondary. I'm over in Australia next year. There's a woman in Australia who wants to launch for schools out there. We've done a prison program. I got a letter recently from an inmate in a prison in Leeds, in Yorkshire who has read the S.U.M.O. book. It's in the prison library. It's not just always about me speaking and being out there. It's just about the message you're getting into people's hands and heads, all the different ways and concepts. It's both exciting, but it's also humbling as well.

Craig White:

Yeah, for sure. I'm very inspired with obviously what you've been doing with S.U.M.O. for schools. I think fundamentally, it's getting right down to the grassroots for the future of leaving a legacy, really, from a younger age, which is so important. Go back 21 years, then. You obviously interviewed yourself and passed with flying colours. What was your goal back then? Where did you start? What did you foresee for the future? Was that the start of S.U.M.O., or did that come along later in life?

Paul McGee:

The phrase S.U.M.O. very much came along later on. I always felt I had a bit of a natural talent to stand up and speak. That had always been something which been proven, I guess, when I'd had opportunities to do so. I always knew that was a talent I had, but I also realised that like a footballer or like a lot of people who've got talent, it can be a talent that's wasted and not developed. The detail was a little sketchy, if I'm honest, Craig, but I was clear that I knew at some stage I would like to speak in front of large audiences. In the early '90s I started writing down goals about where I wanted to be, where I wanted to speak. I remember even, there was a picture taken from the back of a stage of a guy, and you only saw the back of him, the back of his head and body, looking out at a large audience. I actually cut that out and I thought it looked a bit like me from the back. I just had that in my head as, that will happen to me someday. I will do that. It wasn't about, let's go on an ego trip. It was very much about, let's make a difference. I just knew deep down that that difference that I was on this planet to make would involve speaking in front of large groups of people. It's a journey, and I've been in business 21 years. Some people say to me now, oh, you're a great success aren't you, but it took me 21 years to become an overnight success. I think people forget the journey and the work and the effort you have to put into things in order to get to the place you're at now.

Craig White:

Yeah. I think the journey is part of the success, isn't it? If you're doing what you love and you're doing it daily, to me, that's the beginnings of being successful anyway.

Paul McGee:

It's the people you come in contact with as well along the journey, and some can be a challenge, but some are just absolutely awesome. I had a conversation with someone today who read my book Self-Confidence. He's got this idea that he wants to make a video which basically encapsulates a lot of the ideas in that book that he'd give away to every school in the country, to every secondary school in the country. It's his vision, his desire. I've never met this guy before, but he came across the book in the session. It's the possibilities that open up and the people that you meet that's so, so exciting.

Craig White:

Fantastic. That's an exciting vision as well to be able to produce something like that. Great opportunity. Am I right in saying, forgive me if I'm wrong, but I believe you've got obviously the S.U.M.O. book, which I'm most familiar with. Self-Confidence, again a fantastic book which we've just mentioned. Then, you've got your book, How Not to Worry. Are they the three books? Or is there anymore that I'm aware of?

Paul McGee:

There's loads, Craig.

Craig White:

Really?

PAUL MCGEE:

In the '90s, the first one I ever wrote was about CV writing because a lot of my business in the early '90s, I had officially started my business and when we officially went into recession the last time. So, in '91 we were in a recession and people were leaving organisations. I had to let lots of people go. I started off with an out-placement work helping people make the dividends. I wrote a book called Writing a CV That Works. That was my very first one. I've written one called Perfect Public Speaking. I've written one called 59 Minutes to a Calmer Life. The breakthrough was in 2005 when I really got a great publisher, and S.U.M.O. was published. There have been many books. There have been S.U.M.O., Self-Confidence, and then latest one, How Not to Worry. But squeezed in there is a book called S.U.M.O. Relationships, How to Handle Not Strangle the People You Live With. It doesn't have as big of profile as the others, but I know it's had an impact on a lot of people as well. Yeah, there's books coming out in years, and now I've about to sign a deal for them to become audiobooks, which I'm also excited about because I realise not everyone likes to read, but people do like to listen, particularly when they're driving their car.

CRAIG WHITE:

Yeah. Obviously, when people are on the move quite a lot in this day and age. That's exciting. Is it something you'll voiceover yourself?

PAUL MCGEE:

That's the plan. If they've got an opportunity to hire a motivational speaker to actually read the book, then I think it would be a sad reflection on my abilities if they didn't actually book myself.

CRAIG WHITE:

Indeed. It wouldn't be the same without your Mancunian accent, Paul, anyway.

PAUL MCGEE:

Absolutely, Craig. Absolutely. Also, Mancunian motivation is how that today has become a registered trademark. I'm very much planning on the Mancunian aspects of things at times.

CRAIG WHITE:

Brilliant. Let's talk about S.U.M.O., if we can. There's obviously six principles in there, which are really powerful insights for people to shift their mindset, look at things differently and actually take the relevant actions to start making a difference. Are you happy to share your philosophies on that?

PAUL MCGEE:

Absolutely. In a nutshell. I won't go on for too long, but I like to give a metaphor of, we're going to explore the S.U.M.O. house. In each of those rooms of the house, there is a principle. Actually, the house's foundations is built on a formula, E=R=O. The E=R=O, it's the events plus my response that influences the outcome. I think too many people live with an alternative formula, E=O. If that's the event, you know what the outcome is. Actually, it's like, no. We need to put ourselves in this equation. Actually, two people, two teams, two organisations, can have the same reference, the same opportunity, the same challenge, whatever it is, and have very different outcomes to each other. Why is that? Because it's not solely the event. It's not what happens to you. It's all down to your response as well that influences the outcome. That's the foundation, and then I look at six principles.

The first one is called change your t-shirt. It's all about if we're not careful, we can in life wear a victim t-shirt where we play the martyr and we just look to blame someone else for where we're at in life. From a global perspective, people particularly in the UK seem to go, well I blame Tony Blair. I blame Gordon Brown. I blame the coalition government. I blame the Americans, the Germans, the bikes. On a micro level, I blame my partner for my stress. I blame my boss. I blame the traffic. I blame the kids, whatever. It's like, hang on a minute. Take a look at yourself in the mirror, guys and ask yourself, it's actually one of the many reasons why you're at where you're at in life today, down to some of the choices you've actually made and the decisions you've not taken. Although those other factors, the economy and everything play a part, we need to realise that the person that plays the biggest part of your life is yourself, and you need to change your t-shirt if you're wearing that victim t-shirt in order to blame someone else. That's the first principle.

Craig White:

You don't sell them victim t-shirts, do you?

Paul McGee:

I've been asked that. I've been asked 'Paul do you sell those t-shirts, I could flipping sell loads'. He was Welsh. It's like, I'm not selling flipping victim t-shirts no matter how much the demand is out there. I want you to change them. It's great, because schools now, when they do this, they have a change your t-shirt day and kids going to school with different positive messages on their t-shirt. It's very powerful and very visual. That's the first principle, change your t-shirt. It's all about take responsibility. The second one is called develop fruity thinking. It's all around it's talking about our mindset, but rather than just talk about positive thinking, I like people to understand positive thinking's great, but let's just drill down a bit deeper.

So, I've got these seven questions to help you develop more fruity thinking. They range from just the challenge, on a scale from one 10, where 10 is death, where is it? To how can I influence and improve a situation? What can I learn from this? What can I find that's positive? I've got those seven questions, and I'll give you my website later on where people can actually download. Rather than facing a challenge and saying, we'll be positive about it, their question of mine will be, yes, but how? These questions are very much designed to give you a very practical framework to ask yourself these questions that work through your challenges and to bounce back from setbacks. You've got change your t-shirt, develop fruity thinking.

Craig White:

Quickly, just while you're talking about that, before you move onto your next one. I've got a couple that I work with and have done for some years now, and I know one of their younger children, they passed the S.U.M.O. book onto them, I think around about the age of 10 or 11. It was only recently, actually, it was quite funny; they were actually talking to their child. I think not so much giving them a bit of a telling off, just a stern talking to. The response was quite simple. On a scale of one to 10, Mum...I just think it's absolutely fantastic.

Paul McGee:

It's amazing when people start to use your own material on you. Absolutely, as my kids have done with me. So, a good reminder. You always need reminding of this. That's what that is called develop fruity thinking. You've got to keep on working on it daily in many respects. If life is sucking the energy out of you, and the media is bombarding you with negativity, you need to make a conscious decision to work harder. It's like trying to work at your health and fitness, it isn't just something you can do as a one-off. Mindset is something you have to continually revisit. That's principle number two, develop fruity thinking. Hippo time is okay. I ask people, what do hippos do most? They wallow. I talk about actions. Sometimes before you can shut up and move on, you might need some hippo time. You might need to wallow a little bit.

What I mean by that is, sometimes you've had a setback, a challenge, a disappointment. To feel mad, bad, or sad is okay. Just make sure you don't wallow for too long, but it's okay. It is temporary. I think with that principle, Craig, a lot of people find a little bit of realism in that, that actually it's not possible to be on top of the world 100% of the time. If you can have this hippo time, that's actually okay. It sort of legitimises things a bit more for people, makes it a bit more realistic, and that's why I think S.U.M.O. has been embraced by people, even some skeptics and cynics who have seen a bit of that Mancunian-ness come through, tell it as it is, no bull. That's appreciated. That's the third principle. That is something which I know a lot of people regularly use, but the main thing, it's okay, but never forget hippo time is temporary. It's part of the journey. It's not meant to from where you start start to live life from now on.

Craig White:

That recovery time, I think a lot of sports stars often talk about. For example, Michael Owen, he doesn't wallow too long after putting a shot up in the Stafford end. He recovers. He gets on and keeps on fighting.

Paul McGee:

Absolutely. They're the three main principles. The last three, you've got to remember the beach ball, which is a brilliant one, particularly around communication and being in conflict. That's just simply where if there was a big beach ball in the room and you're at one side of the room and I'm at the other side, from my perspective I'm seeing three colours, and it's huge. I'm seeing blue, white, and green. You're looking at the same thing, the same beach ball, but you're seeing red, yellow, and orange. If we're not careful, we'll argue to each other as to why I'm right and you're wrong, rather than go, hang on a minute. Do I need to understand why someone is seeing the beach ball differently from me, and that just because they see it differently doesn't mean that one of us is wrong. We could both be right. If I want to build better relationships, if I want to become more successful in selling, then it's really crucial that I understand other people's side of the beach ball rather than just simply talk about my own. So, it's one I have to say that I've come to very regular, almost on a daily basis and try to understand, hang on a minute. Why have they said that? Why have they done that? What are things looking like from their side of the beach ball and over here on mine? So, very, very visual. Very, very simple, but very, very powerful.

Craig White:

Yeah, agreed. Definitely. I think Anthony Robbins, obviously, famously known, talks about a quote that I love. The quality of our life is within the quality of our relationships.

Paul McGee:

Absolutely.

Craig White:

Understanding this beach ball philosophy, it's a great, as you said, visual way of looking at it to understand not just people around us, but customers, colleagues, etc.

Paul McGee:

There was a conflict situation between some of our franchisees, owners, and the customers. It could have be a big conflict situation, but the woman said, because she's licensed to use my material, she actually brought a beach ball to use in the room and said, I'm going to facilitate this meeting. She just said, right. Tell me your side of the beach ball. Tell me what you're seeing, what you're thinking, and why. She just got everybody to be like, we're all looking at the same thing, we're just seeing it differently, but now we understand each other rather than trying to break each other or you're wrong and I'm right. It was incredibly powerful, and I just love how simple S.U.M.O. is, but also how powerful and effective it can be. Final two principles for you. I learned Latin, which is all about learning the Latin phrase carpe diem, seize the day. In the book, I look at the lot of the reasons why people procrastinate, and that really is a huge factor affecting the way people are succeeding.

They've got all kinds of reasons why they're not going to do something, or they try something once, it doesn't work, and they come up with a list of excuses why they're not going to do this anymore. I looked in that principle at the reasons for that and this whole thing about how to overcome our procrastination and underpin with very much, at the end of the day, you have a certain amount of time on this planet. Let's carpe diem, seize the day, and make things happen. The final one is called ditch Doris Day, which sounds a little bit, what's that about? She's still alive, bless her. She's probably well into her 80s now, but Doris Day sang a song in the 1950s called Que Sera, Sera, whatever will be will be. The future's not ours to see. Que Sera, Sera. You know what? If you want to get the best out of life, going along going, oh well 'whatever will be will be'. Maybe we'll succeed. Maybe we won't. It's all down to fate and luck. That is total garbage. If you have that as an attitude to world poverty or global warming, we'd be in a right mess.

So, make sure you don't have that as your approach to your own life as well. There will be things that you won't understand and you don't foresee happening. Clearly, that will be the case. If you've got your goals, you've got your vision, you've got a plan, got a purpose, you've got your support team, you're working on your attitude, then you can create some very clear goals that you want to achieve in your life. I'm on a lovely property where I am now, very fortunate, but one of the things that was really important to me years ago was that I'd have a really nice large garden, well-established, plenty of colour, everything. Just before this interview I just took a couple of minutes just look out at that and I thought, you know what? I saw this years ago in my head. It wasn't a case of, well, if we're lucky and the housing market is fine. This was very much in my vision years ago. So, let's ditch Doris Day, let's ditch whatever will be will be, and let's take responsibility for our future. That, in a nutshell, is my six principles.

Craig White:

Obviously, I've read the book a few times, actually. So have so many people that I work with. I think the principles, if you can apply them consistently, and I think it goes back to what you were talking about earlier, what Zig Ziglar said about having a wash. It has to be that consistent personal development to consistently work on your mindset to maybe adapt these or adopt them, even, to become second nature almost, but never forgetting to review and reflect.

Paul McGee:

Absolutely. You've got to keep on reminding yourself of this stuff. That's the key. I've just been also speaking to a client this morning. It's a school, and the head teacher and the deputy are hugely into personal development. They have a particular, it's too lengthy to quote, but they have these quote, which is basically about how teachers set the temperature and bring the weather into their own classroom. That is on the back of every toilet door in the whole school. When a teacher or whoever wants to sit down, do their business, whatever, that's staring back at them. It's just a constant reminder. I find it quite amusing, but I also find it very, very powerful that they're not just playing with this, that they're taking it seriously. I think a lot of people play at personal development, but it's a serious business. Life is serious. It's fun, it's a lot of other things, but it's serious business. It's got to be fun, but there's a serious element to it. They're the schools and the tools and resources we need to give us the edge. Sometimes, with just the Self-Confidence book is about how small change can make a big difference. Over time, it can make a huge difference.

Craig White:

I've got to be honest Paul, I absolutely love what you do in the schools. I'm proud of you, to be honest, because I just think, from my point of view having two young daughters, an understanding at that age how we're influenced by society, by our social conditioning. Something that I'm conscious of is to have the right teachers around my children. I might even be moving up to the Northwest, mate.

Paul McGee:

We're doing S.U.M.O. for schools throughout the country. The thing is, actually I always do it myself, because this is also a key thing. I don't want to be—I'm the figurehead of my business. At the end of the day, this about empowering other people to make a difference. There's not, you only get S.U.M.O. if you read the book or hear me speak. I've got a team of associates and we work with teachers because if they don't get S.U.M.O. how are they going to inspire the kids. Some of the head teachers embrace it massively and start running it themselves, and they hardly need support from us. They don't need it. They heard me speak. They got the book. They got the pack, and they run with it. One teacher of his own back has now started a program called S.U.M.O. for Families. This is the whole power of S.U.M.O., not just built on a personality. Yes, I'm going to be associated with it, but once I've gone, S.U.M.O. is still here to stay and still here to make a difference, and that's what's really exciting.

Craig White:

Yeah, definitely. Good on you, mate, good on you. Tell us about this new book thing, How Not to Worry. I've seen it on bookstands on a couple of photos that have been Tweeted.

Paul McGee:

It's exciting. It's obviously very specific. Self-Confidence it obviously just does what it says on the tin. S.U.M.O. is a bit more about general principles for life, but I realised there was an issue, there was a challenge where despite the fact, and this is quite remarkable, isn't it, we're alive on the planet today, then we are likely to live longer, healthier, wealthier lives than we've ever done. Yet, we're worrying more than ever before. The book, again, narrowed down to a practical way, just tries to understand why do we worry? Why worry, and it's such a big deal? How it connects with our anxiety and stress, how that impacts us. Also, what are some of the causes of it? Why do we worry? I tell you what. I wrote a bit deeper, but in a fun way. I even look at our evolutionary ancestors and ask the question, are we wired to worry? Is fear ever a good thing?

One of the things I'm quite chuffed about is quite a lot of research on the subject is about coming up with your own angle. Most people, and probably most of your listeners, are probably thinking worry is always a waste of time. Do you know what? There's a concept I call now worth-it worry and worthless worry. So, if you've got a plane to catch and it's important you catch that plane or else you'll miss out on your family holiday and you're think you're running a little bit late and I've heard there's problems on the motorway, then there's certain people who have anxiety of a little bit of worry may motivate you to speed up and to take action and to get out of that house. That is what I called worth-it worry when it actually motivates you to do something. But if you're then on the plane and then you start to worry, is it going to crash? Then, that is what I call worthless worry. It is totally out of your control.

A lot of people spend a lot of time in worthless worry rather than thinking, okay, maybe there's a little bit of anxiety and stress here, but how can I use that to motivate me to take action? I like people, and I think it's great when someone says, I'm speaking at a conference and I'm feeling nervous. Great, good, because that's your adrenaline that's being released to help you perform at a high standard. You don't just walk up totally complacent and stay chilled and relaxed. You're almost not really in the room. I try and challenge people's misconceptions around this whole subject and give them some practical tools. These first six weeks is the fastest selling new self-help book in the country. That's obviously exciting, and hopefully just some more stuff from me that's getting into people's hands that's helping them maybe just enjoy life a little bit more.

Craig White:

Rock and roll, Paul. You're a good man, mate, and I think everything you've done certainly since I've picked up the S.U.M.O. book, I've been inspired to look at a couple of these other books as well. I'm off into town in a moment myself to do a little bit of organising. I'm going to pick this How Not to Worry book up. I'm confident it will be on the bookshelves in the city of Peterborough.

Paul McGee:

Also, Amazon is a great place to get it as well, and railways and airports seem to have really gotten behind it. I've just had an email a couple of days ago from someone in the Seychelles who I presume didn't buy the book in the Seychelles, but had just been over here and picked it up whilst they were in the UK, although why you live in the Seychelles and need to buy a book called How Not to Worry is beyond me. It just goes to show that even when you've got the sun and the sea and the sand, then some people still get stressed for whatever reason.

Craig White:

Indeed, indeed. Paul, I'm really grateful of your time. I know you're a busy man, and I know the guys that are consistently listening to this show that we've set up this year are going to be really grateful for your show and your principles and your philosophies on personal development. Where's best if people are going to connect with you? We know they can pick your books up obviously from Amazon or The Book Source, etc. What's your website? Where can people connect and what can they gather from that?

Paul McGee:

TheSumoGuy.com, which is fairly straightforward. TheSumoGuy.com. There's all sorts of things there. There's articles to download, the seven questions we mentioned earlier on. They can download those. There's tip sheets. There's videos, podcasts. There's lots of good, free stuff that's there, and they can also subscribe to a weekly newsletter. Also, if you want to follow me on Twitter @TheSumoGuy. They're the best ways to connect with me. The main thing is, I don't want to always be heavy, and this all this about positive, inspirational thinking. I was Tweeting last night about the fact that it was wife's birthday. England are playing, and I'm trying to decide, how can I keep my wife happy by taking her out to dinner but not miss much of the match? I just try and share short challenges and share a few of those, but share some inspirational on the way as well.

Craig White:

A bit of balance there, mate. Did you have a good night, and did Helen enjoy herself?

Paul McGee:

She did. I'll tell you what. I got some brownie points. She liked her present. She liked her meal, and England in the quarter finals. I call that a good night.

Craig White:

Happy days. Hey, Paul, thanks again, mate. I'm going to let you get on. I really do appreciate your time. I hope everyone can get over to your website and follow you on Twitter as do I. I'll see you soon, mate. Thanks very much for your time.

Paul McGee:

All the best to you. Great talking to you, Craig. Thanks, bye.

SUMO www.theSUMOguy.com **MASTERING CHALLENGES ... SKILLS FOR LIFE !™**

PAUL MCGEE – THE SUMO GUY

Paul McGee is one of the UK's leading speakers on the subject of change, workplace relationships and motivation. His provocatively titled book SUMO (Shut Up, Move On) became an **instant best seller** and his book on Self Confidence reached **number one** in the WHSmith's business book chart and remained there for a further **24 weeks**. He has appeared on **BBC Breakfast television** and is a regular contributor to Radio 5live. Building on his background in psychology, Paul's aim is to deliver a practical, relevant message that can make an immediate impact on people's professional and personal lives. His approach is considered both inspirational and humorous as he seeks to deliver a memorable experience that equips people with insights and ideas to increase their personal effectiveness and impact. He's spoken for over **900 organisations** in **36 countries** to date, and from Todmorden to Tehran and from Bradford to Brisbane, Paul's messages have resonated with a global audience.

He has had the privilege of working with one of the world's top management gurus, **the late Dr Stephen Covey**, and his work has been endorsed by the Elite Performance Director of the British Olympic Association, **Sir Clive Woodward**. His clients include prominent blue chip organisations, public sector bodies and a **leading Premiership football club**.

"In our twenty years of running conferences, Paul McGee is the only speaker we have ever invited back. That above all explains the benefit we feel we have gained from hearing Paul's SUMO philosophy."
Doug Perkins, Dame Mary Perkins CBE, Founders of SpecSavers

"I would have no hesitation in recommending Paul McGee and his SUMO philosophy to any organization who wants to engage a large number of staff in a way that provides excellent value for money compared to more conventional ways of training.
The overwhelming feedback has been that the sessions were inspiring, thought provoking, humourous but above all practical in helping my staff make a positive difference."
Julie Spence, Chief Constable, Cambridgeshire Police

"I saw Paul present at an international conference. He uniquely addresses one of the biggest barriers to personal and business development... our own minds. The SUMO philosophy was a unanimous hit. Very, very powerful stuff!"
Simon Newton-Smith, General Manager, Virgin Atlantic, Southern Africa

CHAPTER 11

Craig White It's The Environment

What environment have you created for yourself? Do you inspire others to believe in themselves or are you looking to be inspired? We as individuals influence everything in our lives from health, wealth and happiness. "Change your response, change your outcome" In this podcast, Craig is going to tell you exactly how he achieved this kind of freedom and you can do the same.

During a turbulent time, Craig decided to go to Thailand for a week to spend time alone do discover himself and find peace. Discover how a book he read on this trip and the people he met helped him realise his potential to achieve anything he desired, anything he believed he could be and that this creativity lay within the possibilities before him.

Craig's passion for inspiring others is what shines through the most, challenge yourself to find peace on this journey of development and awareness.

Craig White:

Hi and welcome to today's show. And today, what I wanted to do is really bring you some insights, and really discuss some of my journey, and how, when you make decisions, when you choose to do things, you can be led in paths that open up doors for you to learn, become and develop stronger beliefs, develop amazing synchronicity, which I guess you wouldn't have anticipated or expected when you made that initial decision.

What I want to do from time to time, is bring you these short, sweet and powerful podcasts directly from myself, mainly to raise your expectations, change your thinking, get you to look at things differently. A few years ago, I made the decision, in a turbulent time of my life, to up, pack my bags, and disappear to Thailand for a week. I wanted to get away. I wanted to have peace with myself and discover a little bit about me. Prior to doing so, I'd been on Amazon, and I was looking at purchasing a book. I'm unable to remember what book it was I was purchasing, however, as I'm sure you're aware, when you purchase something at Amazon, it always looks to up sell you and says people who purchased this also purchased this, this, and this.

I found myself looking at a book called, The Biology of Belief, by Bruce H. Lipton, PhD. I simply had to add it to my order because of the title. What this led me to was a book that turned up with an amazing front cover, and it was a big book, it was a thick book. You know when you get these books, you can sometimes be a little bit overwhelmed with—wow, I've got to work my way through that. That was me at the time, and I put it to the side.

When I made the decision to travel to Thailand, I was looking to go to Thailand and I wanted to learn the power of reiki healing. I wanted to discover a little bit of yoga. I wanted to connect with myself, because I was going through this turbulent time in my journey, and I just wanted some peace. I wanted some new direction.

So, what I did is, I booked a trip. A week, two weeks, later, I was jumping on a plane to Thailand by myself for a week, and I found this magical island called Ko Chang, highly recommended if you get the opportunity or decide to create the opportunity to go there. I flew into Bangkok airport, I stayed at the airport for about two hours, got myself this connecting flight on a tiny little propeller plane, and I flew to a place called Trap. I think it's in the middle of Thailand towards the Cambodian border, and we landed at this airport, and this airport was absolutely magnificent. The check-in and arrivals information wasn't on a computer screen, it was written on a white board, and I just thought, wow, I'm here to relax. This is absolutely awesome. I jumped into a taxi, and on the back of jumping into a taxi, I jumped over on a ferry and got over to the Island of Ko Chang. I hadn't really studied the island. The reason I'd gone to this Island is because I found this lady, she was a French lady, lived with her husband on this island of Ko Chang, and it was kind of the northern part of the Gulf of Thailand, and I just felt, I didn't want to go to the commercial holiday maker area.

What I later discovered is that 85% of this island is a national park. There was a big area that was secured off because it's where the King of Thailand goes to holiday. I connected with the local people. I spent a lot of quality time with myself, but what was important, not just the quality time with myself, before I finished packing my bags, this book, The Biology of Belief, was looking at me, and I thought to myself, what better an opportunity, whilst I sat on the beach, relaxing, just accompanied with my own time, to devour this book. To learn what this book has to offer.

So, I packed the bag, and what I found myself realising—I want to explain this journey to you. What I found myself realising since reading that book, is that actually, I can achieve anything I desire. Anything I believe I can be, anything I believe I can create, lies within the possibilities before me. For a long, long time, I've always believed that belief truly is the birthplace of excellence. What we believe to be true, we literally go into the state of mind of it being so. Our beliefs are like commanders of our nervous system, and can be the most powerful force we have for creating good in our lives and other's lives, too. You know, I read a quote very similar to this some ten years ago, twelve years ago, maybe, and it has really stuck with me and become a part of my thoughts, a part of my psyche, and a part of how I live my daily life. Because that's a fact, you know. We live our lives by our daily beliefs. It simply gave me a knowing that my beliefs made a difference, and at all times I have a positive outlook on life, always looking for the silver lining of every cloud.

As a mentor of mine, Jim Rohn, says, "The same wind blows on us all. It's how we choose to set our sail." You see, life, I guess, never has that certainty. It's never perfect. It's almost that philosophy of looking for perfection, and then for a moment, we feel fantastic, and it's that attitude of, "No one breathe, life is perfect!" But then the wind blows, and it's how we choose to set our sail. Napoleon Hill said in his timely classic, Think and Grow Rich, "What man can conceive and believe, he can achieve." So, I really did figure that this book, The Biology of Belief, would give me a deeper understanding of my belief systems, of my system so I could help to inspire others to believe in themselves and their potential they have within, so they can go out and achieve anything they want.

What I found is, this book, The Biology of Belief, took me deeper, deeper. As far as my assumptions go, this wasn't even close on how deep this book has taken me. When the book had first come and I flipped through, and to be honest, I put it down because it was speaking about cellular systems, amino acids, and molecules. It was way over my head, educationally. I felt it was far too deep. Yet, I picked this book up and I packed it. I remember getting in the car, my dad drove me to the airport, and I flew over to Thailand, I found this magical little airport, got on the ferry over to Ko Chang, and went and stayed in this wonderful, wonderful little villa. It was 12 villas around this magical pool, and it was a few minutes-walk from the beach. And this is really where my journey to enlightenment, understanding, and growth started. It was amazing.

So, what I loved about this part of my journey, and I want to tell you a little bit of information out of this book. And I want to tell you the consequences that this journey has had on my life. I want to explain to you how, actually, I've learned to believe that we as individuals influence absolutely everything in our life, from health, wealth, and happiness. So, I'd gone to Thailand, do you know what? I was having the time of my life. I was learning energy healing, reiki, and the spiritual aspects of life and how everything's energy and the chakras and about aligning our chakras and our meridian systems, and I'm really enjoying about learning yoga moves and getting my body into positions I never thought possible. And I felt absolutely fantastic.

One of the things I found is, you know, we go on holiday to relax, and I really, truly believe that you never really relax unless you're in your own company. And I discovered this on my trip. I had the most amazing time learning about yoga, and learning about reiki, and I was reading this book on the beach and what was interesting, what was fascinating, was that everything I was learning from this wonderful French lady in this amazing setting on this beautiful island, from a spiritual aspect and about connecting with the energies of life, I was learning this spiritually, then I was reading this scientific based book that was confirming absolutely everything I'd learned in the morning from a spiritual perspective. It was like synchronicity at its best. I made one decision, to go and develop myself, to find peace, to pack this book, and learn more about my spiritual aspect and then read this book, and for them to come together and really cement the beliefs that I have today, synchronicity at its best. You know what you'll find me doing now? I will never wear Monday socks on a Thursday. I'm a true believer in synchronicity.

So, I was learning this, and one of the things that has come on the back of this is actually, I believe we control everything. I don't know if you've ever listened to How to Get What You Really, Really, Really Want, by Dr. Wayne Dyer and Deepak Chopra, but there's a magical story in there about having the power to reject illness. It's just absolutely magical, and since changing my mindset, you know the philosophy, if somebody sneezes, most of the population of the world go, "Aargh, I'm going to catch that," so they do. You know, I used to get hay fever when the Council would be cutting the grass, and you've got that smell of spring and the smell of freshly cut grass, I used to think, "Aargh, I'm going to start sneezing." And I did.

I remember being out with a really good friend of mine, Richard, and I had a 45-minute sneezing fit. He didn't know what to do. He'd stopped laughing because it was going on so long, he wasn't sure how to deal with me. A 45-minute sneezing fit. That's how bad my hay fever was. And it was bad, do you know why? Because I decided to allow it. Since changing my response, I never get ill because I believe my body, my immune system, is too strong to the environment around me. I've stopped getting hay fever through simply changing my response. If somebody sneezes around me, I think, "That's okay, I'm too strong. It will deflect from my shield." When I'm driving down the road and my windows open and I can see the grass cutter, I breath in and think, "Ah, the wonderful smell of Spring."

So, through changing your response, you can change your outcome. That is all I've done, and now, for over eight years, in fact, over ten years, I haven't had hay fever, and I no longer get a common cold. I'm no longer ill. I'm immune. Yes, I eat healthy. Yes, I go to the gym and keep active, but you know, it's your mind and your belief systems that dictate absolutely everything and control your outcome.

I was reading this book. There's a story in this book called "The Butter and Olive Sandwich." Now, after reading about the magical membrane and seeing this association of how the structure of the membrane works in relation to a butter and olive sandwich, I'm not proclaiming that after reading one book only twice that I fully or even closely understand the science completely. But it backs up my belief systems, and when we believe something to be true, we literally go in the mind of it being so.

I want to empower you to understand it's the environment. One of the titles of a chapter in this magical book is called, "It's the Environment, Stupid." I often talk about and share how I feel the power of association is massive to our life and our outcome, and I talk about it in the Elastic Attitude Audio program. Our beliefs and perceptions come from our experiences, our education, and our environment of the past. This is what fills our subconscious mind. Our auto-pilot, our habits, our attitudes, even. What reading this book did, and this is where personal development challenges your beliefs, it challenges your habits, it challenges your thoughts, what reading this book has done, it's been a massive eye opener to me, and really strengthened my beliefs so that we control our physical and mental health through the environment that we create.

While I was learning so much in Thailand about the spiritual self, and that our bodies are very much energy, and we control through positive thinking, positive actions and beliefs, to then read this book and the science has just confirmed it. Look, spiritually, we are one with our energy. Scientifically we are energy. Our bodies are made up of an energy force. So, I want to share with you a simple thought, because the power we have within is absolutely insane.

Guys, what you need to comprehend is, everything is about the environment. It's our beliefs, it's what we choose, it's how we act, it's how we respond, and I just want to challenge you to challenge your beliefs. I want to challenge you to maybe pick up this book. One of the most articulately written books I've ever come across, it challenged me. But it has inspired me because of the spirituality and the scientific connection when it comes to how important our environment is. Our environment creates our beliefs, and our beliefs create our response, and our response creates our outcome. Wouldn't you love to be healthy? Wouldn't you love to be fit? Wouldn't you love to never, ever suffer a common cold or suffer from hay fever? Why is it that so many people have the ability to repair themselves?

So many people have the ability to fix themselves, to eradicate illness, to remove illness, when the western world suggests that it's impossible. Well, I believe that the mind, I believe that our inner power enables us every possibility. So, remember. It's your environment that creates your beliefs. It's your beliefs that create your response, and it's your response that creates your outcome, in every area of life. So, remember, it's always the environment. I challenge you to find peace with yourself. Guys, you don't need to go to Thailand. You don't need to go to Cambodia. There's no need for you to fly to South America or to Australia. But what you do need to become at peace, to become one with yourself, is you need quality time with yourself.

I briefly was going to touch on it in this short, powerful podcast because this is a mindset-changing podcast, and I've touched on it very, very briefly, and I believe we only truly relax when we only have to worry about ourselves. I go on holiday a lot, and I love to go on holiday and I love to go on holidays with my loved ones, my friends, my colleagues, I love to see the world and different environments. Yet, here's the thing. Whenever you're away, whenever you're in somebody else's company, there is always a part of you, always a part of you that is going to be focused on them. There's always a part of you that's going to wonder have they had a nice day, are they okay, did they enjoy their meal, was this a nice restaurant, is that a nice drink, do you like this beach, are you happy coming on the back of the moped? It's always about ensuring others are happy, too, and more often than not, first.

When you're by yourself, whether that is finding a magical place where you can go for a walk of gratitude every day, sit on a bench and take in this beautiful environment that we have around us, or whether it's you go on a week's holiday to a magical island and you learn things like reiki and yoga and spirituality and about your chakra points, etc. Whatever it may be, I've found, from that one trip, that I am in control because of the beliefs and the environment that I create. I create them from my environment through my choice. I also learned that, actually, you will only ever truly relax when it's just you. When it's just you that you only have to worry about, even if it's just 30 minutes a week, 30 minutes of time that you just spend by yourself, relaxing, maybe even meditating, that's when you will truly, truly relax. My week in Thailand was absolutely magical. I relaxed, I made some new friends, I met a wonderful Thai couple that showed me around the island, I saw areas of the island that people would just never have seen.

So, hey, look, I challenge you to connect with yourself. I challenge you to consistently personally develop. I challenge you to go on a journey of development, a journey of awakening, and I really do hope that this short show has given some power and passion to you.

From a young age, Craig possessed an unrivalled passion to succeed in life. This passion, coupled with an unshakeable work ethic, has enabled him to build a Direct Selling Business that has turned over in excess of a staggering £30million to date.

What now drives Craig is his desire to grow further through self-education and self-improvement and to share this journey with others by showing them the power of self-belief. He wears his heart on his sleeve and finds great reward in seeing others flourish under his guidance. A dedicated family man, Craig puts his children first and teaches them confidence, humility and gratitude as well as supporting them to dream big.

www.craigwhite.com

www.passiontosucceed.com

www.youtube.com/channel/UCnFIJRmcS-nI7-C0vaARetQ

CHAPTER

12 Learn To Unlock Your True Potential

When you look in the mirror, what do you see?

Are you searching for contentment, fulfillment, inner peace? Looking for external means to be fulfilled? What if we said perfection is already within you, everything's perfect you just need to bring attention to it!

We live in a world where everyone's living certain beliefs. Beliefs passed down by our parents, work colleagues or even friends. Ask yourself, are they still relevant to how you are living your life?

Joseph explains why you have to take back power and control of your own beliefs. Banish your limiting beliefs for good as it's a source to limiting beliefs.

In the podcast, Joseph also shares, a few exercises that will open your mind to the possibilities of change. Putting you in the driver's seat, encouraging you to challenge to change yourself.

Craig White:

Hi everyone, good morning. I hope you are well today, and joining me we have a great guy, Joseph Clough. He's an international trainer, a therapist, as well as being a Hay House author. And his goal is quite simple, it's to help people achieve their full potential, something I really got a lot of time for, and I really appreciate you joining us today Joseph. How are you?

Joseph Clough:

I'm very well. I'm incredibly well, in fact. How are you doing?

Craig White:

Yeah, terrific, mate. Thank you, terrific. Now you're based in Cambridge, is that where you've kind of been, you know, from—

Joseph Clough:

Yeah. I'm born here, born in Cambridge. I've moved around to Liverpool and some, but I've come back and I'm just really, wherever my business goes that's where I tend to flow as well. Been in Cambridge for quite a long time now.

Craig White:

Well that's wonderful. Hey guys, I've met Joseph over the last couple of years, and I'm really excited about having him on our podcast show today. And you'll get to see why as we're chatting. Joseph had a successful career in training and as a therapist, and certainly can bring some wisdom and knowledge to really help us make a change, everlasting change, and a difference to our life and our future. Tell us a little bit about your journey, Joseph. Because you've got quite an exciting story, really.

JOSEPH CLOUGH:

Yeah, well, it was a bit on an interesting journey. But I'm sure it's going to be very, very familiar to your listeners. It's one of those cases where, when I was young, I was very, very insecure and very shy. I did absolutely terrible at school. I was told that I wasn't really going to amount to much, and it was just very much a case of not feeling good enough, and having these blushing and self-conscious episodes when I was talking to people. That really continued, all the way until I was about 18 years old. Then, I thought, I can't be doing this anymore. I'm in a terrible job. I don't feel good about myself. I've got these emotional issues, psychological issues, and something has to change. Ultimately, I went on a mission to do as much as I could, to learn as much as I could, to be able to change my own life.

When I started doing that, I actually somehow got into this business and I've been doing seminars and trainings and audio programs, and seeing my clients for the last 10 years now. So, it really started, that whole journey, by making a decision, but look, there's my life. I need to be able to take control of it, take responsibility, because no one else is going to, and going on that mission to really find the answers, to be able to live a happy, fulfilled, and content life. From there, it's kind of led me to this point now, which has been really quite ironic because when you think about it, if I didn't have the issue, I wouldn't be doing what I'm doing right now, which is living, and helping people as much as possible. So, I'm actually very oddly thankful for actually having those very insecure problems. Because that has actually led me, to this new, exciting life over the last 10 years. So, it's a very odd one really.

CRAIG WHITE:

Yeah, it's obviously given you that strength to, you know, make the decisions and choices that you have done over the last few years and leads you to a place where you can, I suppose, associate with people that have had similar experiences, which gives you an understanding to be able to really help, and support, and make a difference with people.

Joseph Clough:

Yeah, I think you're absolutely right, and you'll definitely know this from all your amazing experience. A lot of the time, no matter what the issue can be, usually if we have a belief of not being good enough or worthy, that has such a big effect on our life. Just one belief system can have an effect on your relationships, your career, your health. When we begin to understand what our limiting beliefs are and how important beliefs are, once we get the empowering beliefs, we absolutely transform how we see life and all the opportunities life has to offer us.

Craig White:

Exciting. So, you're actually a certified trainer of the sort of, neuro-linguistic programming?

Joseph Clough:

That's the one.

Craig White:

Timeline therapy, and you're also a master hypnotherapist as well. Which came first for you? Where did you—

Joseph Clough:

They're very interlinked by nature, which we'll get into I'm sure. I actually first started with hypnosis. Now, my dad did it as a hobby, so I was very, very skeptical at first, and also a little bit fearful, thinking that he might hypnotise me one day to do more things when I was younger.

Craig White:

I'm sure he did.

Joseph Clough:

Yeah, as far as I know he may well have done that. He actually told me, you're not in a good place. Just go on this hypnosis course, if anything just to get some head space, get a bit of clarity. So, I got into this hypnosis course, which was based in Scarborough at the time, so it was a long journey from Cambridge. It must have been four or five hours for me and my little one-litre car back then. I took that journey, and on the way back I thought, wow, what a transformational change. When you start to reconnect with the inner resources of yourself, you can make such a difference in your life, and I wanted to be able to share that, so, hypnosis definitely came first. The NLP, which as you said is neurolinguistic programming, is really like a spin-off to hypnosis. It's a way of doing things a little bit more consciously, but you're working with your unconscious mind, and timeline actually came from NLP as well. So, you could say the hypnosis was there; hypnosis has been around for thousands and thousands of years, ultimately. NLP, being about 50 or 60 years old or so now, actually, it was modelled on hypnosis and psychotherapy, and then kind of channeling it into this new kind of type of process.

Craig White:

Amazing. That's interesting, because I know you've got a deep-seated belief that we're always ever-evolving and ever-learning, and people really should be sponges to develop themselves and find out more about their true potential.

Joseph Clough:

That's right. The way I see it, and I think sometimes society can ingrain certain beliefs on ourselves to be like other people, to have all the cars, to be able to look like this certain thing. Ultimately, that can breed fear and feelings of inadequacy. What I want to say in my message is that ultimately, we are all perfect. We can actually may still want to make changes, but ultimately, within you is perfection.

Craig White:

Mm-hmm.

Joseph Clough:

We can put our attention on ourselves, and realise that everything we need is within us. Whether that be contentment, inner fulfilment, peace, confidence, it's all there within us, and it's just ultimately our potentiality. The problem is, we look sometimes for the external means to get it. We go on this searching, I need this to be fulfilled or I need this relationship to know that I am loved. My whole aspect is that actually, it's all there and it always has been there. We just have to put our attention to all those wonderful qualities, to feel gratitude, to be able to understand that we are so worthy, that you can do anything that you want in your life when you put your mind to it. And I think we were born with that. When you think about it Craig, when we're born, we're completely one wholeness. We're completely whole in any way.

We didn't have the understanding of language and labelling. We didn't have any limiting beliefs. We didn't feel at that point lots of negative emotions, or even good emotions, we were just literally a being. Then, through time, as we go through experience, it can create some times, not all the time, but conflicts or limiting beliefs, or certain labels, or having conflicting values or behaviours or habits. What my intention is to really get us back to that source wholeness and resolve conflict, and really acquire that inner belief that, yeah, everything's fine. Everything is perfect. We just have to put our attention to it.

CRAIG WHITE:

I guess this brings us onto the power of our beliefs. I'm certainly a firm believer that we live our daily lives in line with our internal beliefs. What's scary, I think, is when people start to appreciate and understand that our beliefs have typically and generally been created by outside experiences, other people's influences. That social environment that we find us in, what's commonly, I suppose, branded as the power of association. How can people take back the power and control of their own beliefs, and get this right from inside? Which is what you were just mentioning.

JOSEPH CLOUGH:

Well I think the one thing to consider, is, like you said, the power of association and other people's beliefs. I'm always curious to know, where did they get their beliefs from? Now, the chances are they got it from their environment years before we got their beliefs if we're younger than whoever we learned it from. Usually, we get imprinted by our family, our friends, our peers. If we track back where their beliefs come from, the chances are that they were taught that or they were told that life's a certain way. But where did they get their beliefs from? Chances are, the people before them were told that's a certain way of living. Ultimately, we could be actually living limiting beliefs or certain beliefs which are generations old. Just generations old, that we think, actually, when we look at the reality of it, where did this belief come from? Does it empower me? And does it really apply to me? Leading on to that question you just said, I think the first step to realise is, that we must be conscious of the beliefs we believe in, because beliefs do make up our world.

When we become conscious of our beliefs, we have the ability to change it. I remember a great quote, and I think it was, we're only kept in cages we cannot see. So, we're only kept in cages we cannot see. Ultimately, if you're unable, and you just live with these unconscious processes, you're unable to understand the restrictions within that, but when we become conscious of our belief systems, it ultimately means we now have the power back. When we become conscious, we can ultimately take responsibility of them, and when we take responsibility, we get ownership. When we get ownership, we can start to make those fundamental changes. The first step is being conscious of the beliefs that we have within us. We can ask ourselves, if we have a problem or anything like that, we can ask ourselves, what belief do I have about myself which makes this so? If I have the belief of I can't get a relationship. I may have got some anxiety at work. I can ask myself, what is the belief I have which makes me unable to do that? That brings us to the source of that limiting belief.

When we become conscious of that, we can think, well, is this my belief? Was I taught this belief? Let's take the money example. We may have the belief system that money is a bad thing. Or, it leads to evil. Or, I feel guilty. Where does that belief come from? Did we get taught it? Did we just pick it up through some certain experiences, which is very common? If we take my example, I felt not good enough, because I can remember clearly when I was at school when a teacher said, Joseph, you're not good enough to be able to go to the next level if you don't understand this process, which was like going to secondary school. I thought at that moment, wow. The teacher has authority. They know me and know my abilities, and they're saying I'm not good enough. The thing we must consider is, the chances are the limiting beliefs which we have formed were, you could say, formed at a place where we didn't have enough information or knowledge to make the right belief system. If we create a limiting belief at say, 5 years old, or 10 years old, or 15 years old, how much life experience do we have to make that judgement? The chances are, not many. We don't really have life experience.

Maybe that event overpowered us, or someone just told us something, and we just took it on uncritically. I think we don't take on beliefs for fun. We do it for positive intentions. We know that the belief system is there for a reason, but is it still applicable to where I am now in life? Once we get those learnings, then that belief system starts to disappear. And when that disappears, as you said, you change your reality. You perceive a whole new reality from scarcity, from being limited, to absolute optimism, to absolute opportunity. Does that make sense?

Craig White:

Yeah, it does. I understand the power of people being conscious of their beliefs and knowing where they are. I really like they way you've taken that back. We're saying, we could actually be living beliefs of generations of years and years and years ago, which have very little relevance to today, where we are right now. What can people do with regards to obviously, they're conscious of their beliefs and they can ask this question about, what do I have about myself which makes me unable to do that, so to speak? How can then start to replace them with new, empowering beliefs? What actions could you recommend?

Joseph Clough:

There's a couple of ways. I'll try and give you, with the time that we have. One thing is preserving learnings. The reason why we have limiting beliefs—let's take the example of not being good enough, which is very common. The limiting belief of not being good enough is actually a protective mechanism. Like all issues we have, our body does it for a certain reason. If we take the belief of not being good enough, if I have that belief in my mind, it will keep me safe and I won't push myself out there. I won't go into situations in case I get hurt because I don't believe I'm good enough. What if people think this of me because I don't feel I'm good enough? It's very much like a keep me in comfort zone. Or not really comfort, it's just my familiar zone, because it's not very comfortable if you have an issue. It's a very familiar zone, but I'm going to stay here and be protected. The one thing is, once we get our unconscious mind to learn what needs to be learned, the problem will start to disappear, but to make it a little bit more specific and a bit easier for us, if you can imagine, Craig, you have a limiting belief.

As you imagine that limiting belief, how you know that it's true, how you see it in mind or how you feel about it, you keep on asking one of three questions. You'd say, for what purpose do I have this belief? Or for what intention do I have this belief? Or, the third one is, what's this belief trying to get me? Because it's not getting you anything good, but what's the intention or the purpose behind it? The motivation? We dissociate from the behaviour itself and go back to its core intention. Once we get that, say the intention may be, well, it's trying to protect me. We go, for what purpose protection? That might be so I feel safe. For what purpose? Safety and protection. So, I feel comfortable in my environment. We just keep on asking those questions. When you do that and you continually do that for at least 10 to 15 times, your neurology will actually break outside of that belief system. To run it quickly through, it could be the first one is protection. The second one is safety. The next one is comfort. If I feel comfortable and I'm protected, and feel actually quite happy in my situation intentionally. What will that get me? That will give me confidence. We actually become in conflict with the original conflict, the limiting belief. Does that make sense?

Craig White:

Yeah. I'm following you, yeah. Definitely. I think I'd have to listen to you again and practice, I think, is going to be the keys for people to, as you said, look at this 10 to 15 times to really—

Joseph Clough:

Yeah. The way to do it is, if you can imagine that every limiting belief system has a boundary, doesn't it? Like a label, you could say.

Ultimately, by saying for what purpose or intention, we're going to the highest intention why our unconscious mind runs it. When we go there in our mind and we consider it, the unconscious mind will have to reevaluate itself in accordance to that belief system. I know it sounds very technical, but when you apply it, you'll actually see these fundamental changes because you're going, for what purpose? For what purpose? Ultimately, your brain unconsciously will take you to a state of the opposite of that limiting belief system. We're actually keeping the intent of safety but generating a whole new association to an empowering belief of being worthy instead.

Craig White:

Yeah. I understand, mate.

Joseph Clough:

We're breaking through that neurological boundary of that limiting belief.

Craig White:

Yeah. You're becoming conscious of it, and then I suppose you're asking the questions. You're challenging that belief. By doing so, as you said, you're stepping out that boundaries and associating a different belief with that feeling of safety or comfort.

Joseph Clough:

That's right. You're keeping the safety, but you've got this new belief system which supports you in the right way.

Craig White:

Awesome. Fantastic. You mentioned going into, I suppose, NLP, the neurolinguistics program. Am I right in saying this is really just a set of skills that we already have within us that we can very much actively use within our mind, and body, and soul to run our own life much more successful?

JOSEPH CLOUGH:

Yes, it definitely is. The metaphor I paint in my mind is, if you can imagine an overgrown garden, if you go down the one route of that garden, what's begins to happen? It becomes more well-trodden down, doesn't it?

CRAIG WHITE:

Yeah. You clear a pathway.

JOSEPH CLOUGH:

That's right. Think of, if we have a problem, the more times we activate that problem, think it, feel it, act, and react that way, it becomes more ingrained and you go down that pathway. NLP is about interrupting that pattern unconsciously and going down the new pathway. If we just take that metaphor of the garden into the brain like the neuro networks, the more times you think, the more times you feel, the more times you act and react and associate, the neuro networks become stronger. NLP is really getting the unconscious mind to develop a new pathway. Rather thinking this, you think this. Or whenever you're feeling this, you feel that. It ultimately transforms you consciously and unconsciously by giving you the resources that you already have within you and breaking through those limitations.

CRAIG WHITE:

I know we share a passion for personal development, learning more, becoming more and therefore probably experiencing and enjoy more that life has to offer. Do you think this has a real meaning, for somebody very new to personal development or somebody very new to entrepreneurialism, people that are looking to maybe break out of the habits of the past, that negative thinking or that social environment that's not been very empowering. Do you feel that personal development is that first step to start to make new pathways in the brain?

Joseph Clough:

Yeah, it is. When you think of personal development, you're developing yourself. Every time we're growing, we're getting stronger. If we're not growing, as we just briefly spoke before this interview was that if you're not growing, you're ultimately in a way dying. It's like a plant. You need to feed yourself continuously to evolve and grow in life. That's why we're here, after all. The people before us in the genes and so on have had to modify, depending on their environment. What personal development does, it gives you the tools to retrain how your mind works, to access resources like confidence and motivation, to resolve conflicts, let go of stuff, and ultimately master your mind. I think that's one thing I'd love for schools to be able to teach a little bit more.

To really educate young people to think, actually, I can change my emotional state. I can feel empowered, because when we take responsibility for our life, when we become conscious of these limiting beliefs, we actually have an opportunity to do something about it. When we take inspiration and when we take massive action on learning and becoming more, we realise how powerful we are as people. That can only transform our health, relationships, career, and business simply by taking responsibility. Just to take another point, which I think is partly maybe down to society, we can have a lot of reasons and excuses as to why we can't do something, can't we sometimes?

Craig White:

Yep.

Joseph Clough:

We say, I can't do this because of that. I can't do this because of the financial situation or the financial climate. I can't do this because that person won't allow me. Well, I don't live my life that way, and I know you don't at all because we realise that reasons and ultimately excuses hold us back and actually disempowers us. It's like we're buying in to other people's expectations, and that means that we can't take ownership. When we take responsibility for our present situation right here, right now, it means we have ownership over our life and therefore, we have ownership of where we take our life. As we know, our past has led us to this point, so our past behaviour or our past situations, thoughts, and thinking has led us to this point right now. If we take responsibility for our life in this moment, assume that control, and take ownership for our life ownership for our mind, ownership for our reactions, ownership of our environment, then our future will completely transform. Have you ever read the book Man's Search for Meaning at all?

Craig White:

I haven't, no. I'm going to write that down. Man's Search for Meaning.

Joseph Clough:

It's by Victor Frankel, and he was in the concentration camps. He was what the worst of—I know they were all terrible, concentration. I always forget the main name.

Craig White:

Alcatraz? No, not Alcatraz. Auschwitz?

Joseph Clough:

Yeah. It's that one, isn't it? He was there, and he actually survived. He said a quote which goes something like this. It's been a long time since I read it now, but he says, when we are unable to change a situation, we're challenged to change ourselves. Now, think of the situation that he was in. In our lifetime, I'm sure that would never happen again. He saw his family die. He saw people around him die, become depressed, but he came through and survived that experience and came up with that mindset. When we're unable to change our environment or situation, we're challenged to change ourselves. Now, if we can do that in our lives, it just completely takes our problems in such a smaller level that we think, if this guy can do this and survive life and become a better man for it and like to grow as a person from it, we can easily adapt to that philosophy in our mind. When we can't change a situation, we're challenged to change ourselves.

Craig White:

That's a fantastic mindset to have and I think certainly for, I've noticed this being a shift across the UK and Europe at the moment with the current social and economic environment we find ourselves in. I think people are looking for new ways to do things. I think people have that entrepreneurial spirit inside them, and maybe it's rearing its head up and they're thinking, hang on a minute. There's got to be a better way out there. I think people are starting to look to—I know from recently at the Empowerment live event, there's a lot of people there that are running successful businesses in many different arenas as well as people that have come to a point in life where they're thinking, I just need to do something different, and they wanted to be empowered to do so. I think there's been a shift where people aren't looking for that job for life anymore. This attitude of developing a mindset to change and to challenge themselves to change, it's empowering for me and very exciting because I completely agree with you. People very much choose their choices and the actions of the moment of today are what are going to create the future.

Joseph Clough:

That's right, yeah.

Craig White:

I think people can choose their environment. Have you got any simple tips maybe using NLP that can help people to develop this confident, challenging attitude to understand that they are in control of their choices to change their future? Is there anything specific that we can advise people to do?

Joseph Clough:

I'm sure there is. To be honest, the way I see it is ultimately being conscious of this process. It really transformed my life just knowing I'm responsible. I've got to take responsibility to make a change in my life. When I had all those issues, I had to make a decision that this is not good enough, but something has to change and only I can do it. Just reinforcing that belief system that I am the cause of all of the effects in my life. If I'm not happy with the effects of my life, then I must change myself to make that change. When I was writing my book, this sentence came to my mind. It was, rather than being a product of life, allow life to be a product of you. That means rather than life just affecting you, you actually turn it around and go, okay. In my life, this is showing up. If I don't like it, I have got to take responsibility for that and I've got to do whatever it takes to make that change. Then, as we take massive and inspired action to do these changes, it's a continued learning process. As a little process for you, for people out there is to ultimately live more in this moment. This moment is very, very powerful right now. I also understand, we live in a high-paced world and it's very hard to live in the moment. We see the wonderful books like The Power of Now and the Buddhist teachings and some of the spiritual teachings. I think they're absolutely amazing, but also we've got to live in a real life, and we have got stuff happening. To be able to make consistent changes, I do this personally. As I go to sleep at night, I will take 10 or so, 15 minutes, to preserve the learning of this day, the day just gone because I know if I learn from my day, I can take those learnings into the next day. Learnings we actually let go of, emotional and psychological and behavioural issues anyway because we're ultimately updating ourselves. We only have problems because our body thinks they're doing good things. We have a fear of phobias, doing it for protection. We have anxieties. We're trying to control our future too much of all the things we don't want to happen. Ultimately, as you go to sleep at night, take 10, 15 minutes and preserve the learnings from that day. Nothing else. Forget about all the other things. Preserve the learnings. Then, when you wake up in the morning, take 10, 15 minutes to rehearse your day exactly how you would like it to be and really see yourself taking responsibility.

See yourself being empowered. This is good for a couple of reasons. First of all, it's very much like a goal-setting process. Okay, there's my goal for the day. Second of all, by rehearsing it in your mind, your unconscious mind ultimately thinks it is going to happen. The mind cannot distinguish from what is imagined and what is real. When you go there in the mind, you ultimately go there in the body. You're actually firing up the same connections as if you haven't been there. As you rehearse it in your mind, you're ultimately giving your unconscious mind the strategy of how you would like to perform that day. Then, through out the day, every couple hours, take five minutes to sit in your environment and just take it in. Be peaceful for a while. Ultimately, that keeps you bringing back to the now. Every couple hours, just take 10 minutes, five minutes, to sit peacefully and put your attention on this moment because in this moment, you become far more creative. You just live and flow throughout life. As you go to sleep, preserving your learnings, that deals with the past stuff, past-based thinking.

We were transforming our negative past-based thinking into a positive way by preserving learnings and evolving. We're also taking care of our future-based thinking like if we ever get anxious, we're just resolving that by rehearsing our day. Also, every few hours by being in the moment is causing us to live fully in the moment, and that's when you're far more confident and that's when you're far more creative. Also, you're realising that this moment is the most beautiful, most wonderful thing that could ever happen to you. That's no matter wherever we're going. We're just being in this moment and taking responsibility for it. As we do that, we're covering all fields. You could say it's kind of like driving a car. When you're driving the car, you occasionally look in the rearview mirror, which is your past, you can say.

You occasionally look back and you're preserving learnings to make sure you're on track so you know where you've been. You have the big, wide-open window screen in front of you and you're seeing where you're going. That's where you're putting your attention and that's where you're putting your focus, but you're always in the driving seat. You're always in the moment. Yeah, you can keep looking back at the past every so often just to preserve the learnings as you go to sleep at night. You're rehearsing. You know your map. You know where you're going in life by just rehearsing your day, but you're always firmly in the driving seat, directing where you wish to be. You've got to really just utilise that kind of metaphor into our lives.

Craig White:

I love that, Joseph. I think that's a real cracking, useable three-point tip for people to use to really empower themselves daily. I love the philosophy of just preserving the learnings of the day. I think often a lot of people educate themselves through personal development, but maybe this preserving of them learnings, of the experience of the day, I feel can just really empower people to live that enjoyment.

Then, I suppose as you say, in the morning when people are waking up, they're rehearsing their day. I suppose they're rehearsing their very own mission statement to have that day of what would be their greatest day.

JOSEPH CLOUGH:

That's right.

CRAIG WHITE:

I love this taking a few moments as well. I do that myself unconsciously just to enjoy the moment without realising probably the importance of doing so.

JOSEPH CLOUGH:

That's right. The reason why you do so amazing at what you do, Craig, is because you've had to learn. It didn't just happen to you.

CRAIG WHITE:

No, of course not, no.

JOSEPH CLOUGH:

You had to dedicate and you had to learn. Like everyone who is successful, they have to learn. Just by doing that little process before you sleep, you're learning and that means you're growing as a person. As you said, rehearsing in your mind, it's like your own mission statement. You're declaring to yourself, there's how I want my life to be. There's my strategy, and there's where I'm heading. As you live in the moment, you embrace life as well, because people say life is quite short, don't they? You've got to deal with all these things. But it's also the longest thing you will ever do in life, as well. You might as well just live in this moment and enjoy it and really take that responsibility, because wherever you put your attention, that's where you're getting your results. If you're putting your intention and attention on issues, problems, reasons, excuses, that's what you're telling your unconscious mind to look for more of it. When we change our attention and our focus onto what we want, we're telling our unconscious mind, this is where we're heading.

CRAIG WHITE:

Yeah. I love that. I really do appreciate your time. I know you're a busy man. I know you've had a really hectic few months, and I'm sure you deserve some proper chill, recuperation time soon, Joseph.

JOSEPH CLOUGH:

Yeah. That is the plan.

CRAIG WHITE:

I really appreciate. I'm sure that the listeners today and anytime they choose to connect and really listen to this podcast, I think they're going to enjoy the information. I just love the philosophy to get people understanding that everything they need to have, be, become, and enjoy the moment of life, they already have within them and the opportunity to make the choices to develop the mindset to just challenge and change themselves. Ever-evolving, ever-learning, just to enjoy everything that they've got within them to create the abundance and fulfilment in their life's quest.

JOSEPH CLOUGH:

Perfectly put.

CRAIG WHITE:

I really do thank you very much for joining us.

JOSEPH CLOUGH:

My pleasure.

CRAIG WHITE:

Where can people connect with you if they want to connect, find out a little bit more about you, Joseph?

JOSEPH CLOUGH:

One of my mission statements is just to give. On Facebook, I just give loads of free audio programs. I've got an eight-hour audio program for confidence. If you want to join me there, it's just Facebook.com/JosephsFanPage. On Twitter, I've got Twitter.com/JosephClough. Or JosephClough.com. I've got loads of free resources to help people. That's what I'm really about.

CRAIG WHITE:

Yeah. That's wicked, mate, and we've got a lot of time for that. Also guys, Joseph's book, as I said, he's a Hay House author, soon to become very successful author I'm sure. It's called Be Your Potential, and it's going to come out in July. Myself being a product of personal development and somebody that's got a belief that it's the key to our personal growth, I'll certainly be picking up the book and highly recommend that others do, too. The more we learn, the more we become. Hey, Joseph, thank you very much. I look forward to connecting with you and catching up with you soon, buddy.

JOSEPH CLOUGH:

Absolutely. It was absolutely a pleasure speaking to you, as always.

CRAIG WHITE:

Cheers, mate.

JOSEPH CLOUGH:

All right. Have a great day.

#1 best-selling Hay House author, and creator of over 200 hours of Free Hypnosis and Coaching MP3s and videos that are being downloaded over 3,000,000 times every year and listened to over 250,000 times a month and international Speaker, Celebrity Coach and Hypnotherapist.

Joseph's goal in life is to help each person achieve their full potential and that includes you. He combines advanced techniques of Eastern and Western inner transformation, and his own techniques and Hypnotherapy, and have worked with celebrities and professional athlete clients.

www.josephclough.com

CHAPTER 13 Go Pro

Do you have what it takes to become a "Network Marketer"? How do you become a pro, mastering a new skill set like an Olympian athlete through total dedication?

Eric, author of the international bestselling book Go Pro – 7 Steps to Becoming a Network Marketing Professional, is someone who understands this journey. In this podcast, Eric shares some principles and fundamental skills needed to develop an entrepreneurial spirit through network marketing.

Eric Worre has been a leader in the Network Marketing profession for 28 years, this podcast is a must hear for anyone who is serious about building their network marketing business.

Craig White:

Hi everyone and thanks for joining us again today. I'm extremely happy to be chatting with Eric Worre from Network Marketing Pro. Eric now has been involved with our amazing network marketing business for well over 25 years, creating a substantial income of in excess of, I believe $15 million of income, which is quite mind-blowing, really. But when you get to understand the industry, you can really understand why and how that's possible. I know Eric is extremely well-known through the industry for the value that he's given over the years, but also now he does a lot and he's focused on his website, Network Marketing Pro, which gives daily value to inspire in ordinary people the opportunity to stand on the shoulders of giants. I've been inspired by a lot of what I've seen over the last 12 to 18 months, and it's really great to have Eric with us today. Eric, we have an amazing following of listeners from every walk of life, we have some students, some athletes, some entrepreneurs, and many people associated with our network marketing industry. But, you know, I think successful fundamentals are transferrable. Would you agree?

Eric Worre:

Absolutely, and if they're not transferrable, we've got a problem with our business. First of all, I just want to say thanks for having me on. It's fun to be able to chat with you and talk about ideas on how to be successful. To your question regarding ideas being transferrable, it's just like any skill set. It's like any profession. If you're going to be good at any profession, there are skills inside of the profession that you need to develop, and one of the things we talk about in Marketing Pro all the time is this idea of going pro, this idea of becoming a professional. Getting rid of the word industry and replacing it with the word profession. Just deciding that, yes, we're going to figure out what the skills are, we're going to learn them together, we're going to use them to help a lot of people and to create freedom in our lives.

Craig White:

It's that shift, isn't it, to look at it from a professional point of view, and it's that shift that it kind of has on the inside and it's like our perception of our projection, I suppose. Today we're going to specifically focus on this industry of network marketing, as you're aware and many people listening, but many may not be aware, but I think there's more millionaires created through this individual industry than any other individual industry in the world. I know you often say, I totally believe, I think we do have a better way. I know these shows are transferrable, and I'm really grateful for you joining us today. It seems quite timely. When I first contacted you about doing a show, Eric, I wasn't aware of this new book that you've just launched. So, we can come to that later. It's great to get you on the show at, I suppose, a perfect time considering you've just launched this new book, Go Pro. I know it's smashed some records on Amazon, which is great to see.

Eric Worre:

It's a lot of fun. I haven't written a book for 25 years. It's the first time I've written something. I've had different information products, audio programs, video programs, events, those types of things, but it took a long time for me to get my head around offering up what I knew for $12. It's a little bit of a challenge, mentally. But, I'm at a little bit different stage of my life, legacy stage, contribution stage. I want to see our profession raise itself up, because so many amateurs are giving us a black eye in the public's perception. If we have more professionals involved, we're all going to be better off. You know? Better products, better companies, better distributors inside of those. People can be proud of this as a profession, instead of kind of dodging around it. Right?

Craig White:

Yes, I know, I agree. I suppose it's what you're saying about the skill sets. If people can embrace them and learn them, it's the philosophy, the more you learn, the more you earn. So how long have you been involved in this industry? I mean, give us a quick lowdown of how you got involved and where you're at etc.

Eric Worre:

I got involved when I was 23 years old, 1988, and I was in a situation where I was barely making enough money to survive, I had a young family started, and starting to feel a little bit desperate. Behind on my bills, behind on my promises. And I was fortunate to be introduced by somebody I respected, to the network marketing profession. At the beginning, I was like, no, listen, I've heard about those things, I'm not interested, you know, whatever. Big know-it-all 23-year-old, and then they said, well that's fine, but we're going to do it anyway. And these were people I respected and I didn't want to get left behind, so I borrowed some money from my father, and got my first little product order, and I started. And I had some decent success. My first couple months I made some money.

Enough, I quit doing what I was doing, I was selling real estate at the time. So, I quit selling real estate, and by the third month, my money completely went away. I mean, month one was great, month two was great, I was in the right place at the right time, and then month three was nothing. So, I was desperate, and I was really mad, to be honest with you. I started blaming the profession, I said this thing doesn't work, my upline doesn't help me. They say upline sells itself, my downline doesn't do anything, this won't duplicate. How do they expect anybody to do this without any training, and all this blame list. The blame list was fine, it worked up to that point in my life, but frankly, I could blame all I wanted, but it wasn't going to make me any money that month. So, the only place I could go make money that month was to go back into network marketing and go to work. So, I did, and I started building up a little bit more, little bit more, little bit more, but I will tell you, I rebuilt my organisation seven different times in my first three years. I built it up, it would crash, I'd build it up, it would crash, I'd built it up, it would crash. Never had any duplication, never had any residual income at all, and then I had a little bit of a defining moment. A little epiphany. Actually, what happened, I narrowed it down to just one particular moment in my life. One thing that I was taught early on was never to miss a company convention, so I didn't. I was always at the company convention, three times a year with that company. So, one way or another, I drove, or I slept in my car, or whatever I had to do to be able to make it happen, but I was in the hotel room the night before convention, I was watching CNN, and there was this crazy expert that was being interviewed on CNN. I don't know if you have the shows where you are. These shows were where people were trying to value a certain thing, so they'd bring in an expert. And, how do you value this old sword that we found? How do you value this piece of ceramics that we found in our attic, or whatever? So, they find this expert, right? It was an expert like that.

I remember thinking, how does a person become an expert at that? And I said, well, I suppose they have a lot of experience with it, maybe they've read everything there is to read on it, they probably interviewed everybody there is to interview on it, and there came a time when they became expert, and people were going to call them to find out how much their piece of ceramics was worth, and they would call them. So, nothing happened that night. It just went through my mind. The next day I'm at the convention, and I'm sitting in the audience. You've been involved with networking marketing for a long time, so you know what I'm talking about when I say this. The big shots were going across the stage, and they're getting their big oversized cheques, and they're getting their flowers, and they're getting their trophies, and doing their tearful thank you speeches, they're doing all these things, and that was really inspirational for me for the first couple of years. Then it started to not be inspirational for me, after that, because I was getting frustrated; why were they having the success that I'm not having? They don't look that much different from me. I'm working as hard as they're working, what's going on? So, I'm watching this, big shot after big shot, when is this going to be over, when am I going to get some training, la la la la la, and it was like getting hit by lightning, literally. It was like an audible click in my brain, where I went wait a minute.

What if I decided, like that guy on CNN last night, what if I decided to be a professional in network marketing? What if I decided that I was going to develop all the skills in network marketing, and I was going to master them? Not just conceptually, intellectually, but in practical use. If I did that instead of— you know, see, up to that point in my life in my career in networking marketing, I was focused on timing, positioning, I was very fear based, I was going to miss it, I was going to miss out, and I will tell you, in an instant, my fear went away. I went, I got this. I will figure out what the skills are and I'll learn them, I'll let go of luck and timing, and guess what? I have to be up on that stage, soon, because I'm going to become great at the skills necessary.

So, my focus completely changed, versus trying to figure out the secret or the angle, to try and figure out the skills. And it was very calm. I had a little bit of a relaxed intensity, and that changed everything. Within about two years after that, I had made a million dollars in a year. I was 29, that year I made $980,000 in commissions, and just a couple of years later. I'm the same guy, just my focus changed, from luck and timing and lottery and what everybody kind of plays around in network marketing, to saying I'm going to do this like a professional athlete would do this. Like a football player would do this.

Craig White:

Total dedication.

Eric Worre:

Total focus, dedication, I'm going to become known as a talented professional, like a doctor, like a whatever. So I did. And that created a career for me. And ever since that, I've been trying to tell people, let go of the lottery and step into the profession. Let go of the industry, step into the profession. Decide to be a network marketing professional. Decide to go pro. That will change everything for you. You'll attract people to you, it will grow an organisation, and you'll never have to worry about money again, if you develop these skills, you don't have to worry about it anymore.

Craig White:

It's a good position to be in. I remember some advice I was given early on. My parents had been involved in the industry, and that's one of the reasons why I was looking at it initially, and then I remember when I was 18, I remember my first kind of experience to the business, and it was some friends of mine that lived around the corner, and one of their guys come around and was doing the presentation, drawing the circles on a flip chart. And I was quite a young 18. I was immature, I was in the party zone, I just wanted it over, I wasn't taking it in, wasn't interested. When I look back, I think wow, I was introduced to the business, but for me it was about timing and stumbling across the right opportunity, and then I was given some advice. When I came in, going back to like the football world cup, soccer, you guys call it over in the States, and I remember there was a Coca-Cola ad and it talked about "Eat, sleep, dream Coca-Cola."

So, when I got involved in this business, I was passionate, and I wasn't used to goal-setting, however, I'd come back from travelling, I was 23, like yourself, and I had one core goal. I needed two grand a month, I'd never earned two grand a month doing anything in the past, however, I needed two grand a month to be able to move back out of my parents. And that was like a burning desire. So, I was positioned to kind of eat, sleep, dream the industry, but I remember somebody talking about personal development, I suppose learning the skills, it was something I didn't necessarily believe in back then. I didn't see the necessity.

I never missed an event, however, I remember my mum gave me the advice, but you never listen to your parents, do you? And there was another guy, quite a young guy, very successful, good friend of mine called Rob, and he said to me, "Look, Craig, energy, excitement and expectation will only take you so far, but you're going to hit your glass ceiling, and the only thing to break you through the glass ceiling is to develop some skills, to develop some skills which are the fundamentals." Obviously, we're coming from the same mindset. For the listeners to kind of unleash some of your wisdom and experience, Eric, what would you say the core fundamental skills are for people to focus on? I believe you cover some of these in your book. I haven't got a copy yet, I'm waiting for it to come.

ERIC WORRE:

Yes, I cover all of them, but let me give you five principles first, and then I'll give you the seven skills that you need to develop. Five principles that I've come to accept that are just fundamental:

1. Network marketing isn't perfect. There are challenges. It's emotional. You have to deal with the ignorance of the public. You have to go through a lot of challenges. Inside of this business it's lonely sometimes. It's frustrating sometimes. It's not perfect, but it's better. For freedom for the average person, it's better than any other way that I've seen in the world to create freedom. Lifestyle and income, which those two don't often go together. People have income but they don't have lifestyle, right? Number 1, network marketing isn't perfect.

2. If you're going to do it, decide to be a professional. Decide to go pro. You're going to do it anyway.

3. Like any profession, there are skills you need to develop. Just understand that. Accept it. Embrace it.

4. It's going to take some time. You're not going to be able to replace your income in a month. You're not going to be able to have total financial freedom—you can't go to the gym and workout one time, and expect to be in shape for the rest of your life but that's what people expect inside of network marketing. They're going to get involved, if they don't make money immediately in the first week then they're done. Well, come on, it's going to take a little time to develop some skills.

5. It's worth it. It's worth it for all kinds of reasons, but it's worth it.

The seven skills that you need to develop, there's not 70 or 700, just seven fundamental skills:

1. Finding people to talk to. That's a skill. I didn't think that was a skill for a long time. I thought that was a natural resource. You either knew a lot of people or you didn't. If you knew a lot of people, you could make money. If you didn't know a lot of people, you couldn't make money. That's what people say, well, "I don't know enough people, so I'm not going to join." That's irrelevant, knowing people. Completely irrelevant, because the professionals learn how to find people to talk to. Most of the top earners in any company, the majority of the people that they've sponsored into those companies are people they met after they joined that company. They didn't even know them prior to joining the company, because they're professionals, that's what they do. That's one of their skills.

2. Inviting. Inviting people to take a look at your product or opportunity, and doing that in a professional way. This is one of the most horrifying skill sets in network marketing, because people are just awful at it, and they make people uncomfortable, they make the profession look bad, and it's pretty simple to do it right and make everybody feel good. So, inviting people is number two.

3. Presenting. How do you present in a way that not only works, but will duplicate? Because you can present in a way that works but it won't duplicate, and you won't have freedom. So, presenting is skill set number three.

4. Following up. How do you do this in a way to keep the prospect engaged in the process, so you don't have to start over and over and over and over. How do you follow-up effectively, answer questions, overcome objections, those kind of things?

5. Closing. How do you help a person make the decision that they want to make? Not twisting people's arms or pressuring people at all, but acting as the consultant, helping a person make the decision.

6. How to get somebody started effectively. How to help them get moving and give them the best chance for success.

7. How to promote events. How to put butts in seats, how to get people to attend events of every sort, being a promoter. That's the highest paid skill in network marketing, by the way, skillset number seven.

Craig White:

I've heard you say that before, and in the twelve years of being in the business, it's something that I've heard time and time again, and

I've promoted myself from a leadership perspective, and bums on seats is the key. Going into that in a little bit more detail, being as you kind of confidently stated it is the highest paid skill in the industry, share with us some tips on how people can really focus on getting more people to events, whether it's prospects, whether it's team, what's your philosophy on that?

Eric Worre:

We talk about it a lot, we have a whole chapter in the book, but I'll tell you that getting people to attend an event in your home is one particular discipline. Getting people to attend a local event for your company, an opportunity or training event is another thing. Getting your downline to attend a training event, to get them focused again is another skill.

Craig White:

You drag them along kicking and screaming.

Eric Worre:

Yes, yes. One of the highest paid is getting a person to a destination event. Somebody has to leave their home, go somewhere, stay in a hotel or something, and be totally focused on their dreams for a weekend, you know? That's the highest pay of all. To make that happen in your organisation, there's a lot of things that you need to learn how to do, but you just need to think about—any promoter, if somebody's promoting a sporting event, what would they do. If somebody's promoting a Broadway show, what would they do? If somebody's promoting a movie, what would they do? One, you've got to make a decision that this is important. Two, you've got to lead by example. Three, you have to be more committed than everybody else. Four, you've got to bring so much enthusiasm and excitement and you've got to be able to portray a vision to people as to what is in it for them if they'll attend. You have to help them get all the obstacles out of the way. You have to help them focus their brain on away from the smallness of their life to the bigness of their dreams. Get them to go, say, come on, we'll do it together. And we're going to do this, and we're going to do this, and we're going to do this. "Yes, but there's a birthday party that weekend." "Listen, you know that that birthday party can change. You know that." If you played for—what's your favourite football team?

Craig White:

Liverpool.

Eric Worre:

If you played for Liverpool and there was a birthday party on a game day, would you miss the game?

Craig White:

Of course not.

Eric Worre:

Of course not. You're not going to miss the game. You'll move the birthday. It's not that you don't love that person, but it's game day. It's all about your focus. It's all about what if there was a wedding on a game day. If they wanted you to attend they'd change the wedding, wouldn't they? Because you're going to be playing. And your whole world will understand that.

Craig White:

Priorities, as you said about kind of removing all the objects and getting to see their vision and focus on the right thing. Yes.

Eric Worre:

Total focus, total commitment. Total bring the group of people with you and tell stories about how people have breakthroughs and everything else. So just really, a total commitment to it, and just decide how many people you're going to have at that next event, and then make it happen. And then decide that the next one's going to be bigger and the next one's going to be bigger and the next one's going to be bigger. If you were a publicly traded company, you as a person, we would be buying or selling your stock based upon how many people you had at the event.

Craig White:

Okay. I get you. Yes, yes, yes, of course. It's like getting people to have that mindset of making it happen. We often hear that in the industry, but people, when they've got that emotional connection to why, making it happen is just second nature, isn't it?

Eric Worre:

Usually I say, one of our chief wants in life is for someone to show up and make us do what we're capable of doing. That's one of our big wants in life. But here's the thing. What if they don't show up? Most leaders in network marketing, we're waiting for someone to show up and make it happen, and that person didn't show up, so they said, "I guess I have to be the one to show up for someone else." And then their whole life changed. Most leaders didn't grow up saying, "I'm going to be a leader." There was just a need and they stepped in because nobody else was stepping in.

Craig White:

Yes, of course. It's insane, really. You talk about the emotional connection to being a pro, and I know you have a vision where we're all kind of superheroes, which I loved that. I was listening to it recently.

Some of the guys who may have not come across you as yet, I noticed a few people that follow me on Facebook are following you, but not many in comparison to the volume. So, explain your vision of kind of superheroes and what you were sharing most recently.

ERIC WORRE:

Well, you have to remind me. I do so many shows I forget which one you are talking about.

CRAIG WHITE:

I think it's just a case of you talking about being a superhero, and having a better way, and being able to positively influence—

ERIC WORRE:

Yes, I'll tell you. Just the fact I admire people in network marketing probably more than any other group, and I'll tell you why. One, they're entrepreneurial to their core. They're just entrepreneurial. They have huge hearts, they want to help people, they're going against the traffic, you know?

CRAIG WHITE:

Yes, against the grain.

ERIC WORRE:

Everybody else is going with the traffic, they're going the other way. Suddenly there's a four-lane highway. Everybody's going one way and they're trying to figure out a way to go the opposite way up that highway. And they get a lot of people honking horns at them, and shaking fists at them, and threatening to beat them up, and everything else. But they say, "I have a better way. I'm going to help people. Eventually some other people are going to follow me up this road, and eventually everybody's going to realise that they're all going the wrong way. And we're going to turn them around." So, what we've got inside of our profession, the people have unbelievable powers, they really do. The powers of influence, powers of giving, powers of connection to other human beings. Because most jobs, people go sit at a desk or they sit in a cubicle, and they just—they're working with people they don't like, and they're doing things that they don't want to do, and it's kind of like they're the Clark Kent, compared to the Superman, right?

Craig White:

Yes, yes, yes, yes.

Eric Worre:

Yes, they put on their jobs and they go do this thing that other people told them they were supposed to do, and then, inside of our business, they learn how to be what they're supposed to be. And they have the freedom to do it. The freedom to say, "You know what? The heck with you. I'm not going to do what you tell me I have to do anymore. I'm not going to follow because you tell me I have to follow. No. I disagree and I wish you well. I'm going to go this other way."

Craig White:

It's like social conditioning, isn't it, because I know when I joined the business, it was a case of—used to work in that 9 to 5 and having that office mentality. You know, you find out you want to get in and get out as quickly as you can. I suppose it's part of your journey. For me, myself, now I've kind of lived the dreams I had and work for the dreams I have. I know when I got involved in the business, it was pure selfish indulgence, it was a case of greed, I wanted that two grand a month, 24 grand a year, wouldn't get out of bed for it now. However, and then the further you climb the further you see, and then the power of association, spending your time with entrepreneurial superheroes, people that are positively influencing you. The business, and I know the financial reward to be able to do the things that you do with the people you love is very important. You know, money is second to oxygen as much as it makes the world go around. We need it to be able to do quality things with the people we love. However, one of the things I've learned over the years is built upon relationships, and I was an event recently with a lot of leaders in my organisation, and you know, it's a case of I'm here for the duration, you guys have got me for life.

That excites me to know that collectively, we get the opportunity to create an empowering environment for others to willingly follow. Even those that join our business just for that extra 500 quid a month, they're valuable, and knowing that you're making a difference and influencing people is just quite inspiring. Yes, I'm still driven by my own goals and things that I want to do, you know, world tour with my children and all sorts of magical things you can do with the people you love and care about, but I think enabling other people to feel inspired to develop their vision and start to walk the path of their dreams. This is the better way, isn't it, Eric? There isn't anything else.

Eric Worre:

Yes. What I talked about last chapter of the book is it's all worth it. And it's not just worth it for the income. I don't even talk, I don't think, about the income in that chapter. For the career you create, yes, absolutely, because career is great. A career is better than having a little bit of money because it's more fulfilling, it's more rewarding, it's more long-term. For the people that you'll meet, the most amazing, unbelievable people. The places that you'll see, travel the world. I've been able to see places that are just stunning. I can't even believe that I've been honoured to be able to see it. For the causes you can contribute to. There's causes you want to give to, the ability to give and to leverage your influence for important causes. For the person that you're going to become, you know, because you've got to become something in order to earn in our business.

And that was the biggest blessing for me, because I was a 23 year-old kid with a lot of software viruses, in my brain. I needed to figure some stuff out. There were some things that I thought were red and they were really blue. I was messed up in the head, and network marketing helped me face my bad habits. Face my limiting beliefs, and it polished me up, and it still does it today. I'm surely not finished. You're either growing or you're dying, right?

Craig White:

Yes, damn right. I know, it's one of those things that the involvement in the industry enables you to become more, because of the environment, because of the association.

Eric Worre:

It doesn't enable you, it forces you. And then it enables you. But you don't have a choice. If you're going to be around, you're going to be in network marketing, guess what? You're going to grow. And if you're not going to grow, you're going to leave. It's super simple.

Craig White:

Growing or dying, I love that. I remember being—I mean I've benefitted from so many great experiences from this business, from travelling like yourself. But I remember being at something the company organised. It was an event for some leaders and had a guy called Colin Jackson, and he's an Olympic gold medalist in hurdling. From Wales, so running for Great Britain. And he was the speaker and did a fantastic sort of speech, very funny, very informative, and however, when we were sat down after dinner and we were just chatting he was just saying to me, you know, people—it's just like you were just saying to me about going to the gym and giving it time. It's not just going to the gym, it's what you're putting in to that time.

I mean, I go to the gym. I understand the importance of consistency, perseverance, etc., but it's also—recently, I had a cracked rib from a snowboarding incident. So, I've gone to the gym, but I almost felt like a fake because I wasn't fully in. I couldn't fully commit to do what I needed to do because of that. So, I suppose it's almost like the business. There's a lot of people that have got their toe in the water, and they can have their toe in the water for five years, but unless they go fully committed, unless they make the decision, as you say, to go pro, it's having that, it's not just time, it's doing the right things.

Eric Worre:

Right. Yes, I will tell you, what I've learned in this business is it takes 100% throttle to get an airplane off the ground, but you don't have to keep it at 100% to keep it going. You could throttle back to 50%. So, what I will tell you is network marketing is a little different. You don't have to stay at 100%. If you're afraid to go to 100% because you don't know if you can stay there, you don't have to stay there. But you have to do it in a burst, maybe 90 days to start your business, maybe 90 days a year where you just go crazy, where your life is swung out of balance, where you're like in training camp for Liverpool. Every day, you're working out for six to seven hours, you're just preparing, you're working like crazy to get ready for the game. There's going to be that time, every year, where you do that. But then, you can throttle back. You can have lifestyle, you can have freedom, you can have other things. You don't have to be white hot 24/7. But, in order to get to the other side, you've got to go to 100% first.

Craig White:

From my experience, you can go to 100%, and the last couple of years I've enjoyed some of the fruits of my labor. Had some quality time with my little girls, I think last year I had 56 flights in and out of the UK, and it's a case of you can choose at any time to recommit and go full throttle again. I suppose it's why it's a better way. That's why we have that freedom, but as you said—

Eric Worre:

In most businesses, if they're going to pay us the money we're getting right now, they're going to expect 100% all the time. But inside of our business, we don't have to give 100%, we can give 100% for a period of time, then throttle back if we like it, or throttle up if we want to get a little bit more, helping more people, or whatever. So, yes, you have choices here. You're not being controlled by somebody else, which is awesome.

Craig White:

You've just got to love that. Well, Eric, I know you're a really busy guy. I know your new book is being very successful, and you've got a lot of travelling ahead of you, so I really do appreciate you connecting with us and sharing some of your wisdom and experience of the last 25 years. For people's opportunity to connect with you, your website is NetworkMarketingPro.com. People can connect with you through there. And I know your book's available. I'm looking forward to receiving my copy, so hopefully that'll be landing on my doorstep shortly. But Eric, I'm very grateful and appreciative of your time. You're obviously a great guy for the value you give. Thanks very much for joining us today. It's much appreciated.

Eric Worre:

It's my pleasure and I will also tell you that if people want to get a Kindle version right away, of Go Pro, you can do that at GoPro-Kindle.com. Straight to Amazon, and I think it's seven dollars U.S. It's nothing, pretty inexpensive, so you can start reading that within a few minutes.

Craig White:

We'll certainly do that. Again, I think you for your time and I really appreciate you for joining us here. Have a fantastic day.

Eric Worre:

My pleasure. You too.

ERIC WORRE- GO PRO

Eric Worre has been a leader in the Network Marketing profession for 28 years. Although he's now retired from being a distributor and focused exclusively on Network Marketing Pro, his career has given him a broad range of experience. He's been a top field producer, building sales organisations totaling over 500,000 distributors in more than 60 countries; the President of a $200 million Network Marketing company; a co-founder and president of his own company, TPN- The Peoples Network; and a high-level marketing consultant to the Network Marketing profession. Eric is the author of the international bestselling book Go Pro – 7 Steps to Becoming a Network Marketing Professional, which has sold over 1,500,000 copies and has become a "must-read" for anyone who is serious about building their network marketing business.

https://networkmarketingpro.com/

https://www.youtube.com/user/ericworre

CHAPTER 14 Knowledge Is King

As you grow you see things differently. Have you recognised how far you have come, how much you have grown as an individual and the benefit of that? Do you have any books that inspire you or have inspired you in the past that you refer back to periodically? Are you putting what you read into action?

Barry worked in an industry for 18 years before building his own team in partnership with his family in Network Marketing and Personal Development. He had established good contacts and this move seemed like a natural progression. 14 years later he has created an online store, providing people with all their network marketing and motivation material they could ever need!

Barry's passion for inspiring others is what shines through the most so don't miss this amazing opportunity to soak up his knowledge and get inspired.

Craig White:

Hi everyone, and welcome to another podcast show. I hope you're having an absolutely wicked day today. Joining me today we've got an amazing guy, somebody I've worked with and been inspired by. He's become a good friend. Great guy called Barry Phillips. How are you today, Barry?

Barry Phillips:

Yeah, brilliant, Craig. Thanks.

Craig White:

Good stuff. Good, good, good. Guys, for those of you that don't know Barry, Barry commonly known as Barry the Book, has been running a fantastic company called Knowledge is King now for over 18 years. They're very much responsible for providing thousands upon thousands of people within our industry hot and up-to-date personal development material from all over the world. In many cases, I know you've brought some world-renowned leaders and authors and speakers from around the world to the UK stages, which has been really great Barry. I know we share a passion for personal development and connecting with ourselves, and I'm sure we'll discuss that at some point today, but how did it all start for you? I know you've been involved in the industry now for 20+ years. Where did the idea of Knowledge is King come from, and how does it work for you, really?

Barry Phillips:

Good question, Craig. Ultimately, what it was, 22 years ago I was actually a network marketer myself. I was working with a company, an American company called Envirotech that had a whole range of waterless technology products, which were way, way before their time. Within that, we were building, myself and my dad were actually building quite a large team ourselves. To support them, we started to bring in the good books and the good CDs from America because at that time, you could not find them anywhere for love or money. You just couldn't get ahold of them in the UK. We'd already started to establish a few connections with people like Jim Rohn and a couple of the other big American companies that were at the time selling both network marketing and personal development materials. We were bringing it over, and we were helping support our growing team with this material. Unfortunately, what they chose to do a couple of years into Envirotech in the UK, they chose to go back to a traditional direct sales model, which meant that overnight, we lost our royalty income.

However, what we had done is, when we'd established some great connections with people in personal development and network marketing who had great material, we'd also realised the importance of it as well. One of the things I remember in those early days is that I recognised something I think Jim Rohn said, which is that your business will only grow as you grow. I recognised that myself. I saw it in my own experience. I loved the books and the CDs anyway. Still love reading all the material myself. We also saw it happening in our team. We saw our team growing, building and obviously them benefitting from growing and helping them to grow their businesses. So, although overnight we were no longer in a network, we had established some good contacts, including contacts with a few other companies. It was almost a natural progression to move from being a network marketer to supporting the industry with that material, and that's literally how it started, and Knowledge is King has now been running for 18 years.

Craig White:

It's awesome, really, because I know you look to keep in tune with the British attitudes, and look to bring in the relevant resources. Obviously, I'd imagine you're scouring the world and you've got them connections. I'm a firm believer as well, we do become what we study.

Barry Phillips:

Absolutely.

Craig White:

I'd imagine you've got an extensive library yourself, Barry that's spanned 18 years. I can just visualise and imagine what it looks like.

Barry Phillips:

Yeah. Unfortunately, there's so many that sometimes you forget some of the best ones. I know we've talked about this before. I had a conversation with a customer this morning who'd just gone back over Questions Are the Answers by Allan Pease and just said, wow. I can't believe how much good material is in there. I know I've been using this stuff, but I bought this in '98, he told me. 1998 he bought it, and he's just revisited it and started using it again. That's often the case with it. Sometimes it's one of those situations where you can't remember all of the good stuff that you've read and listened to over the years unless you've implemented it and it's made a massive change in your life.

Craig White:

I think that's the key aspect, isn't it? Obviously, I've got that hunger and appetite for personal growth and personal development, as I know you have. I think, as you said, a lot of the time, it's the importance of not just learning the information but acting upon it so that it becomes part of you.

Barry Phillips:

Yeah, absolutely.

Craig White:

I think if you're just reading the information—I think maybe from my early experiences, and I'm sure you've maybe experienced the same sort of thing, but the early experiences of reading a lot of books but probably not putting a high enough percentage of it into action, I was never actually really learning. I know you've said before, do the thing and have the power. I think we've discussed at some point. It's always very important to keep fresh with what's hot and what's in the market today, what's relevant to today's industry, but there is some all-time classics that you can just consistently keep reading again and again, isn't there?

Barry Phillips:

Absolutely. As I said, each time I speak with people, especially people who've been around the industry for quite a while like yourself, that's very, very common. Sometimes, we do have to do that. I do it personally. Think and Grow Rich was one of the reasons I actually formulated Knowledge is King, in fact. That's actually what happened whilst I was in between jobs after Envirotech went back to direct sales. I was working very briefly for a company down in Bristol, and I used to commute on a daily basis to Bristol, which is about 90 minutes there and back. I had, it was an old audio tape at the time of Think and Grow Rich by Napoleon Hill. I used to listen to it every day on the way down there, on the way back. Almost to the point where, firstly I wore the casing out. You couldn't read the exterior where it used to say Think and Grow Rich. But I could almost at that time, talk to you about it verbatim and giving you exactly what he was saying on the CDs. And, Lo and behold, within about two months of starting this Bristol commute, I formed Knowledge is King.

Craig White:

The joys of being a busy man.

Barry Phillips:

Absolutely.

Craig White:

You formulated Knowledge is King really from the back end of that, then. That's awesome.

Barry Phillips:

I do believe that, yeah. That's one of the ones that I revisit on a yearly basis. Normally in January, I always go back over that. My copy's well highlighted and I just go back over the relevant bits. It's interesting because even then, some of the bits that I've forgotten or I haven't necessarily implemented.

Craig White:

Do you think it's as you grow, you start to see things differently, I suppose through your personal growth? Different things fall into place at different times in your life, I suppose.

Barry Phillips:

Definitely. It's also good to keep track of things like that as well. One of the other things that I remember, again going back to the early, early days, I spoke to a lot of people that were ex-Amway. They all used to tell me that even if they hadn't made any money from Amway, the biggest benefit that they gained was getting involved in some great reading and listening material, because that's something that Amway used to do a lot, promote a lot. Again, Jim Rohn comes to mind there, where he says it's not what you get, it's what you become. Sometimes we don't necessarily recognise how far we have moved on. We've read a lot. We've implemented certain things from different books. It's very easy sometimes not to actually acknowledge just how far you have come and how much you have grown and the benefit of that, because it's not just your own benefit. Obviously, if you're working with a team, the teams see it and they replicate it. It's the same when you've got kids. When you see your kids taking note of what you're doing and duplicating you, copying you, and it's positive stuff, stuff you learnt from books. That to me is icing on the cake. That's the real nitty-gritty of personal development in its entirety.

Craig White:

I suppose you're very much creating that empowering environment, starting with your own self, because it's the inside that creates the outside, isn't it? I suppose from doing so and studying, I get that message that obviously certainly with Think and Grow Rich, you've studied that program from the book to the audio CD, that a lot of it would be part of your deep-seated beliefs and second nature to you, become very much built around that. I can understand creating that environment for your kids. Obviously, I've got a couple of young kids, and actually I tell you, Barry. My youngest, it's quite funny because I've got a real good environment. Obviously, the personal development has allowed me to have that same effect on her. She's got a philosophy of I can and you keep on keeping on and practice makes perfect. She's only four and a half, but she's got a great little attitude. We went kite flying the other day, and she looked at me and she said, Daddy, you really need practice to get good at this. I just thought that's brilliant. I suppose our industry, it's worth practicing. It's worth getting good at, because it'll change people's lives, won't it?

Barry Phillips:

Absolutely. Good point, as well. Good point that you just brought up there. You probably heard, I can't remember exactly where it came from. There was a study done and to master anything, they were talking about 10,000 hours of practice. It's been followed up recently with a very, very smart book called Bounce by an English guy in fact, called Matthew Syed. Matthew Syed was an England table tennis player. He studied it from a sports angle, but he's then now studied it from a business point of view. Again, it's no different, and I think that's one of the biggest challenges that people face when they join our industry, the direct sales network marketing industry, that they don't realise that if that's all they do is just keep practicing, they will be successful. If they don't get overnight success or quick success sometimes, unfortunately some people tend to go elsewhere or they look elsewhere. They actually sometimes think it doesn't work, but if they realise right from the outset that it's just a case of getting good at a few very, very simple skills and they're pretty much the same across the board, whichever company you're working with, then you can become whatever you want to become through that industry, through that company. Which is phenomenal. Nothing like it out there, Craig.

Craig White:

It's that, I suppose, the key of perseverance, isn't it? I'm trying to remember what book it was I read. It was recommended by a good friend and colleague of mine, Steven, and it was talking about the difference between mediocrity and the top performers in any industry and any sport and any area is life, is one hard-hitting word and that's chronic inconsistency. I suppose it's that perseverance, as you said, learning them core skills. I suppose one of the things I've learnt with my personal development, I think Jim Rohn was famous for saying there's no new fundamentals. Anybody who says, I've found a brand-new way, a new fundamental here, you need to go in the other direction. I suppose that's the same in life, in our business, in personal growth, whether people want to be a great footballer or a great rower or a great mum or dad or whatever it may be, it's that perseverance with implementing the basic skills and looking to just be the very best they can be.

Barry Phillips:

Absolutely. Then, just the practice. Again, going back to the sports, I remember when Beckham was at his peak, renowned and recognised as one of the best players, if not the best player in the world at one point. People used to talk about his free kicks. Everyone used to marvel at them. Obviously, that was something he was well known for, but I also remember reading about how he'd finish training, all the others would go home and for the next three hours, he'd be out at Old Trafford practicing corners and free kicks. He'd have one other person with him, just throwing the ball back to him. That, to me, again emphasises why he was so good. He was prepared to do. That's the other thing which again, you just touched on there, which I think is really, really key. I remember not too long after I started, I met a very, very influential couple of leaders from another company. I did a semi-interview with them, just purely wanted to find out about them, what was making them so successful?

Bear in mind, this was 12+ years ago now. They are now earning over a million pound a year in the industry. They're both from the UK. I remember I was sat there, and it was so simple, what she said to me, but I didn't really grasp it at the time. I wrote it down and I've been back over the notes several times. She turned around and she said, the difference that makes the difference is being able to be prepared to do whatever it takes. It's something that's a very, very, it's almost a throwaway comment, but when you really, really think about that, if people were totally prepared to do whatever it takes, firstly they'll never have to do everything they think they're going to have to do. But more importantly, they would reach the top of whatever their top of whatever network they're in or whatever industry they're in or whatever business they're in. You touched on persistence there. That is one of the major, major keys.

Craig White:

I suppose that commitment, going back to doing what it takes and the philosophy of Beckham. I suppose so many people in our industry or in the sports, they see the success and the see the fruits of people's labour. They see the lifestyle. They see the great lifestyle, the great cars, houses, holidays. All the shiny things that come along with success. They see the person people have become, even. But what they often don't see is this commitment to have that attitude, I suppose, of doing what it takes from the point of—. I remember talking a while ago, I think it was a training I did and I was talking about the similarity. Are premiership footballers worth the millions they're paid? I think they are, because I think they've made themselves worth it, maybe right from an early age, when if you take someone like David Beckham, he probably wasn't out in the street robbing cars. He wasn't eating McDonald's. He was on a strict diet. He was on a strict training program. He was committed to his goal, his passion, and he had a passion to learn and as you said, make it happen.

Barry Phillips:

Absolutely.

Craig White:

I suppose that's the same in everything, isn't it?

Barry Phillips:

I agree, yeah. Sport is a great analogy in many respects. The other one that instantly comes to mind there is, you know I'm a keen golfer and Tiger Woods. Tiger Woods has been nurtured from the age of two to three to four, I think, to be the greatest golfer the world's ever seen, which is what he has become. The benefit and the level, the different level that he took golf to, again at his peak. When

I say his peak, he's just won a game this weekend just gone. U.S. Open coming up in two weeks' time. You never know, he might be winning another major. Again, I've read several of his books, and the dedication, most people to be fair, wouldn't be prepared to put that in. But that is to be the pinnacle, the best in the world. Not everyone's trying to be the best in the world in this industry. If they just realised that it is a case of committing, being persistent and practicing until they get good. If you keep practicing, you will get good. It doesn't matter what aspects it is, whether it's phoning people, whether it's cold calling. Meeting people on the street doing presentations. It doesn't matter what it is. If you practice, you will get good, and that's your mastery.

CRAIG WHITE:

Yeah, agreed. Agreed. I know one of the things that we share in common is a kind of passion to connect with ourselves and keep fresh to what matters to us. I suppose the power of goal setting, we know the importance of goals and why, and I'm sure maybe you could recommend a couple of great books to people to really nail this. As you know, it's like what we're talking about with the sports stars and Tiger Woods. It's the dedication to achieve what they've set out to achieve, what goals they set, what they're passionate about, what matters to them. I think you need that to be able to make that decision to do whatever it takes.

BARRY PHILLIPS:

Definitely.

CRAIG WHITE:

I'd like to chat with you, because I know we both went away last year for our own reasons, but it was really empowering. What would you recommend on a book point of view? I know there's loads, Barry, but from your experience, for somebody quite early on in their business or relatively new to goal setting or maybe even someone that's not mastered the importance of goal setting yet. What would be one or two cracking books for them to study and implement?

Barry Phillips:

There are two that instantly come to mind, Craig. Again, this is probably more, it's based on my opinion but also more on what I know has helped so many people over the last two or three years, has been The Slight Edge by Jeff Olson and The Compound Effect by Darren Hardy. They're not specifically set out, hey, this is how to set goals. The principles of them are all about setting your goals, having your plans, and then working it, but doing it really small. One bite at a time, just those little things that make the difference. You can change those habits. Then, even if you are not prepared to sit down and set massive goals, you will notice a difference in all aspects of your life. Again, the feedback and the results that we've seen people get over the last couple of years with those two particular items has been phenomenal. That would be a strong recommendation from me.

Craig White:

Brilliant. That's interesting. I wouldn't have expected you recommend them, but I can see why. Obviously, having read and studied the both of them myself, I understand why. But it wasn't what I expected, so you pulled that out of the bag there. I went away last year. I think it was last year. Time flies when you're having fun, doesn't it? I know we share a common vibe, I suppose, or common feeling of the importance of spending time with yourself and connecting with yourself. Where was it that you went, again? I can't remember now.

BARRY PHILLIPS:

It was actually for my 50th last October. I'd always wanted to go to Asia. It was somewhere I'd never been before. I had this goal of visiting several of the Asian countries. Basically, I took a month out of the business for my 50th. I visited the Philippines, Vietnam, and Hong Kong, China. It was pretty amazing, and kind of did that on my own. Met a few interesting people along the way, but it was phenomenal. I know what you're getting at. It's sometimes hard to quantify just how important time out from business, from work, from everything, can be. These days, as we know we're so much busier. We're bombarded with a lot more information due to technology. You've got your phones and every other form of technology that you use. I do feel that even more so now, people need to get away, even if it's just a couple of days. To just spend time on themselves doing nothing, Craig. I know we talked about this. For me, it wasn't necessarily what I was doing while I was away. It was just the fact that I was totally freed up. I had nobody trying to get hold of me. The phone was left in the room every day, and I got so in touch with what I wanted to do. I had inspiration. That's the one for me, the biggest one for me, is when I totally shut down from everything, I get inspired. I'll sometimes wake up with an idea or I'll just be cycling and I'll have an idea. I'll be near the sea. I tend to get a lot of ideas there. It's just that whole experience of being away from it all, clearing your mind. To me, I look upon it as a mental shower. Completely emptying the head and letting new stuff come in.

CRAIG WHITE:

And truly relax. I think that's the key as well.

BARRY PHILLIPS:

Yeah. I know when you were telling me about when, it was Thailand, wasn't it?

Craig White:

Yes. That's right, yeah.

Barry Phillips:

In that respect, based on what I've just said, what did you also experience? Was it similar?

Craig White:

Yeah. I went away because I'd always wanted to learn to meditate and I wanted to do yoga. I just reached a point, and it was early last year. I just thought to myself, do you know what? I'm going away for a week. I found this tiny little island. I think it was two weeks before I booked everything. The beauty of having a royalty income and the freedom of choice, hey?

Barry Phillips:

Absolutely.

Craig White:

I just went away and connected with this wonderful French couple who live out in this beautiful little island near the Cambodian border. It was very out of the way in Thailand. It wasn't commercialised. It was real Thai. It was great, but what I found was, I'll be honest. The fear. I remember when I was travelling down the airport and I got the airport, and I love people, and I love spending time with people. I just remember thinking to myself, what have I done? Then, actually when I got out there and I do love that time. Sometimes, I'm the same as yourself, Barry, just that free time when you don't have to worry about anybody else. It may sound a little bit selfish, but I think we often talk about people go on holiday to relax, but you go on holiday with your loved ones. I believe that actually, you never relax on holiday because I think people care about people generally, and I think when you go away on holiday with your loved ones, you're always concerned about them.

You're always wondering, are they having a good time? Do they need anything? Can I help them? I don't think you actually truly have that mental shower or that you truly relax. What I found with going away was, I didn't have to worry about anybody else again. No one was contacting me. I didn't have my phone. I got up, I did my meditation. I did my yoga, which was all very new to me, but it was really empowering. I'd walk down the beach. I was just in my own world. I read a fantastic book called The Biology of Belief, and it was amazing, really. I was learning a lot of things on a spiritual side, and then I was reading the scientific side behind all this. I just thought, this is amazing. I just connected with myself, just that quality time with just me, which was difficult as a people person, to be honest, but empowering.

Barry Phillips:

We don't do it often enough, Craig. You've touched on that fear. I know exactly what you mean. To be fair, you're actually stepping out your comfort zone when you do something like that, especially when you do it on your own, because you're also in a position where you've got to—if you want to get on when you're half around the other side of the world, you're going to have step out your comfort zone. You're going to have to ask people questions, sometimes people that don't speak your language. You've got to adapt. There's quite a bit of stretching, as well, involved in it. I always feel that I've stretched myself when I come back from something like that as well. I think that's an additional bonus. It's not necessarily what you're going for, but it does actually help as well. What do you think?

Craig White:

Oh, without a doubt. I think you do come back feeling revitalised, reenergised. As you said earlier, inspired with a new focus. I just come back and people—I remember people saying to me, you look great. I was only away a week. Okay, I was eating beautiful seafood, drinking a lot of water, but I felt great, and I suppose it's that philosophy when you feel good, you portray that positive, good feeling, don't you? That vibe. And people noticed. I know not everyone can go away on holiday, but I still think it's not necessarily the fact that you went to Asia and I went to Asia. It's the power of the doing that, even as you said earlier, Barry. Even if it's little moments of quality time. Like you said, when you're out on your bike or if you go for a walk on a Sunday afternoon or if you want to learn to meditate. Or if you give yourself time every week where you decide, look, this is my time. I'm going to shut down and I'm going to go and spend some quality time with me just to, I suppose reconnect with what's important to you.

Barry Phillips:

Definitely. You mentioned something that I really relate to, where you said about it almost sounds a bit selfish. I do remember the first few times. I've been doing it now for about the last four years, but the first few times, I did feel a little bit selfish, and I had to get in touch with that. Part of me wanted to understand why I felt like that, but I also didn't want to feel like that. I did some reading along those lines, and I came up with what I now use. Instead of selfish, I use self-focused, and I think everybody needs time, like you said, just for themselves to just focus on you. What do you need at this moment? Whether it be some time away on your own, a massage, a bike ride, go on an inspirational walk, go on a course. Do something new. Take up something new, but do it just for you, and that be your own time. Then, stick to it. Commit to it. Use The Slight Edge, The Compound Effect principles, of using and doing something on a regular basis that does revitalise you, as you said. You paint a picture to me there when you said about, when you got back a lot of people commented on how well you looked and obviously the fact that you looked well meant you felt well. You were exuberating that kind of inner confidence and that inner peace, and that's what people want. Like you said, we are trying to attract people to us in our business. Again, great tip there. If you're on top of your form and you feel at peace, then you're going to attract that kind of person as well.

Craig White:

Yeah. I really like the fact where you've obviously, as you said, you've looked into this and acquired that it's that self-focus. I do love that concept, because I think that's really important for people to be able to tap into the inner power that we know everyone possesses and to feel good about life. Do you remember, was it Jim Rohn that used to talk six days on and one day off? That's something that I listened to, where you've got six days, that's how you want to work your business. Six days where you're focused and you're in your zone and you're having fun doing what you do and creating a legacy. And certainly in our business, having the power being able to develop and make a difference to people's lives from personal development through to the networking industry. It's all personal development, isn't it? Let's be honest. I think that's what our business is core to. To be able to spend that quality time with yourself and have that self-focus so that when you are having your own time, you keep to them principles you were talking about, and you make it your own time. You have that quality time. Whether it be with your family, whether it be with your friends, your loved ones, but you also have a little bit of time just for you.

Barry Phillips:

Yeah, absolutely. So, so key, and personally, it makes such a difference. It really does. Certainly, I've experienced that, and I know I've shared it with other people. I know other people that started more recently and commented back that, hey, that was fantastic. The other thing again, as I say, I like this one because it's not the one you do it for, but it's a big, big benefit. It does take you outside your comfort zone, a lot of what you do. Even meditation. I remember when I first started meditation, it was so uncomfortable, Craig. To actually try and quiet my mind for five minutes, let alone the time I'm being recommended. It was really, really tough. Even now, if I'm not on it regularly, then I have to go back and it's almost like starting again, because we've all got so many things going on in our heads.

Craig White:

Yeah. It's amazing, mate, isn't it? You're just making me chuckle there, because I'm remembering just trying to quieten my mind. It's near-on impossible. You think you've mastered it, and then you realise that actually, everything's flowing all over. Brilliant. Is meditation still something you try to quiet your mind and have a little bit of quality time there? Is that something—

Barry Phillips:

I don't, Craig. It's a good question. Interesting, because I'm one of those people, I love the concept. I've read so many people. Wayne Dyer was probably the biggest influence in my own personal life over the years, and he's someone that, every day, 20 minutes in the morning, 20 minutes in the evening, swears by it, talks about it all the time. I got involved in it. I started doing it and did notice, by the way, lots and lots of very, very positive results. But I still struggle with it. If I'm honest, I didn't practice it enough, going back to what we were saying about practice. I wouldn't say I mastered it, but what I did find is, I can do it in a different way now. What I tend to do is, I do it what I'm out on my bike on my own. I can just totally lose myself. I'm very fortunate in that I live on the River Thames. So, I'm two minutes away from the paths around the Thames. I very often, especially after work, I'll just shoot off, even if it's only for half an hour like last night. I was busy but I fit half an hour in. Again, I can come back from that and I could have let go of everything, and my mind will almost be empty. Just that focus on pushing myself on a bike and just being in nature, being in a very quiet environment. Most people wouldn't call that meditation, but for me, that's my meditation.

Craig White:

Do you know what, Barry? You've just inspired me, because I live not too far away from a beautiful park, some amazing parts in the Peterborough area, actually. I've bought myself a bike for that exact reason, and then it started raining a lot. So, I actually haven't fulfilled, I'm obviously a fair-weather biker, but you've just inspired me to actually. This evening, I'm going to go out on my bike and just let go.

Barry Phillips:

Brilliant.

Craig White:

So, next time I see you, make sure you ask me how am I getting on with my bike riding.

Barry Phillips:

I will, definitely. Just on that note, I actually go out when it is raining. I don't know about you, but you've been anywhere in the countryside or in the forest or wherever, there's always that clean smell, when it is chucking down, the rain. Although it isn't always raining here, whenever it's raining, I actually I'd rather go out when it's raining than if it's lovely and sunny, personally. Again, there tends to be nobody else out. Where I go, there won't be—yesterday, it was chucking with rain. There was no one by the river. I was the only person down there. It's so lovely down there. It's beautiful. Okay, I got wet, but hey. Even that sometimes getting wet is quite refreshing. So, lots of different ways you can do it, isn't there?

Craig White:

Yeah, mate. I'm inspired. You remind me, every time, because I travel a lot like yourself. Every time I come back to the UK, I always love coming back to the cold, fresh air early in the morning. It just reminds me that I'm back home. Yeah, I can see the attraction. It's raining today, mate. I'm going to make a commitment to go out in pursuit of my happiness. Hey, Barry. I really appreciate your time. I know you're a busy man. It's great to chat with you. I certainly feel inspired, and I knew that we'd be able to share some value with everyone that listens to this podcast show. What I'll do is, I'll get this out to everybody. If everyone wants to connect with Barry, you can do it. Their website, KnowledgeIsKing.co.uk. They've got an amazing resource of personal growth and network marketing material from books, CDs, and DVDs. There's a great thing. I think you write it as well, Barry. You've got that little section. Is it called Something to Think About?

Barry Phillips:

That's the one, yeah.

Craig White:

And that's something that you put together from your findings from your own personal development. Is that right?

Barry Phillips:

Yeah.

Craig White:

Brilliant. Guys, get onto the website. Barry, I really appreciate your time, mate. I know you're a busy guy. I look forward to speaking to you soon.

Barry Phillips:

You're welcome, Craig. Great. Pleasure as always, mate. Take care and I'll see you soon.

Knowledge is King is a family owned partnership managed by Barry Phillips, affectionately known as "Barry the Book."

Barry has always had a voracious appetite for motivational and network marketing materials, especially resources which are more in tune with British attitudes. His extensive personal library was so often used by friends and colleagues both in network marketing and in direct sales that he recognised a need that he could fulfill by supplying the best and latest books and audios to people in network marketing, direct sales and others looking for personal growth.

Our beliefs

One of Knowledge is King's strongest personal beliefs is that you become what you study: if you study law you can become a lawyer; if you study people skills you can become a great communicator ; if you study wealth and investing you can become financially free.

Take Network Marketing – if you study the industry, the successful people within it and how they did it, you will have all the information required to carve out your own success story.

Whatever you wish being a better parent, raising happier children, being a better golfer or whatever else. We believe we can help you become that BETTER YOU.

www.knowledgeisking.co.uk

CHAPTER 15

iCann- Yes You Can

Are you at a turning point in your life where you want to take action to either change a situation or improve it? "I Can" are two words that will change everything!!

In this podcast, Richard McCann shares, not only his story of how his mom was tragically killed by the Yorkshire Ripper but also how this tragedy transformed his life. Discover how someone lacking in confidence or self-belief learnt to unleash their inspirational potential to inspire others. Today Richard is one of the busiest inspirational speakers in the UK.

Adapt your mind set and turn your dreams into reality and go onto what you set out to achieve by using Richards shared philosophy and inspirational approach with his "Key Principles of I Can"

Craig White:

Hi, everyone, hope you're well and having a wicked day, and thank you for joining us on another podcast show. Joining me today we've got an amazing guy, someone who has certainly been an inspiration to me since I recently met him. I've had the pleasure of seeing Richard speak on stage and having read his recent book, I Can, I'm really pleased to bring in Richard, a best-selling author and sought-after international speaker to join us today. Welcome to our show, Mr Richard McCann, how are you?

Richard McCann:

I'm fine, Craig, thank you for having me.

Craig White:

Yes, it's an absolute pleasure. It must be a few months now, or six months to twelve months since I met you when you were speaking at a conference here in the UK. I suppose you've had a really exciting journey since then.

Richard McCann:

It has. I mean, the last few years have been very interesting and exciting, you know partly the speaking journey I've been on, but it's about a year since we met, and I remember being inspired when you won that award the Direct Selling Association conference, the Distributor of the Year. So, yes, you inspired me, actually, back then. Thank you for saying that I inspired you.

Craig White:

Likewise, mate, and it's amazing, I think relationships is what the quality of your life is built on, and I think, you know, people come into our lives for reasons and we get the opportunity to make a difference. And I know that's one of your core principles now, of what you do. But you've got a different, shall we say, story, a different background really, and there's going to be a lot of people listening to our show today that know who Richard McCann is and they've had the pleasure of seeing you and reading some of your material. I know you've had three best-selling books now. But for those who haven't got that affiliation or that knowledge of your background and your story, can you give us a bit of an insight into where you come from, Richard, and how you've become this best-selling author and, as I said, a sought-after, international speaker.

RICHARD MCCANN:

Thank you. Well, I think what makes my story different, although not too dissimilar to some people I've come across is, I was brought up in poverty, on a sink estate, a council estate in Leeds, and many people have, but what makes mine slightly different is that when I was five, my mom was tragically murdered by the serial killer, Peter Sutcliffe. For those living outside the UK, Peter Sutcliffe became known as the Yorkshire Ripper, who murdered 13 women, in fact, but my mum was the first. That's what, I guess, gives me that unique story, and it sent me on a downward spiral for many, many years, and because I was brought up in poverty anyway, I didn't feel too good about myself, on top of the death of my mum, which was in the public eye throughout my childhood. I was lacking in confidence, no self-esteem, and these are some of the things that people can relate to, for whatever reason.

So, that's where I started from, and I went through life not doing a great deal, in fact, dead end jobs, you know, ironing trousers you learn from the presentation, washing plates in a hotel, I worked in shoe shops, so I've done a lot of menial work. So, doing what I do now, being a best-selling author and the books around the world, that inspirational speaker. You know, Craig, I couldn't have dreamt of where I am today for many years. Even just six, seven years ago,

I couldn't have dreamt of me doing the work I do today. So yes, such a pleasure to be able to do this work and to meet wonderful people like yourself and wonderful people that are out there doing great work.

Craig White:

It's amazing to think that your journey from where you've come, because it's quite a different background to most, to have that experience in your life at such an early age, and I suppose it had a compound way it influenced your early years. What was the point of view—there must have been a change in your mind, there must have been something that happened that all of a sudden changed your direction from where you were going, what you were used to, the environment you was in to the journey that you've had over the last six, seven years. There must have been something, or a series of things, that started to compound that you to the point of making a different choice and choosing a different route.

Richard McCann:

Yes, and I get asked this quite often, and people do ask that question, what was the turning point, where did you turn around? It'd be nice to be able to say, "Oh yes, it was February 2004 when this happened," but you know, if I actually think about my whole life, the mindset that's been required to get me where I am today was there way back when. Because actually, when my mum first died, although we weren't told how she died, we knew she'd been taken, and I can remember just a few months after she died, in the time I spent in the children's' home, where I'd been laying there asking myself, "Why has this happened? Why has this happened?" coming up with this scenario in my young mind. "It's happened to give me a better life." You know, I'd not listened to 20 motivational speakers. I'd not read any books on the subject. But somehow, I came up with this meaning that I decided to apply to what happened to

Mum and I told myself it happened to have a start in your life and my father left when I was five. That's what I told myself. He had a new girlfriend, I thought she could be my new mum. That mindset, whatever it is, wherever it came from, I think it's the thing that's helped me to become the person I am today eventually. And I've needed to tap into that mindset from time to time along the way, where certain setbacks have occurred and I've been able to kind of tap into that. And there was a couple of turning points, but actually, it's kind of been with me ever since.

What's been with me is that ability to look at a situation, and finding a way of improving it, be it get a job as a speaker, or write a book, or set up your own business, or just think about what's happened and think about it in a particular way. Even before my mum died Craig, while having no money, drink and drugs, deprivation and all that stuff, despite all that negativity, I worked out if I go and—I forget her name, bless her, but there was an old lady that lived next door. This is age five! I'd go around to her house and she would send me to the shop on an errand to get some shopping, took her forever, and she'd give me a few pence for going. That didn't happen once, that happened multiple occasions, so I kind of worked out if I did something, and took some action, I can improve my situation, and she'd give me some money, I'd get some sweets.

So, I guess there was a massive turning point and that was when I came out of prison in 1997, but whatever it is, it's kind of been with me throughout my life.

Craig White:

I'll say it's an amazing kind of innocent philosophy to have at such an early age, this has happened to give you a better life. I suppose sometimes that's the innocence we have as children, we always look to believe in ourselves, believe in our dreams at a younger age, the things that you want, desire and wish for. And I suppose that innocence and the social conditioning that we experience as we grow up that sometimes beats that out of us, or gives us a low self-esteem. I suppose you don't have that at such an early age, and it's a great philosophy to have kept with you all these years.

Richard McCann:

Yes, and it might be a bit naïve, well, I'm saying that. I don't think it was naïve, because actually I do believe my mum died to give me a better life and me to go and do the work that I now do, and that's a little bit deep and it's not something I normally share from the stage, but I do believe I chose this life and it was always going to happen. So actually, it's not naïve, it's something I've carried with me and it's served me very, very well, and some very strange things have happened in my life that suggest to me that there is more to this world than we can fully explain. Some very strange coincidences and things have occurred that left me thinking, "Bloody hell, what happened, where did that person come from?" Anyway, that's probably a different subject for a different time. But you know, it's a funny old world that we live in.

Craig White:

Yes, I know, we were talking and have done in the past, you know obviously if you decide what you want, the universe will find a way of connecting the dots, I suppose, won't it?

Richard McCann:

Yes, although, that concept, of having the goal and the universe bringing it to me. That's quite a recent understanding of mine. Well, having said that, if I looked back throughout my life. I've kind of always understood that aswell, maybe. What I'm talking about and you won't know this from the stage show, when I used to lay in bed, as little as I was, a seven or eight-year-old kid, and being beaten for whatever triviality in the house by my dad, who was often very violent, the thing I'd say to myself is this. I'd say, Richard, about what's taking place because when you're older, you'll be able to help people around the world."

I have no idea what I meant by that, or what that would look like, but once again it was me trying to put some positive slant on what was taking place, and it's funny isn't it, now I do inspire people around the world, my books are out in different countries and I have heard from people in Mexico and New Zealand, or wherever else, that have been inspired by reading my books. So, gosh what did that seven or eight-year-old boy know? You know, as I spoke to you, I was speaking in South Africa a few weeks ago, inspiring people in South Africa. That thing wasn't me setting a goal, back 30 years ago, or was it me understanding what was going to take place eventually, and who knows? What I do know is, I thought about something aged seven or eight, and it's now happening, which is strange.

Now when I think about goals and goal-setting, which is one of the big parts of my book, what I do understand now, is when you have a goal, your awareness is heightened and you start spotting things that are going to make this goal turn into reality, I suppose. I heard one of your recordings recently, Allan Pease, was it? And he was talking about that when you buy a car and then you start seeing the same cars everywhere and it's so true, I've experienced that. And that can be applied to not just cars, but whatever we're going on to achieve.

Craig White:

I think it just brings out awareness into your mindset, doesn't it? And you're able to, as you rightfully say, Richard, see more opportunities that are in line with the goals and the targets that you set. But I think it's amazing, going back to what you're saying about lying in bed, seven, eight years-old, and how your life's materialised in what you said all them years ago. Maybe there is something in that. You hear stories time and time again of different stories, but similar kind of examples where people have dreamt from an early age, and believed in themselves and their life has materialised. I suppose it's staying true to that is the important thing.

Richard McCann:

Staying true to that and having that belief that it will happen, despite it appearing not to happen, initially. You know, one of the areas of my books, and it's been said by many people, but never giving up. It's about hanging in there and keeping going. There's no real facts to suggest you're going to achieve this thing, and just keeping going because often, as you know in some of the work that you do, that often people just give up and success is just around the corner. I have to say that I almost gave up when it comes to the book, well my first book, anyway. I was writing off to publishers and they weren't interested, or agents, sorry, they weren't interested. But I kept going and I'm so glad that I did keep going because 400,000 copies later and books around the world, and it all started and opened the door for my speaking career. I'm so glad that I kept going, I didn't give up.

Craig White:

You persevered. That book, in particular, was that the book About a Boy?

Richard McCann:

Just a Boy, that's the first book, about my childhood, I guess and early adulthood. You know that was one of the most terrifying things I've ever done. Up until that point, I'd been ashamed of my past, and I was worried about will people find out, shall I tell people? Shall I tell my girlfriend? I'm writing the book, I thought, this is just going to reflect badly on me. I guess mainly because I've been to prison. I'd been to prison on a drugs charge back in 1997. I thought, gosh, if I write about this, this is going to harm my future career prospects. But I had the courage to say, you know what, I'm going to do this. And I'm so glad I found my courage because, well the rest is history.

Craig White:

Just talking to you now, I think, you know I've read your book, the I Can book, and the key principles in your book are the importance of positivity, that courage creates success, achievement begins with a goal, and then that never give up philosophy. And just chatting with you right now, you're evidently somebody that's not just writing a book, you're actually living your own principles. And I've got a lot of respect for that. It's obvious that you've come from tough beginnings and you've now got the opportunity to make a difference, which is inspiring and that's why I think so many people have been inspired by you from stage, and obviously for those of you that have connected with Richard by reading his books or through social media or your blog or whatever it may be, I'm sure they see too, that you very much kind of live, breathe your own principles which I think's important when you're sharing a story and a message.

Richard McCann:

Yes, thank you, Craig. And I'm thinking what you said earlier. Just last night, and I've got three wonderful children now, and I was reading to Sky, she was laying on the top bunk of their bunk beds. She's only five, and we were talking about businesses and setting up businesses and I asked what she wanted to do when she was older and she wanted to be a hairdresser, and I said, "No, no, no, you have to be a hairdresser to begin with but let's have your own hair salon." And I started talking about my work and how people will say to me they want to be a hairdresser, and I try and encourage them to have their own salon, so yes, I do live this from the stage and in my own life, and I'm trying and push it onto my children all the time. I think it's so important, and I'm living proof of that. I didn't get any encouragement as a child, and the way that I saw myself as a child fitting into society or not fitting in, in fact, was quite detrimental to me, going for those very basic jobs. I just want my children to live and breathe this themselves it's starting to work... They're great kids and you hear them repeating some of the things that I've said which means so much to me.

Craig White:

I think it's really important, because I've been lucky enough to have an influence and to be influencing myself now through choice, through the personal development and the understanding that we are what we read and what we study we become. I see that, I've got two young daughters, as well. One's not talking yet, just goo-ing and ga-ing, but Isabella—it's funny you should say that, because you've now got the opportunity to have an environment and create an environment that you didn't have as a kid. And give that influence and that legacy that's really important to you.

Richard McCann:

It's so true, so true. I'm re-living my life through my children, and I don't have favourites, but I've got two girls and a boy, and it's just so fantastic to see them grow and thrive in the way they're doing. Which I never got and they take it for granted, well, let them take it for granted and I'm sure we'll find a way of showing them what the real world's about and how much hardship is out there. In fact, they do know about hardship. They know about homeless people, and they know about charity shops and they know about other people who don't have a great deal. And it's just fantastic that we, as parents, have the ability to educate them and empower them in a way that some people didn't get, especially me.

Craig White:

The kind of thought of gratitude that we're able to teach our children, and just the environment they're in with your philosophies, your personal development, but also your belief, it's still not common. I mean, you know, children and families might not have it tough as you had it when you were younger, but they still have it tough, and they might not have that positive influence, whereas you are able to turn your daughter's dream and say, hey look, she wants to be a hairdresser, to plant a seed about having her own salon. You know, that's not commonplace. People wouldn't commonly do that. But because of your growth, you're able to do that. You foresee that, hey, why not? Because you believe in yourself and you've got that attitude of making things happen.

Richard McCann:

Sure. And on a long day, continuous laughing.

Craig White:

We've both got completely different upbringings, haven't we, really, yet still have a passion to succeed, a passion to make a difference. You've had a tough upbringing and yet it's had a positive influence on your life. I was very lucky on the complete opposite end of the scale, where my parents instilled this positive attitude into me that you and I are instilling into our children. So, from either ends of the scale, the influence, can still be turned around to be positive, can't it?

Richard McCann:

Yes, and as you're saying that, I'm thinking about, what's her name? Shelly Rose? Can't remember her name. I saw her speak recently, last year in fact, on NLP, and I haven't got an LP training. But I was listening to this session and this trainer was talking about we have goals, often, and some of them are go-to goals, and some of them are go-away-from goals, and if we can think about what she said, it sounds like you have success, or your family did, and you wanted more of that and that's what you've done, so you've gone toward success. Whereas, we who didn't have any success, from poverty and lack of money and I've done everything that I can to move away from that, and I just wonder am I moving away from or am I moving to? I must have a look at the material again. It's interesting that we both, as you said, come from different backgrounds but we've kind of, now anyway, having a similar journey, aren't we?

Craig White:

Yes.

Richard McCann:

In enjoying the success that we do.

Craig White:

It's amazing. I love that thought. You learn so much in life and you forget some of the things you've learned. I've heard that somewhere before, probably from an NLP practitioner, but the go-to goals and the go-away-from goals, it makes sense, I suppose, doesn't it? But what drives you now, because obviously, initially you had that go-away-from goals, and I'd imagine you're a million miles away from that now, so do you now have go-to goals? I know your family's a priority to you, and security, etc. What drives you at the moment?

Richard McCann:

Security is one of my biggest drives, security, but also seeing other people grow. I tell you what's always been big in my life, I was always like the underdog, the kid in school that had the secondhand clothes that couldn't go on the school trip and whatever else was going on as a child. I also have a soft spot for the underdogs, which is why, I know people scoff at these X-factor programs, but I always like to see those X-factor programs where the kids come from nothing and they've got this opportunity on stage. I just love to see that. And I love to see people that are a certain place, and that we can grow them in some way, be it give them the inspiration to set up their own business and be it give them some communication skills from a stage, and that's such a big drive in my life. So, security and seeing other people grow, especially the underdog, that doesn't believe in themselves, they are what drives me.

As far as goals are concerned, my goal is to speak globally. I want to be a global speaker. I want to do more of what that seven, eight-year-old kid believed was possible, that my message would go around the world, and I'm on that journey anyway, so next stop Vancouver, hopefully, which was a goal of mine. It's funny how the weird universe works, because I knew there was a potential opportunity in Vancouver in 2013 for the Global Speakers Summit. It happens every two years around the world. So, I knew this took place, and I had the postcard somewhere in the in the office.

So, I spoke in South Africa, I don't know, three or four weeks ago, and suddenly that's part of the Global Speakers Federation. Janelle Barlow, in fact she's the President, was at that conference, and she's part of the decision-making committee that might be able to make that happen. Isn't it strange how we do these things. What I'm talking about here is the goal I've got to speak in Vancouver, looks like it will be a reality because I spoke in South Africa. But my goal is to do more international work.

But also, my more recent goal is I want to make a difference in prisons. I mean, I've been to prison, and I know only too well how difficult it is to turn your life around when you come out of prison, because nobody would give me a job. You may recall, Craig, from the presentation, I was in there on a drugs charge. Nobody would give me a job, I was about to get my house repossessed, I almost took my life, formed a suicide pact with my sister, and I thought there was just no point. Thankfully we didn't go through with it, and I actually got a job and saved my house at the last minute.

So, I think there's an important need there to give offenders a second chance. It almost cost me my life and I don't think there's enough being done out there right now. So, my goal at the moment is to create a program to go into prisons and not only inspire them, and give them the skills and tools to help them grow as an individual, but also to change the mindsets of employers or potential employers when it comes to considering ex-offenders to be employed. So, that's kind of the goal of the moment, so that is new goal of mine.

Craig White:

Sounds exciting.

Richard McMann:

I just love it. I love the work that I'm involved with and my latest goal is to create a book full of impactful stories. I'll never forget the words of the police officer that told me, when I was five, in the children's home that mum had been taken to heaven and that I wasn't going to see her again. Those words have been in me throughout my life. 36 years later. Also, I've got other words that I've heard in my life that had a massive impact in my life. The words of Desmond Tutu, just less than two years ago, when he shared from the stage when he was speaking about forgiveness, when he came out with this sentence, "You could never force a person to forgive another, but when it occurs it has the capacity to change a situation." Those words hit me like a tidal wave of energy, and at that moment I forgave the person that murdered my mum. My new book is about words that you've heard that had a massive impact in your life, and that's one of my goals at the moment, and I'm right in the middle of doing all that. You know, collating the stories and editing them down and I want to get that out there, because I know how important the words that we hear are, which is why you do this podcast, of course.

Craig White:

Well, yes, it's the environment that's created around us, isn't it? Through words, tonality, that power of association is so very important. I just remember, actually, I'm sure it's in your book, you talked about actually forgiveness is what set you free. And that's quite empowering, looking back, that obviously, Desmond Tutu's words had that influence on yourself and, you know, made this book be with us very soon, my friends.

Richard McMann:

It did set me free. What I mean by setting me free is, for 36 years I'd been angry and bitter about what he did, about him taking Mum's life. Yes, it's good to experience anger and get it out of your system, but for 36 years I've been, you know, wanting revenge and all the rest of it, he doesn't even know why I feel this way, so where has that energy gone? It's just gone inside and imploded in me and done me damage. So, for him to say those words, Desmond Tutu, you're right, it did set me free. And not just with regards to Peter Sutcliffe, but in all the smaller ways as well, and life wasn't the way I had fallouts at home with my wife about the weather and the person that cuts you up on the road. We could be angry about that, or we could just let it go. And so, when things happen now, I can think about what he did, forgiving Peter Sutcliffe, well if I can do that, I can forgive this person as well.

Craig White:

Yes, I can see something so big can be associated with some of the smaller forgivenesses of life are so important to just keep us true, keep us happy, keep us focused on what matters and not the negatives surrounding us on occasion. Just kind of for those that are listening, obviously, I've read your book, and many will have done, but you've talked about how some the principles have enabled you to turn your life around and how you want to impact prisons etc., and impacting other people from inspiration and communication point of view. But for those people listening, if you look at your four core principles in your book that you discussed and expanded on, what advice can you give people to kind of either turn their life around and make new decisions and start working towards what matters to them, or for those that are already on the journey, like ourselves and many others, how can they accelerate their success by implementing these four core principles?

RICHARD McCANN:

Well, the first principle is the importance of positivity. That's a massive principle and it can cover many aspects of life, business and everything else. For me, positivity is about looking at any situation being negative or the one idea that stops the negative, it could be better, it could be greater, it could be better results. It's just about focus on well, what things can I do that will give me greater success or less negativity or make the situation appear better than it had done had I not thought positively. It's also about looking about the people around us for the leaders that are out there, and finding the good in them. Because when you find good in somebody, I know this because I have experienced it in years gone by, when you find something good in someone you let them know. That can be life changing.

I can remember one of my warehouse supervisors saying to me on one occasion, "Richard, you're management material." Now when he said that to me, I'm in the warehouse, I started wearing a shirt and tie to work, and before I knew it I was running the computer system, so the positivity is not just about us and what we're thinking about a situation, it's about what we can do for other people as well. It's a massive principle, but basically, we have the ability to put whatever meaning we want to a situation, and find a positive in it, and that's something I've instilled in not just my audiences and my children and everybody I come into contact with. That's positivity.

Now what that means to your audience, well they'll know. Do I need to be more positive, do I need to raise the bar and do more, do I need to ask for the help of other people if I'm a leader, do I need to start finding the good in people rather than criticising them all the time. So, that's the positivity.

The second one is courage to create success. Courage is often confused with confidence. The thing about courage, you don't need confidence to do it. It's about doing something without the confidence, and you'll remember from my presentation that the first time I believe I was courageous was when I got on the stage, age 13, with no confidence at the time, and took part in

the public speaking competition at school. You know that was life-changing, although I didn't know it. But in the short term it changed the way that I saw myself fitting in, and I won the competition, it was fantastic! When we talk about situations that feel uncomfortable, if we can find the courage, which is free of charge by the way, if we can find the courage to do that thing, it can often take us to a place that we never knew existed. And I tested it my first professional speaking engagement back in 2005. I was terrified. Absolutely terrified, but I did it, and it lead on to one engagement after another and before I knew it I had done 1250. And in writing the book, I found the courage to write the book. For some people listening to this, they'll be working part-time in some jobs and full-time in other jobs, they have ideas about businesses they want to start and conversations they need to have, you know, courage means different things to different people and different people will need it for different things. It's just about doing that thing, seeing where it goes. And you know, it might not work out, when I'm talking about setting up business here, it might not work out, but you'll learn something in the process, and you'll apply it to the next attempt and you'll do it slightly differently next time you have cause to do it. And go on what your gut instinct tells you you should be doing.

Craig White:

Having the power, yes.

Richard McCann:

We've all got the power. We don't have the confidence, we just need to do it, and stop listening to that little voice that we have in our brain that'll try and talk us out of it, thinking it's looking after us, when it's not, it's holding us back.

And the third one, of course, is achievement begins with a goal. There's many things being said about goal-setting, nothing really new out there. But my take on that is, when we have a goal, we spot the things that help us get there, but if we raise the bar and have a bigger goal than we had previously, we start coming out with bigger ideas. I did a workshop recently and one of the things that I said, I said to one side of the room, "Can you give us some ideas on how we can raise £50 for charity?" So, they started to write down the things they would do to raise £50. I said to the other side of the room, "You've got to raise £50,000." They came up with different ideas. Now, the people who were raising the £50, they could only come up with suggestions that would help them raise £50. If you raise that goal, your brain comes up with bigger, juicier, more interesting, more creative ideas.

So, when it comes to goals and goal-setting, let's have them, raise the bar, but also get a picture of what they might want to achieve. You know we think in pictures, we don't think in text, so get some pictures, like the Vancouver poster that I'm looking at on my wall, and a picture for the car. I know you know about this stuff, Craig, because I've spoken to you before. But, some people are unaware of this stuff. The car I drive was the screen saver on my computer, and one of those speaker bureaus that I now work for, they weren't interested, so I did that by printing out the page of speakers that we have that talk about overcoming adversity, put it in my noticeboard on my wall, I cut out my photograph from my business card and I stuck it on there as if I was one of their speakers. And when you look at something enough times, your brain will find a way to make it a reality and by the way I did make it a reality because I ran that speaker bureau up and got on their books about a year and a half later.

And last, of course, is the never giving up. I did think about giving up and throughout my life, on many occasions, and almost did, and I'm so glad that I didn't, because the book and the speaking and the family that I have got is just a fantastic place to be. That book that I wrote took me, I think 40 proposals before I finally got myself an agent, and then, obviously got the book published. The speaking, when I first started out, I spoke three times in the first year, wasn't much of a speaking career, but I kept going and the second year it was 11 times, not much of a speaking career, but I kept going, and I kept going, and now, all these speaking engagements later, I am glad that I didn't throw the towel in. Being part of the Professional Speakers Association, honestly, I come across speakers all the time that have got fantastic stories to tell, and they give up because they don't get an engagement straight away. Nothing gets given on a plate and we give up far, far too easily. I'm so glad that I didn't. Not just for that, not just for the speaking, various things throughout my life.

There's nothing new in the world, but it's one of the principles that I live my life by and I know that my children know I live by it as well. My son was taking part in his sports day recently, and he had two races. The first race was the egg and spoon—no, it was beanbag race, sorry, and he lost that and he was in tears and I was comforting him and then a few minutes later, or twenty minutes later they had the second race, which was the running race, and "Come on, son, you can do it!" and he won the race. He got this little gold medal, I've still got it. Not only did he have a goal but he didn't give up and he kept going, that was in the book in fact, that story. In the I Can book. So, I hope my children in years to come will read about how inspirational I thought they were.

Craig White:

You know what, mate, I'm really glad you never gave up, and I think it's been a pleasure chatting with you today, and I'm sure everyone listening to the podcast will get great value from it. And for those of you that would like to connect with Richard, you can do at his website, RichardMcCann.co.uk. Highly recommend you pick up one of these books, I Can, and any of Richard's other books from his first book through to his one on its way. You know, I'm really pleased that you've spent some of your time to chat with us, Richard, but I'm sure it's kind of the attitude that you've created for yourself, and I'm really happy that you're able to influence your kids, even though I don't know them and leave a legacy for them, because I know how important it is to me to do the same, so I know how important it must be for you to make that positive difference. I really appreciate you connecting with us, mate, and sharing your words of wisdom and some of your experiences with us.

Richard McCann:

Craig, a real pleasure, and thank you for having me. I look forward to connecting with you again. And listen, everybody, have a great day.

On a cold and misty morning in October 1975, Richard McCann woke to discover his mother was missing. He was just five years old. She was the first victim of the notorious Yorkshire Ripper, Peter Sutcliffe.

Despite other tragic losses, and a period of dabbling with drugs and prison, Richard decided to turn his life around. He grew to become a motivational speaker and loving family man, with a film of his life in development. Today, Richard has delivered over 2,000 presentations around the world, inspiring audiences with his story of overcoming adversity, and sharing his powerful iCan approach.

In 2009 he founded the iCanSpeak Academy, training individuals and teams to enhance their presentation skills and communicate their message authentically and with confidence so they achieve more effective results. See the iCanSpeak Academy for details of upcoming events.

http://www.richardmccann.co.uk/

21536959R00182

Printed in Great Britain
by Amazon